August 17, 2011

MVFOL

Heywood Gould Novels:

ONE DEAD DEBUTANTE (1975)
FORT APACHE, THE BRONX (1981)
GLITTERBURN (1981)
COCKTAIL (1984)
DOUBLE BANG (1988)
LEADING LADY (2008)
THE SERIAL KILLER'S DAUGHTER (2011)

Heywood Gould Screenplays:

ROLLING THUNDER (1977 movie starring William Devane and Tommy Lee Jones)

THE BOYS FROM BRAZIL (1978 movie starring Gregory Peck and Laurence Olivier)

FORT APACHE, THE BRONX (1981 movie starring Paul Newman, Edward Asner, Ken Wahl, and Danny Aiello)

STREETS OF GOLD (1986 movie starring Klaus Maria Brandauer, Wesley Snipes, and Adrian Pasdar)

COCKTAIL (1988 movie starring Tom Cruise, Bryan Brown, and Elisabeth Shue)

ONE GOOD COP (1991 movie starring Michael Keaton and Rene Russo; directed by Heywood Gould)

TRIAL BY JURY (1994 movie starring Armand Assante, Gabriel Byrne, and William Hurt; directed by Heywood Gould)

MISTRIAL (1996 movie starring Bill Pullman and Robert Loggia; directed by Heywood Gould)

DOUBLE BANG (2001 movie starring William Baldwin and Adam Baldwin; directed by Heywood Gould)

The Serial Killer's Daughter

THE
SERIAL
KILLER'S
DAUGHTER

a novel

Heywood Gould

Nightbird
Publishing

2011

This is a work of fiction. The events described are imaginary.
The characters and settings are fictitious. Any references to
real persons or places are included only to lend authenticity to
the story.

THE SERIAL KILLER'S DAUGHTER

FIRST EDITION

All rights reserved.

ISBN: 978-0-9819572-5-8

Nightbird Publishing
P.O. Box 159
Norcross, Georgia 30091

Website: www.nightbirdpubs.com
e-mail: info@nightbirdpubs.com

PRINTED IN THE UNITED STATES OF AMERICA

First Printing: April 2011

10 9 8 7 6 5 4 3 2 1

For Pattie

I Didn't Ask For This

I'm sitting cross-legged on the shag carpet of a Motel 6 (I can't say where) pecking away in the glow of my laptop. The shades are drawn. The pencil-flash between my teeth is shining on the keys.

A minute ago I was coming back with a pizza and thought I saw one of them. It could have just been a random guy, but he was lurking between the cars and it looked like he was watching my unit.

I parked behind him. He felt my eyes and turned. Staring straight ahead, I took the gun out of the laundry bag and put it on the seat. He stood there for a second, like he was trying to decide what to do. Then, he about-faced and walked around behind the units. A minute later, a white Focus peeled out onto the freeway. I couldn't see who was driving.

So, I came in here and started writing.

It's like I'm putting a message in a bottle. If something happens they'll find the whole story on my hard drive. It's also on my USB stick, which I'll keep on a chain around my neck.

Have to hurry. The dying sun is seeping under the shades. Shadows cross-hatch the floor.

Have to get it all down before the room goes black . . .

Me

I was good, but I had never been lucky. My buzzer-beater would roll off the rim. My walk-off line drive would scream over the third-base bag, but the left fielder would always make a diving catch and become the hero instead of me.

The other benchwarmers went geeky or Gothic, or just got tragic on drugs. I kept trying. I wanted to be the All-American boy. Star on the field, brain in the classroom. The dude in the flashy tux escorting the Prom Queen.

There were 1,100 in the senior class of 2003 at John C. Fremont High. Graduation day we lined up in the heat on the football field, all capped and gowned and giggly from bong hits behind the gym.

My name is Peter Vogel (in the class photo I'm the oblivion sandwich in the last row.) The kid in front of me was Felipe Velez, the star striker of the soccer team. He got a roar from his teammates and "whoo-whoos" from the hoochies who thought he was hot. I walked out to a pathetic smattering from my mom, my faculty advisor, and the few good souls who applauded every grad. On my heels came Jenny Voorspan, the editor of the newspaper, volunteer in the Feeding the Homeless project, scholarship to Princeton. She got a standing ovation. The kiss-ass teachers on the dais stood and cheered.

I spent the summer working at Blockbuster, getting blasted and watching the worst movies I could find. The Tuesday after Labor Day I started at a big UC (can't say which one). I had no plans. My ambition was to stay drunk and have meaningless sex. Girls walked by me like I was invisible.

Tutoring My Fetish

A university campus is a universe of parallel galaxies—jock world, frat world, geeks and politicos. English majors whirl in aimless nebulae, disdained yet left in peace. We have a pleasant life pretending to write, learning to drink and trying to hook up, which is tough when you have no money and can only talk about dead authors and old movies.

Senior year, a girl appeared in my American Lit class. She was almost as tall as me. Pale and skinny with big breasts that stirred at her slightest movement.

I tried to be cool and unimpressed around women, but couldn't stop sneaking sidelong looks at her. She had long legs that led to a tight, perfect ass. I'd seen that body type a thousand times in porno flicks and knew exactly what she looked like naked. She daydreamed in lectures, eyes half closed, mouth half open. There were coffee stains on her blouse and wisps of black hair curling out of the stubble in her armpits. At night I was tormented by a vision of her eyes widening and her mouth flopping open in astonishment as I stood over her, naked and masterful. My body would throb and it would feel as if my brains were going to burst out of my head. Next morning I would pass her in class like nothing had happened and shoot her a casual "hi." I got a dismissive smile in return.

And then one day she chased me down in the quadrangle.

"Is William Dean Howells the most pointless shit in the world?"

I had read that if you masturbated thinking of the same girl every night she would feel your energy and be drawn to you. Had that happened? Her eyes were dark, almost black and impossible to read.

"All writers with three names are boring," I said. "Wait until you get to Ralph Waldo Emerson."

She squinted like she didn't get the joke. "I'm an Economics major and I've been putting off taking these Lit classes, but now I need them to graduate."

"Don't worry, this is English. You don't have to know anything. Just show up and hand in a paper."

She jumped in front of me, walking backwards. "I have to get at least a B to keep my three-point-five so I can get into a decent law school. I've been watching you in class. Professor Katz always perks up when you start to talk."

"I'm an English major. I know the code."

"You get A's on all your papers. Even an A-plus." She laughed and answered the question I was about to ask. "My roommate is seeing Katz's teaching assistant. He says you're the smartest guy in the class."

"I want people to love me for my body, not my mind."

"Your body is workable." When she leaned forward I could see the imprint of her nipple on her sleeveless blouse.

"I need someone to write my papers for me," she said. "Will you do it?"

"People are getting three- or four-hundred bucks to ghost papers," I said.

"I can't pay you, I'm broke," she said. "I'll let you fuck me. That's the best I can do."

I was shocked at how casually she said it. "Let me get this straight," I said with a knowing smile that implied I fielded propositions like this all the time. "You'll let me . . ." I wanted to say *fuck* with the same nonchalance, but couldn't get it out ". . . *sleep* with you if I help you write a paper."

"Only if I get an A."

It had to be a prank. My stupid friends had put her up to it. I was supposed to start slobbering and agree to everything and then they'd jump out of the bushes, yelling "punk'd!"

I played along. "How do I know I can trust you? Say I

write the paper and you show up with your boyfriend, who's the captain of the Lacrosse team, and say the deal is off?"

"I can see why you're an English major. Don't worry I'm not creative enough to come up with an idea like that."

"If this were a porn movie, I'd be following you into the bedroom right now," I said.

She grabbed my hand. "Life can be a porn movie sometimes."

She took me to an apartment a few blocks off campus. A Subaru sat in the driveway. "My roommate is home," she said.

She led me into the garage, to a vintage Ford pickup draped with a tarp. I kept waiting for my friends to jump out at me. She lifted the tarp and we both crawled under. She pushed me back down onto the cold cement floor and unbuttoned her blouse.

I was afraid to look down or touch her, because I wanted this to last. But it didn't, and a minute later she was checking herself out in the smudgy mirror over the worktable.

"You'll have to give me a few smart things to say in class," she said. "Participation is part of the grade."

"The way you participate, it won't be a problem," I said.

She offered her hand. Her grasp was warm. She grazed the inside of my wrist with a long nail and I felt a chill to the top of my head.

"Hi, Peter," she said. "I'm Hannah."

LoveLust

Professor Katz had announced on the first day that plagiarism, copying, or ghostwriting, "are capital crimes punishable by an instant F and possible expulsion from the University." He put me to work, checking all papers for what he called "sudden outbursts of eloquence," or "suspiciously sound insights." I was his favorite, but had no qualms about betraying him.

I worked out a simple method. Hannah would write the paper and I'd smarten it up just enough to show that she'd been listening. Then I'd add some uninformed yet sincere reaction to the stories to show that she cared.

In class I passed her notes with questions for Katz. He liked it when the pretty girls played up to him.

The first assignment was an essay comparing "Daisy Miller" and "Rappaccini's Daughter," two stories about romantic young women.

"That Hawthorne is a sick bastard," Hannah said. "To write about a girl who dies in her father's garden of beautiful poisoned flowers. It's so unfair."

"It's an allegory," I said.

"Beatrice didn't deserve to die," she said with surprising vehemence. "I hate it when writers kill women for no reason."

"So you think the male use of the female as a symbol objectifies her and deprives her of her humanity."

She blinked. "Is that what I just said?"

"Yeah. Also that Rappaccini's Daughter isn't believable and Hawthorne is just using her to express his ideas about the danger of scientific rationality. But also Beatrice is the name of Dante's heroine, so what's up with that? Then you'll say that it looked like Henry James was following Daisy

Miller around, taking down everything she did and said, but he didn't seem to care about her, just wanted to show how naïve Americans were. Also, you'll say Daisy is named after a flower that dies in the winter and Beatrice dies in a garden, so both authors kill off young, beautiful women."

"Wow, I'm smarter than I thought," Hannah said.

The next week Katz e-mailed the grades. I couldn't catch her eye during class, so I slipped her a note. "What did you get?" She scribbled over it, crumpled it and threw it back. "A, I'll call you later." Then ran out a few minutes before class ended.

That night I waited for hours. My suitemates laughed at me. "She was playin' you, dude."

At midnight she called my cell. "My roommate had a fight with her boyfriend, so she's staying in."

"You could come over here," I said.

"You told your roommates about me, didn't you?" she said. "Don't lie. Guys only have sex so they can brag about it to their friends."

"So that means there's no deal?"

"I didn't say that. We'll do it tomorrow."

I went out. Bars closed at one, so I had to make up for lost time. Six or maybe seven tequila shooters later, she called again.

"They made up and she's going to his house. Come over now."

I stumbled the few blocks to her house, but once I got out of the fresh air I puked the tequila and the nachos all over her bedroom.

I crawled into the bathroom to finish the job. When I came out, she had spread paper towels over the floor.

"I better go home," I said.

"It's okay, you can stay."

"But if I just sleep here that won't count as payment?"

"It won't count, don't worry," she said. She sat me down on her bed and pulled my pants off. Holding my shirt at arm's length, she took it into the bathroom. I closed my eyes and got the spins so bad I had to open them and sit up. She came back and slid into bed. She was wearing a XXX basketball T-shirt with nothing underneath.

"Shouldn't get that drunk. People will take advantage of you."

She woke me early.

"You smell like throw-up. Take a shower."

When I came out of the bathroom, she was bending over, making the bed.

"I think I'm ready now," I said.

She turned and looked at me. "Yes, I can see that." And sighed. "I have a class at eight-thirty."

It was fast and frenzied, like trying to stay on the bucking bronco at a country music club. When it was over, I struggled against the question you weren't supposed to ask, and lost.

"Did you get off?"

"Not really. I'm undersexed."

"Well, maybe, if we went a little slower."

She patted me on the cheek. "Isn't the girl supposed to say that? Don't worry, you're a wonderful lover." She jumped out of bed. "And just to prove it I'll throw in a cup of coffee for extra credit."

I was dizzy from the tequila and the sudden, unsatisfactory exertion. I put my boxers on and felt my way into the living room. Hannah's roommate came in. "Ooh, free show."

She was a trim, tan little blonde with a brash laugh. I had seen her in the bars partying with the jocks. Hannah shot her a secret giggle look, which I pretended not to see. I went into the bedroom to get dressed and heard the roommate say: "He's cute."

"Get your own nerd," Hannah said. And there were more smothered giggles.

Katz wanted a paper on every story we read, so I was at Hannah's house every night. She always had food for me, take out, or even something she had cooked. After every 'A' paper, she paid promptly and mechanically.

I tried everything. She wouldn't smoke weed, and wine made her drowsy. She didn't respond to massages. Even oral foreplay was a non-starter.

She seemed preoccupied. I decided she was thinking about an ex-boyfriend, although she never talked about him and girls usually told you the whole, boring story.

Maybe she had a lover. A hunky jock who came in and rocked her world after I had slunk away with my laptop.

I thought about her constantly. All I had to do was close my eyes and I would see her naked, crouched over me, her black, bottomless eyes boring into me. It was so intense I could even smell her.

One night I saw a guy duck behind a tree. Was this the boyfriend waiting for me to leave? I crossed the street.

"You a friend of Hannah's?"

He was a gawky guy with hair falling over his face. He raised his hands to ward me off.

His voice broke. "I don't know any Hannah."

"Then what are you doing in front of her house?"

"I don't know whose house this is." He took a lurching step toward me. "And anyway, I don't have to tell you what I'm doing here."

He was creepy, like an overwrought teenager who spent too much time in sicko chat rooms and posted cryptic hints of violence on his Facebook status. He was scrawny, too, but scary. I stepped back with a patronizing smile. "Sleep out here. I don't care."

"Go fuck yourself!" he snarled as I walked away. I gave him the finger without turning and speeded up, hoping he wouldn't come after me.

The next night after we finished working, I asked Hannah out for a drink.

"I hate bars," she said.

"Coffee then?"

"Don't drink coffee at night."

"What's the matter, don't you want to be seen in public with your nerd English tutor?"

"How'd you guess?"

"Or maybe you have a boyfriend. I saw that dude hanging around outside waiting for me to leave."

"I don't have a boyfriend," she said.

"Then you have a stalker."

"I don't have a stalker, either. I'm a deprived child."

At the end of the term, Katz was late posting the final grades. A week went by and I hadn't heard from her. Before winter break I got loaded at a sorority party. I was drinking Popov, the vodka that comes in a plastic bottle. I sat in a corner trying to make a compound word out of "slut" and "sorority," but nothing really scanned.

I called Hannah's cell. "This is Peter, the nerd tutor," I said to her voice mail. "I didn't get my Christmas bonus. I'm coming over to collect."

My phone rang a few seconds later. She was actually laughing.

"You don't qualify for a bonus. You've been with the firm less than a year."

"Did you get your grade?"

"Not yet."

"Where are you?"

"Far away."

"I wanna come see you."

"You're drunk," she said.

"I'll get on a plane."

"Look, go find a girl," she said.

"I found one."

"Find one in the same room. Don't scrunch your shoulders up, don't put yourself down, and don't make stupid jokes that nobody understands."

When spring term began, I checked at the English Department. She wasn't registered for any classes. I called her cell, but she didn't answer. I used my friend's phone so my name wouldn't come up on her Caller ID. Still no answer.

I waited outside her apartment one night. Before dawn,

her roommate drove up with a fat guy with shoulder-length red hair. She tripped getting out of the car and blinked to get me into focus.

"Hey, Peter," she said

"Hey." I realized I didn't know her name. "I'm looking for Hannah."

"She quit school."

"But she only had one more semester."

"I know. Weird, huh?"

"Do you know where she went?"

"Sorry, Peter."

I followed her to the door. "Hey, I'm not gonna bother her."

The fat guy turned and squared off on me. I could see the prickly blonde hairs on his fat red fists. "Back off, dude."

Hannah's roommate stepped between us. "It's okay." She wobbled and coughed and took a second to pull herself together. "Hannah is strange, Peter. She was working in some really cheesy strip joint, pole dancing and whatever."

A few hours later, lying on my bed in a welter of Bud cans, I had a vision of Hannah, the darkness welling out of her eyes and flowing over me until I was lost, plunging deeper and deeper into her nothingness.

Maybe it was the beer, but I felt like I was hurtling through space, my life breaking into chunks of debris. I had been counting on going through the semester with her. Now I would never see her again.

Teaching For America

G raduation was a bust. There were ominous rumors of plans to disrupt the ceremonies with anti-war chants. "Mecha" and the Chicano Liberation Front talked about rushing the platform to symbolically retake California. The Rainbow Coalition wanted to launch kites. Palestinian Rights and Hillel were threatening counter demos. In the end, most of the 3,000-odd people who were graduating showed up with hangovers, wearing shorts and sneakers under their robes. The amplified echoes of the commencement speakers sounded like the lineup announcements at a ballpark. I saw my mother among the thousands of well-wishers, holding a bouquet. My father worked his way through the crowd to her. I had been drinking cognac all semester and was convinced that it made me more perceptive. Watching the two of them greet each other with a polite hug, I thought of how these two lonely people had come together briefly and produced another lonely person, who might go on to produce yet another lonely person some day.

My parents had separated when I was seven. My father had been a draftsman at Hughes Tool. Now he dealt "Hold 'em" at Hollywood Park. He lived in a studio in Venice over an alley where homeless people squabbled day and night. I didn't see a lot of him and whenever I did I was worried by our resemblance. I was skinny and dark-haired like him. I had tried bulking up with weights and protein shakes, but my body rejected muscles like they were foreign transplants. He was an alcoholic and I wondered if my taste for booze was more genetic than literary.

He gave me an envelope with five hundreds in it. His hands were trembling and he looked down to hide his bleary eyes. My mom stood there with a long-suffering look.

"All these big corporations have booths," he said. "You oughta line something up."

"There's this program, Teaching For America," I said. "You sign up for two years and they send you to teach in inner-city schools."

He looked at me bleakly. "How much do they pay?"

"Fourteen-five to start. It goes to seventeen the next year."

"You can't live on that."

"He's not doing it for the money," my mom said, speaking slowly, as if explaining to a child. "He wants to do something constructive."

He turned away from her and appealed to me. "These programs are bogus. They don't care about these people. They have Mexicans to do their jobs for half the price, with no benefits."

"That's a terrible thing to say," my mother said.

My father threw up his hands in a hopeless gesture.

Limbo, Texas

I wanted to go to Bed Stuy in Brooklyn, but they needed people in Houston. Hurricane Katrina had dumped thousands of New Orleans kids into the school system. Crime and violence had surged.

"Houston is the best place to test your commitment," the recruiter told us.

We would undergo twelve weeks of intensive training in order to be ready for the start of the school year in September. They found us cheap apartments on the fringe of the Fifth Ward, the ghetto, where we would be teaching. I was in a low-slung two-story complex that had a rickety stairway leading up to a common balcony. The apartments were like warrens, one little room leading to another—sooty blinds, rust stains in the bathtub. There were a few students, but mostly it was Mexican families, illegals jammed ten to a room. Early in the morning you could hear doors slamming and motors coughing as they went to work. An obese white lady, who wore housedresses and flopped around in mules, dealt crack at the other end of the balcony. We had five people living in four bedrooms with one bathroom. Three guys had their own rooms and two girls shared. People came and went all night long. The crackheads broke into our cars and stole our radios.

I had never been out of California in my life and was a total weather wimp. Houston was like a pizza oven. It grabbed me in a bear hug as soon as I walked out the door, squeezing the breath out of me. We put up thick shades to block the sun and keep our neighbors from looking inside. There was an ancient, shuddering air-conditioner in the living room. We kept the casement windows tightly shut to keep in the AC, but the cool air seemed to stop at my bedroom threshold. After a night of drinking, it felt as if I had a cement block on my chest.

I hit the college hangouts in Rice Village looking for a night job, but they only used waitresses and every busboy was a Mexican. After getting turned down in six bars with a Dos Equis in every one, I bitched to a manager, "If they ever close the border this city will be buried under a pile of dirty dishes."

He was a big guy with slicked-back black hair and a cut-off work shirt to display his guns. He shook my hand in a big soft grip. "I'm Steve," he said. "I need an English speaker to work the door."

"I'm Peter, and I'm not a bouncer."

"Just take money and keep out the single guys. Anything physical goes down I've got three linemen from the University of Houston."

Old campus habits died hard. Thursday was still party night, even for people who had to make it to work Friday morning. I sat on a barstool at the door taking money, checking IDs and stamping hands. Two of Steve's linemen shouldered through the crowd, silencing the rowdies. Rory, a moon-faced hulk from a ranch in Abilene loomed up behind me if anyone got out of line. They paid me fifty bucks a night, plus a burger and a going-off drink. Somebody always had some funky weed that gave me palpitations on the first puff. After hours, we'd go to all-night taco joints and watch the drunks battle in the parking lots. At four in the morning it would cool off as the breeze brought the dew from the bayous. But I'd wake at nine in a hot sweat, anxious from dreams I couldn't remember.

The Worst Night of My Life Begins

B eer seemed like a good idea on the humid days. It was cool going down, but a few hours later it started to percolate into blurry waves of steam. Beer took all the fun out of weed, like dousing a fire down to acrid smoke.

One day on the bus going to class, I noticed American flags fluttering off the office buildings. It was the July Fourth weekend. I had been in Houston for six weeks, one day following another with no sense of time passing.

A burly blond guy in an army uniform was standing outside my building when I came home. The sun glinted off the steel frames of his glasses. He smiled pleasantly at my curious glance.

"Lost my parade," he said.

The bar was frantic that night. Steve had formed a line. They were coming at me one-by-one. Five dollars. Stamp the hand. Next . . .

High school girls, all dolled up, flirted and teased, trying to get in with phony proof. There were scuffles inside—stools toppling, glasses smashing. Cursing, red-faced drunks swung wildly as the bouncers shoved them out.

I took a few tokes and a shot of Patrón. It felt like my heart was going to explode in my chest

A face rose up. "Hi, Peter."

It took me a second. Those black eyes boring into me. She seemed out of breath, as if she'd been running. "Don't I get a kiss?"

Before I could answer, she wrapped her arms around my neck, lips cool against my throat. There were whoops and whistles. Somebody yelled, "Get a room, you're holding up the line."

She was wearing floppy jeans and a man's white shirt. She thrust a five at me. I pushed it back.

"No, no, it's okay . . . Steve, this is Hannah."

"Go on in, Hannah," Steve said.

She put her mouth to my ear. "You're not tutoring anyone else, are you?"

"What are you doing here?"

"Long story."

They took her to a spot at the end of the bar, where all the friends of the staff congregated. I got distracted dealing with another rush. When I got a chance to turn back, she was hunched over the bar staring into a pink cocktail.

"No day-dreamin' on my party time, dude."

First thing I saw was the blue NYFD T-shirt. He had a black NYPD cap on backwards, but didn't look like a cop or a patriot. He was big and rangy, towering over me, and I'm six-one. Tattoos crawled up his arms to his neck—knives, snakes, grinning heads. He had matted dirty blond hippie hair down to his shoulders, green eyes glittering, a thin, braided beard dropping from the cleft in his chin onto his chest. He wasn't Southern. Maybe one of those California boys who had dropped out of high school to go surfing.

"It's couples-only tonight," I said. "No single males."

"That's sexual discrimination."

He wasn't drunk and he wasn't kidding.

"What if two guys come up and say they're a couple? You gonna let them in?"

I struggled to keep my voice from breaking. "Sorry, man, house rules. You can wait for the manager."

"I ain't talkin' to the manager, I'm talkin' to *you*." He smelled of soap and mouthwash. It was scarier than if he had stunk of booze.

"Couples only," I repeated, hoping I didn't have that pleading look you got with a bully.

He raised his hand so quickly I flinched. He smirked and patted my shoulder. "Okay, son." He turned with a wink at the people behind him. "I guess a good-looking dude like me can find himself a date, huh?"

The crowd parted to let him through. No props for me. Nobody thought I had backed him down.

Steve showed up with a guilty look. "Everything cool?"

Rory was suddenly back, too, and real belligerent. Pushing people away from the door, daring the college kids to start something.

Hannah was still hunched over, staring into her pink drink like she hadn't moved.

It was like nothing had happened. But when I turned, the Nightmare was back in my face. "I'm legal now, dude."

He was with one of those dolled-up high school girls. She was so loaded he had to hold her around the waist to keep her from falling. "Like you to meet my fiancée," he said with an exaggerated redneck twang.

I took his crumpled ten and tried to cover with sarcasm. "I hope you two are very happy together."

"We're plannin' on it," he said.

As soon as he got inside, he put her down and walked away. "Hey," she called. She bounced off a few people, then fell flat on her face. The two linemen carried her out by her armpits.

Next thing I knew he was at the end of the bar, standing over Hannah. He seemed to be talking to her, but I couldn't tell. She just kept staring into her drink until he stepped back into the darkness.

The Snatch

L ast call was chaos. Everybody rushed the bar screaming for drinks, then spilled out into the streets looking for the next party. The Houston cops cruised by checking for drunks to "de-key." You had to be comatose to get their attention. Shrieking on two wheels out of the parking lot didn't count. Neither did mooning or baring your boobs or puking into the potted plants in the mall.

I fought against the flow, looking for Hannah. There was a line outside the ladies room. Two silhouettes were rising out of a booth.

It was the Nightmare. He had Hannah. She lunged at me, sloppy drunk and slurring. "Save me from this lady-killer, Peter. He slipped something into my drink."

"I slipped another drink into your drink, honey," the Nightmare said.

My knees were shaking, "Do you want to go with him, Hannah?" I asked.

"Well, that's the stupidest question in the world," she said. "Of course not, you silly goof." She fell on me, wrapping her arms around my shoulders, pressing her soft lips into my neck. "I want to go with you."

I took a breath and faced him. "It is what it is, man," I said. "You can total me, I guess, and try to drag her out, but there's people all over the place."

The Nightmare shook his head, unconcerned. "Bitch is trouble, brother. Cut her loose. I ain't never gonna fight over no bitch. I won't even get my hands dirty. It's about you and me now."

"I don't have a beef with you," I said.

He looked almost sad. "You do now, baby."

Little Blue Bug

Hannah was in a drooling doze. Steve looked her over with an expert's eye. "He roofied her."

I had never heard the word, but made a good guess. "Date rape drug?"

"Yeah." He shook her gently. "She'll sleep it off, but she'll be sick as a dog in the morning. Don't count on gettin' much. Even if you didn't do it they get into this attitude where they feel like they've been violated."

I put Hannah's arm around my shoulder and picked her up. Her head lolled back. "My hero."

"Do you have a car?"

"My beautiful periwinkle Bug. It's a chick car, Peter, but it's a stick. A chick stick. Do you have a chick stick?"

"That dude is a jailbird," Rory said. "See that Harley tat on his neck. That's the biker's symbol. Means you killed somebody."

"I never heard that," one of the linemen said.

"It's true," Rory said. "My uncle was a guard at Pelican Bay prison in California. The bikers run every jail they're in, he says."

"That's the Aryan Brotherhood, man."

"Same thing," Rory said. "You mess with a guy with that secret sign, you get the whole gang on your ass."

Steve pointed to a blue Volkswagen under a light. "That it?"

Hannah lifted her head. "My little blue Bug."

I propped her against the car and found the keys in her pocket. I slid her into the front seat. I had only driven a stick shift once in my life, a Honda Civic. I started the car, trying to remember the gear sequence. Push for first, pull for second, up and to the side for third, and pull for fourth.

Outside, the guys were watching me.
Be calm, I told myself. Be calm.

Home Invasion

The date-rape drug had been big with the jocks and the frat boys. They just wanted to knock chicks out so they could get their rocks off and take videos. But we English majors were romantics in the great tradition of Lord Byron. We wanted poetry and communion while we got our rocks off and took videos.

I parked in the supermarket lot next to my building and tried to shake Hannah awake. "Gotta get up now."

I opened the door and pulled her out by her feet. She had a lumpy backpack and a big Nike traveling bag bursting at the seams. "This weighs a ton. What do you have in here?"

"Shoes."

I had to fireman-carry her up the stairs. Every light was off along the balcony.

The apartment was dark. My roommates had gone with a group to South Padre Island for the weekend. I had never bothered to set up my bed, just dropped the mattress on the dusty floor. The room smelled of dirty socks. I apologized.

"Sorry for the mess." She waved, irritably. When you're that drunk, you don't want to talk or listen. I knew this, but couldn't shut up. "You can take the boy out of the dorm, but you can't take the dorm out of the boy." She collapsed on the unmade mattress and drew her legs up in the fetal position.

I lay down next to her. "Do you want to take your clothes off?"

She groaned. "Later . . . I've been driving for days."

Her hand was as soft and warm as I remembered it. I lay in the darkness, listening to her breathe.

I don't know how much time passed. I could have dozed off, or maybe I was awake all the time. I just slowly became aware of the voices. Maybe I had been hearing them all along. People came and went all night long. But these voices were constant, as if they were standing outside my door.

It had to be those dumb crackheads. They must have seen everybody leaving for the weekend and thought the apartment was empty.

I eased off the mattress and out into the living room. Shadows were mingling behind the shades. I couldn't tell if there were two or three.

The doorknob turned. There was a scraping sound, as if somebody were trying to lift the lock with a credit card.

I took out my phone to call 911, but the battery was dead. My knees were shaking so bad I could hardly stand. If they got in they wouldn't turn around and say, "sorry man, we thought nobody was home." They would stay and tie us up. And then kill us so we couldn't identify them.

I wanted to yell, "Get the fuck outta here. I'm calling the cops," but my mouth was dead dry.

They were coming in.

I ducked into the kitchen and grabbed a steak knife. Snatched a frying pan with somebody's burnt breakfast off the stove. A hand came out of the shadow and punched at the casement window. The glass tinkled onto the floor. Another hand came through, reaching for the window handle.

I grasped the knife tightly and stabbed through the shade. Caught a knuckle and heard a gasp. Stabbed harder. Once . . . twice. Warm blood trickled down the back of my hand. A shadow loomed. I swung the frying pan and sent it crashing through the window, yelling, "I'm getting my gun, mother-fuckers!"

There was a low growl of rage. Something crashed against the door and the room shook like in an earthquake. There were hurried footsteps along the balcony and down the steps.

"No!"

Hannah was standing in my bedroom doorway pressing her hands against her temples, as if she were trying to push the skin off her face.

"It's okay, they're gone, Hannah," I said.
"No!" She screamed.
And kept screaming until the cops came.

A Major Case

T he first cops to arrive looked like theater majors in a student film. They walked all over the crime scene, crunching the broken glass. I had a gash on my palm, which I had wrapped in a bloody paper towel, but they didn't call an ambulance. Hannah was hunched over on my mattress, staring blankly. One of the cops went in to get a statement "She's in shock," I told him, and he backed away with a frightened look.

A Sergeant showed up, a heavyset black guy with sweat stains on his tunic. He berated the rookies for not calling the paramedics, then sent them for yellow crime-scene tape.

He took my statement down in a dog-eared notebook, looking me in the eye as if trying to catch me in a lie.

"You know these people?"

"Don't think so."

"What do you mean you don't think so?"

"I never really saw their faces."

"You were close enough to stab one of 'em."

"It was dark and the shade was down. They were just shadows."

"Why do you think they picked your place?"

"I guess they thought nobody was home."

"Do you keep a lot of money around?"

"I don't have any money," I said.

"Anything else they might be after?"

He was talking about drugs. He thought somebody was dealing out of the house. He was like the campus cops. We called them "square badges." They'd show up to a party, handcuff us and make us stand outside while they searched our rooms. "Looking for a big seizure?" we'd jeer.

"It's better to tell me," the sergeant said, "because if we

find something we can charge you with obstruction."

"Search my room if you want," I said.

He gave me a sharp look. "Are you giving me permission?"

"You can't use nothin' you find in a warrantless search," a voice behind me said.

A big man was taking up the whole doorway, his face obscured in the shadows.

The sergeant kept his eyes on me. "Man's giving me permission."

"Man's home is invaded and his girlfriend sent into a catatonic state," the big man said. "You could find a ton of heroin under the bed and the search would be thrown out." He stepped into the room. "I'm Detective McVickers, Major Case Squad," he said to me. "You Mr. Peter Vogel?"

His face was red and puffy and pocked with acne scars. He wore his light hair long and slick. It was two AM on a suffocating night, but he was cool in a light-colored suit, blue shirt and red tie, like he had tried to dress for the Fourth. The only signs of the heat were the few damp strands of hair plastered against the back of his neck over his collar. He pointed to a chunky man in a HOUSTON PD windbreaker, prowling the balcony. "That's my associate, Detective Herrera. You need to post some people in the parking area," he said to the sergeant.

"I've only got two men," the sergeant said.

"Get some more bodies over here, then." McVickers stepped into the light. His eyes were the color of faded dungarees. "It's been a busy Fourth, Mr. Vogel—drunk drivers and brawling and whatnot. Did you call for an ambulance, sergeant?"

"Soon as I got here."

"Better call for another one when you get outside."

The sergeant lowered his eyes and brushed by me as he went to the door.

McVickers came closer, squinting like he was trying to get me into focus. A mound of belly poked out of his suit jacket. He put a heavy hand on my elbow. "Step out here with me for a second."

"I don't think I should leave my friend alone."

He looked back at Hannah, squatting on the mattress, staring at the wall. "We'll send an officer in to watch her." He pulled me along, gently. "Come on," he said in a confidential whisper. "I want to show you something."

The building manager had shown up. He was a hugely fat guy, fatter than the lady who sold crack, and white as a ghost in a soiled white shirt.

He labored up the steps with a resentful look. "Tomorrow's a holiday," he said. "We won't be able to replace the window until Tuesday."

"I've got all my stuff in there. What if they come back?"

"Don't worry, Mr. Vogel," McVickers said. "I'll have an officer on guard here tonight."

My thumb started to shake. I was falling apart, but I didn't want this cop to see it. I put my hand behind my back and tried to cover with a wisecrack. "This isn't much of a major case."

McVickers gave me a closed mouth smile. "Oh, it'll do."

In the Dumpster

The sergeant was kneeling over something on the steps.

"Give us a minute," McVickers said. The sergeant got up and stepped aside. McVickers shone his pencil-flash on a roll of black duct tape.

"Home invader's tool of the trade, Peter," he said, switching to my first name. "They were fixin' to tie you up and spend some time in your place lookin' for somethin'."

I thought of all those slasher films with victims writhing helplessly in duct tape before they were horribly murdered. "But there's nothing to find," I said.

"Just 'cause this is Houston don't mean these people are rocket scientists. They go to the wrong places all the time." McVickers crouched on the step, bouncing easily on the balls of his feet like a catcher. "So far there's nothin' unusual goin' on here. Even if they had gotten in and killed you and your girlfriend, it wouldn't be unusual, I hate to say."

He grabbed the banister and pulled himself up with a groan. "Gettin' old. Gotta find me an easier way to make a living."

He shone the light on the next step. There were dark spots leading all the way down to the ground. "Blood, we call it spatter in the trade. Looks like you cut these boys pretty good."

"I barely scratched one guy's hand," I said.

He tilted his head at me. "Don't take much. I once saw a guy with a buttock wound bleed to death in the ER while everybody was laughin' at him for gettin' shot in the ass. He was laughin' harder than everyone else, and then all of a sudden his eyes went up in his head."

Detective Herrera was walking a path in the parking lot.

The two rookies followed him, laying out crime scene tape.

"Stop sightseein' and get that list of tenants," McVickers said.

Herrera gave him a left-handed salute. "Okay, *jefe.*"

At the end of the lot was a clump of bushes. McVickers held the flash between us, so we could see each other's faces.

"Had a lot of experience with the police, Peter?"

"The usual . . . Traffic stops, wild parties . . ."

"Ever been arrested?"

"No."

"Ever do anything wrong?"

"You mean criminal?"

"That's a harsh word. Let's just say somethin' that's illegal today, but won't be tomorrow."

My heart started to thump and flutter. "Then I'll wait until tomorrow to do it," I said. I couldn't see his dungaree eyes in the dark.

"What's behind those bushes?" he asked.

"A supermarket."

I followed him through a dusty thicket of dead shrubs, the branches scratching my face. We came out in an alley behind the supermarket. It was a place where the homeless foraged and slept. Blankets, bottles and fast food wrappers were scattered on the ground.

McVickers lifted the lid of a dumpster. There was a body half buried in the trash. McVickers shone his flash down on the face. "Know this boy?"

He was one of those runty crack-heads who were always outside the fat lady's apartment, sitting on the steps or knocking at her door. Without knowing why, I decided to lie and shook my head. "No."

"Killer cut his throat. Almost beheaded him." He dropped the lid with a crash. "Propped him up against the side here. See the spatter pattern? Then *swoosh*, slashed him. The boy slumped, head hanging off his neck. Killer left him and came over here." McVickers walked into a dark space between the dumpsters. Lying on the ground, his feet drawn up like he was trying to crawl away, was a Mexican kid I had seen around the building. He had a thick, jagged gash on the back of his neck. His shirt was dark with blood.

"Know him, Peter?"

I shook my head again.

"This boy tried to run. The killer backhanded him, you can tell by the wound." McVickers pointed to a blotch on the ground. "He goes down and starts to crawl away. But the killer don't slash him again. He knows that boy ain't goin' nowhere. Knows he's gonna bleed to death. So he comes back and tosses the white boy into the dumpster. He's gonna throw the other kid in, too, but sees a pile of rags stirrin' in the corner. A wino sleepin' it off. He turns and walks back through the bushes. Pretty cool killer. Ever seen a dead body before, Peter?"

"Never," I said.

"Feel like you wanna throw up?"

"No." I wasn't sick. I wasn't repelled or fascinated. I wasn't feeling anything. But my arm was shaking and I couldn't stop it.

Hannah Won't Go

A police car sat in the parking lot, lights flashing. McVickers opened the back door so I could sit down. I saw dents and scratches in the bullet-proof shield.

"Somebody really put up a fight," I said.

"Nobody ever wants to get into a police car," he said. "Not even a policeman."

He started giving orders. "Turn them lights off. Canvass the building. Get this boy a bottle of water." He stood over me, his jacket open over his big gut, his gun jammed into his belt, and shook my knee gently. "What's the lady's name, Peter?"

"Hannah Seeley."

"She your girlfriend?"

"I knew her at school. She just drove in tonight."

"So, these boys couldn't have been after something they thought she had."

"No . . . Nobody knows she's here. I didn't even know she was coming."

The cops had everybody out on the balcony. The fat lady was blocking her doorway, arms folded, snarling at Herrera: "I don't have to let nobody in my house without a warrant."

The Mexicans were huddled in their rooms. They knew somebody was going to be taken away for something. "Everybody has to come outside," the cops were saying. "*Todo el mundo aqui, ahorita.*" Their Texas drawls seemed to get thicker when they spoke Spanish.

They had closed off my apartment with yellow tape. There was a cop standing by my broken window. As we walked in, Herrera came out of one of my roommate's bedrooms. He nodded at McVickers. "Uh-huh, yeah."

"I thought you said you couldn't search the apartment," I said.

"This isn't a search," McVickers said. "It's a canvass of the crime scene to make sure one of the perpetrators isn't hiding inside."

A policewoman with the buff, breastless look of a body-builder stood, arms folded, outside my room. "The young lady refuses to get into the ambulance, sir," she said.

I went in and sat down next to Hannah. Her hands were ice cold.

"It's over," I said. "It was some neighborhood crack-heads who thought nobody was home." I decided to leave out the part about the dead guys.

She looked at my hand. "You cut yourself."

She blinked as if she was going to burst into tears.

"Hannah, you should go to the hospital," I said.

"I'm not going anywhere with them."

McVickers stood in the doorway, hands on hips.

"You'll have to come down to headquarters in the morning," he said. "We need to know a lot more about what happened here."

He stepped away without a "good night." Footsteps, a jumble of voices, motors starting and the caravan of police cars pulled out. Doors slammed. The balcony was empty except for the lonely cop outside my window. In the parking lot, another cop guarded the path of yellow tape that led to dumpsters. The red-and-blue ambulance lights blinked behind the bushes as they took the bodies away. Then it was quiet.

When I turned off the lights the apartment got so dark I had to feel my way into the bedroom. Then I realized the bad guys had taken the bulbs out of the lights outside the apartment. They had really planned this thing out.

I lay down next to Hannah. "Welcome to Houston."

"I brought trouble with me as usual," she said.

"Hurricane Hannah."

She turned over and put her head on my shoulder. "I missed your silly jokes."

Her body was warm against mine. She put her arm around me and we hugged, my lips pressed against her forehead. "Did you think about me every day?" I asked.

"Every day," she murmured. "Sometimes twice a day."

"I thought about you."

I slid down and nuzzled her. For weeks I had been looking at Texas girls, blonde, tan and all done up. I had forgotten that she never wore perfume or much makeup. Never really did anything to make herself attractive. "I haven't been with another girl since I last saw you," I said. Was that the right thing to say? Women didn't like guys who couldn't get other women.

But Hannah hadn't heard me anyway. She was fast asleep.

Weird News

had forgotten to draw the shades and woke up with the sun glaring on my face. Blood was seeping through the bandage the paramedics had slapped on me. Hannah was asleep with a pillow over her head.

My roommates had returned. They had flattened a cardboard box and put it in the broken window. The girls were spraying the flies that had come in during the night.

They stared in amazement as I told them what had happened.

"That's it, I'm out of here," Donna (Communications Major from Mt. Holyoke) said to her friend Naomi, (Women's Studies, Berkley).

Mike (Event Planning, Arizona State), came out of his room. He was a weed-brain who had taken an instant dislike to me. "My bong is gone, man. I thought you said those dudes didn't come inside."

"They didn't. The cops must have taken it."

"The cops? Did they search our rooms?"

"I think they thought we were big time drug dealers and had kilos of shit," I said.

My other roommate, Andrew (Divinity, SMU), came out of his room carrying a pistol that was right out of a Western movie, with a long silver barrel and an ivory handle. "They didn't take this."

"They took Mike's bong, but left your gun?" Donna said.

"Firearms are legal in Texas," he said, soberly.

Donna looked at Naomi. "I am *so* out of here."

My cell phone rang. I didn't remember charging it.

It was Detective Herrera. "I'm downstairs, Mr. Vogel."

The girls promised they would stay with Hannah, but warned me to be back by sundown. "We're not spending the night in this place."

Herrera sat behind the wheel of a black Crown Victoria. He wore a short-sleeved shirt with hula girls and coconut palms. He had small hands with stubby fingers at the end of thick, hairy forearms. His hairline began about two inches above his thick, black brows. He had the AC on high, but there were still beads of sweat on his forehead.

"Hot enough for you?" he asked. "Wait'll we get into hurricane season. You'll miss this weather."

Police headquarters was in a steel-and-glass skyscraper downtown on Travis Street. The cop at the door nodded to Herrera, but made me walk through the metal detector. There was a black kid in handcuffs standing by the newsstand, people rushing by him without a look. I got in the elevator with attorneys rummaging in brown legal folders, cops with badges drooping out of their pockets.

We got off at the Robbery Squad. A fat lady cop bulging out of an electric blue pantsuit got up from a desk. "I'm Detective Willis, Mr. Vogel," she said. Her buttocks bobbling, she led me down a line of cubicles, past large men in shirtsleeves, holsters hanging from coat racks, staring into computer screens.

McVickers was in a conference room at the coffee maker. In the daylight his red face was even more chewed up with acne potholes. He gave me a second look, too, as if he were seeing something he hadn't noticed in the dark.

"Cop coffee," he said, pouring it into a Houston PD cup. "Take a pot that hasn't been washed for weeks, put in three pouches instead of one and let it sit all night. Use this artificial sweetener, which causes cancer in rats. Drink it for twenty years, along with a coupla thousand Taco Cabana burritos and about a million cigarettes, and you won't live long enough to collect your pension, which is exactly what the City of Houston wants."

He shoved a manila envelope across the table at me. "Sure you don't know these boys?" Inside were stark black-and-white morgue photos. The gashes on the boys' necks were black and thick like Magic Marker lines.

"The Mexican kid lived downstairs from you," Mc-Vickers said. "The white boy was always around that crack lady's house, neighbors told us."

"I never made eye contact with the people outside that lady's door," I said. I pretended to look at the Mexican kid again. "This kid looks like so many other people in the complex. Maybe I saw him. I don't know."

McVickers gave me a long look, like he wanted me to know he knew I was lying. "You can always tell what a murder victim was thinking in his last moments," he said. "Check out the white kid's eyes. Watchful, but not scared, like somebody just called him and he's lookin' over his shoulder. Now look at our Mexican friend. Eyes bulgin', he's shittin' his pants. That tells me the white boy was taken by surprise. He knew his killer and wasn't afraid. The Mexican kid saw him get it and tried to run. You still say you don't know nothin' about this?"

"Yes."

"We'll see about that." He closed the door and came toward me, fists clenched. Then stopped and laughed. "Had you goin', huh? You thought I was gonna pull a Guantanamo . . . I just wanted some privacy." He took a crumpled box of Marlboros out of his pocket. "We're not supposed to smoke in this building. But my mind don't work without tobacco. A coupla lines of coke would get the old brain in gear, just like Sherlock Holmes."

"I wouldn't know," I said.

"Or meth. That shit really gets the sparks flyin'."

He was trying to sucker me. It was so obvious it was scary, but that was the point. He had the power. He didn't have to be slick.

"We're getting a lot more cases of college kids bringin' meth up from Mexico," he said. "My daughter's in her freshman year at TCU. DEA broke up a ring there that was directly connected to the Mexican Mafia in Cancun. You believe that? *Texas Christian University*."

McVickers sucked his cigarette, burning through nearly half of it with one long puff. "Hate to see that, Peter," he said. "A nice white boy goes to jail, he could find out some things about himself he coulda gone a lifetime without knowing. You know how the rap goes: Better be a Nazi, a nigger, or a *narco-trafficante* if you wanna survive in a federal penitentiary. I'm not about lockin' up the wrong folks, even if they do break a rule. I know who prison is for, Peter."

He had me pegged as an amateur drug dealer. He was like those campus square badges.

"I have to get back home," I said. "I left my friend with my roommates and they have to leave."

"Oh, yeah, Hannah Seeley. Know her long?"

"Six months."

"Not your fiancée or anything like that?"

"Nothing like that."

"She just showed up without calling."

"Just dropped in."

"Guess I'm old fashioned, but I just can't see how you can be friends with a woman if you're not bangin' her, excuse my French." He stared glumly out of the window. "My daughter says I'm a fossil. She says it was my sexist attitudes that broke up my marriage to her mom." He turned and squinted, like he had forgotten who I was for a moment. "Sorry, Peter, I went off into my own world."

There was a soft knock. McVickers slipped the lit cigarette into a desk drawer.

Detective Willis peeked in. "You'll wanna see this," she said and handed him a printout. "Somethin' burnin' in here?" she asked with a wink at me.

McVickers looked at the printout and put it in his desk drawer. He took out a legal pad. "Just wanna do a timeline, Peter, okay? Let's go back to yesterday afternoon. Where were you?"

"In my room reading," I said. "We were supposed to have class, but they canceled because everybody was going away for the Fourth."

"Later, you went to work at the bar."

"Right."

"Then about midnight, Miss Seeley came in."

"Right."

"Anything happen after that?"

"Nothing really," I said. "The usual drunks. One real scary wacko."

"Why scary?"

"Just a big guy with a lot of tattoos. The motorcycle wheel on the neck, which some of the guys said was a jailhouse thing."

McVickers nodded and started writing.

"What did he do?"

"Tried to bull his way in alone and it was couples only. Then, he grabbed some drunken girl and we had to let him in. At the end of the night he tried to leave with Hannah. I think he slipped her something."

"What did he look like?"

"Blond ponytail. Big, about six-five maybe. Thin braid of beard hanging down from his chin. He wore an FDNY cap and NYPD sweatshirt. Really overdoing the patriotic thing."

"Right," McVickers said. He lit a fresh cigarette off the old one and dropped the butt into the dregs of his coffee. Then he sat back and watched the smoke dribble through his fingers. "How much do you know about your girlfriend?"

"She's not my girlfriend," I said.

He blew a smoke ring. It hovered like skywriting in the dead air. Sweat glistened in the potholes on his face. "Did you ever hear of Arnold Seeley?" he asked.

The name nagged like an itch at the back of my mind.

"He was a serial killer," McVickers said. "Took out eleven women in California in the '90s. Tied 'em up, raped 'em, tortured them, then choked them to death with an article of their clothing. Wrote taunting letters to the police."

I guessed it was coming, but when he said it my heart thumped anyway.

"Your girlfriend Hannah is his daughter."

The bottom dropped out of my gut. "She's *not* my girl-friend," was all I could say.

McVickers rummaged through his desk. "Miss Seeley dropped her driver's license. Detective Herrera found it on the floor of your room and we looked her up."

He slid Hannah's license across the table. "Funny she didn't tell you who she was."

"Why should she?" I said. "It's not like her dad won the Nobel Peace Prize."

He gave me that squinty close-mouthed smile again. "Can't choose your parents. I got a daughter who'll tell ya that. But if Hannah didn't tell you about her dad, there might be other things she's hidin'."

"Like what?"

"Like maybe this big psycho was after her all along. Maybe he followed you home and got those two crackheads to help him bust into your place. Then killed 'em when it went south."

"That's pretty farfetched."

"Farfetched," McVickers said. "Nice word."

McVickers stubbed out his cigarette. "Homicide's a big deal in this town, Peter. They want you to solve murders right quick, so people will feel safe and keep spendin' at the Galleria. You give me somethin' that'll help solve this, I'll keep you out of it."

"I've told you everything I know," I said.

He got up slowly and hitched his pants up over his gut. "You don't have to get your ass in trouble protectin' some-body who's not bein' honest with you."

"I'm not protecting anybody."

He held out a blue card with an embossed shield over his name: *Detective Sergeant John McVickers, Major Case Squad, Houston Police Department.* "You're in my world now, Peter," he said. "Try not to stay too long."

A Happy Family

Herrera was at the elevator, twirling his car keys. "Is there a library or an Internet café around here?" I asked.

He poked his head into Detective Willis's cubicle. "Can Mr. Vogel use your computer?"

"Sure can." She came out, struggling into her jacket. "I'm goin' to lunch. No porn, now."

"Like you couldn't recommend a few sites," Herrera said.

And they laughed walking down the hall.

The chair was still warm from her ass. I Googled *Arnold Seeley*. He was on 117,000 sites. I wasn't ready for the gory story, so I went to Page 10 and found a site that said: ROBBINSGATE . . . SEELEY REELECTED . . .

Arnold Seeley's Google history went back to before anyone knew he was a sex murderer. This story was from the *Redlands Courier*, announcing his reelection to a third consecutive term as Chief Compliance Officer of Robbinsgate, California. "A Compliance Officer is employed by towns and small municipalities to ensure compliance with local ordinances, covering everything from construction codes to unleashed pets."

Robbinsgate had begun as a garden apartment complex built on two subdivisions in the '60s, but had grown on foreclosed farmland into an incorporated town with a K-12 school system, a mall and a "thriving religious community," the story announced.

Mayor Fran Leonard was quoted as saying that Arnold Seeley was "the kind of public servant every young city needs." He and his wife Rose were active members of St. Paul's Lutheran. A Navy veteran, Arnold was a deacon of the church. Rose was Treasurer of the Parents Association. Their daughter Hannah was the star forward of the Robbinsgate High girls soccer team. Rachel, their youngest, played the flute in the marching band.

In Seeley's acceptance speech, he said: "I don't see myself as a policeman, but a guardian, protecting the quality of life in a town I love."

But according to some other stories, he soon became a feared and hated man. People dreaded seeing his black Tundra on their block. He measured hedges with a ruler and gave out violations if they were an inch too high. He cited homeowners who didn't take in their trash containers after collection, and would disallow building permits for the smallest infraction. Once, he wouldn't even let a family give a birthday party for their cancer-stricken son because the tent they wanted to put up was too close to the fence and didn't give "proper egress in case of fire."

One woman had a Golden Retriever who kept running away. Seeley had caught the dog in a snare and taken it away to be "put down." She recalled her daughter's hysterical screams and how her husband had left work and rushed to the pound just as Seeley was taking it to be gassed. He wouldn't release the dog until they had paid triple the fine.

Another woman said Seeley had prowled around her house for weeks, collecting specimens of dried turds to prove that her Siamese was slipping out at night. Now she shuddered to realize that his prowling might have had a more sinister intent.

There was a story about a young woman who had sued Robbinsgate for wrongful termination, saying that Seeley had verbally abused her, lied on her employee evaluations and locked her in her office during lunch to make her finish a job. On the stand she told a chilling story about how he closed the door of his office one day and walked toward her "like a zombie," she said, "his eyes all red and weird" until she screamed and he let her out.

Robbinsgate settled with her for five-hundred-thousand

dollars. Millions of dollars were paid out to the families when it was established that Seeley had used city files to get his victims' addresses and a city vehicle to stalk them. The city had declared bankruptcy. The Office of Compliance had been shut down.

I couldn't postpone it any longer. I clicked on the *LA Times* story: SERIAL KILLER PLEADS GUILTY. There was a photo of Seeley in an orange jump suit, manacled and shackled, a slight, balding, goateed middle-aged man dwarfed between two paunchy court officers. He wasn't big, didn't look strong. You had to wonder how he had overpowered all these women.

He stood before the judge and said "Guilty," in a "clear calm voice" as the bailiff read off the names of the victims. The families were in court, but the judge admonished them to stay silent during this phase, promising, "you'll have your chance to speak."

The prosecutor read excerpts from Seeley's confession. His father had been a school bus driver, his mother a beautician. After they divorced, he was sent to stay with his grandparents on their small farm in Wisconsin. One day he saw his grandmother in the barn wringing the necks of chickens. The image of the chickens squawking and struggling in her merciless grasp excited him to masturbation that night, and stayed in his mind.

Had that brief scene in the barn been enough to ignite Seeley's latent fantasies? Was that all it took to create a monster who would bring so much misery into the world?

Seeley called his murders "seductions" and divided them into three stages. The first was what he called *love at first sight*. He would see a woman and suddenly feel an *urge*. Age wasn't a factor. One of his victims had been sixty-one, another only eleven. He couldn't explain what drew him to his victims, only that it was instant and powerful. He followed them home or to their schools or jobs, found out their names and then went into the next phase, which he called *foreplay*. He would stalk the women for weeks until he knew every minute of their daily routines.

Then came the final stage, what he called "the *consummation*."

Seeley had spent twenty years working for a company that made alarms and he knew how to disable any security system. His method would vary. Sometimes he would sneak into his victim's houses when they left and would be waiting when they came home. Or he would break in late at night and take them by surprise in their beds.

He had a venetian blind cord, a hunting knife, and a wooden chair leg in his Compliance Office backpack. He would put on latex gloves and threaten them with the knife, while explaining slowly and reasonably that if they let him fulfill his fantasies he would leave without harming them.

"People want to believe," he told police.

Most of his victims would let him tie them hand-and-foot. But there were those who struggled fiercely. He would beat them with the chair leg until they submitted or just passed out. One woman was getting the best of him, he said, but then her son came home. Seeley put the knife to the boy's throat and threatened to kill him unless she submitted. Then, he locked the boy in a closet. Later, he strangled him with the same stocking he had used on his mother.

Once he had his victims secured he would find an article of their clothing, a scarf or panty hose. He would choke them into unconsciousness, revive them and choke them again. At a certain point they would lose their fear, he said, thinking he was just going to choke them again. That's when he would double the knot and crouch over them, so he could see their faces at what he called *the exquisite moment*, when they realized that this time they were going to die.

When it was over he would masturbate with the scarf or panty hose and leave.

After his confession he led police to a trunk in his basement where they found the club, the gloves, the pieces of clothing he had used to kill, plus Polaroids he had taken of his victims and what he called *keepsakes*—small items like ashtrays or pencils or hair clips that he had taken to "remember them by."

Seeley terrorized the Robbinsgate area from '88 to '95. The local police were frustrated. They called in the FBI, psychics, *America's Most Wanted.*

Then the killings stopped. The media speculated that the murderer might have been a drifter who had moved on. Talking heads said that these psychopaths often outgrew their need to kill. The local sheriff, smarting from his failure, said the killer had sensed that they were on his trail and stopped out of fear of being caught.

But suddenly, ten years after the last murder, it happened again. Alexandra Baines, a high school senior, captain of the cheerleaders, star of the drama department was found in her bedroom, bound, gagged, and strangled. She had been attacked in her bed while her mother and brother were asleep in adjoining bedrooms. The murderer had gotten in through a French door leading into the house from the backyard. The house was wired, but a piece of tin foil secured with chewing gum had been placed over the electric eye, disabling the alarm. DNA tests on the gum revealed it had been chewed and discarded by the victim.

ROBBINSGATE RELIVES A NIGHTMARE, a headline read. "Carefully planned," the local news anchors stated, calling attention to the fact that the killer had stalked Alexandra and retrieved her chewing gum.

The news stations camped outside the house, pouncing on the neighbors for interviews. The family next door—the Seeleys—was particularly traumatized, the stories said. Alexandra Baines and Hannah Seeley had been inseparable friends since childhood. Hannah was the star of the girls soccer team. The week before, Alexandra had led a delegation to the Athletic Department, protesting that the squad only cheered for the boys teams and demanding that they be allowed to cheer when the girls team played in the regionals.

"We feel so helpless," Hannah's father, Arnold, had told Fox News. "Hannah lost her best friend. How do you bounce back from this?"

After a week the story died. But a day after the mobile units pulled out of town, they had to turn around to cover a bigger story. Arnold Seeley had been arrested.

In his confession Seeley said he was annoyed that the police hadn't made the obvious connection between the Baines murder and the earlier killings. He stole a laptop from the Town Clerk's office, which was just down the hall from the Compliance Department, hacked the password and went to the Starbucks to write another letter.

He was seen on surveillance cameras set up to catch credit card scammers using the WiFi. The cops weren't suspicious, but ran a routine check on the laptop and found a letter boasting of the murder and promising more.

They moved carefully. A detective obtained a pair of Hannah's soccer shorts from the high school athletic department. The DNA from the shorts matched samples taken from the victims' bodies. They matched that to the DNA on Seeley's Compliance Office coffee mug. Then they confronted Seeley with this evidence. He confessed in the police car on the way to the station.

Seeley told police he had been busy raising his daughters for the past ten years and had "lost the urge." But one day he was getting out of his car as "Zandy" Baines was coming out of her house. He had known her since childhood, but this time when their eyes met "it was love at first sight."

He murdered her two nights later.

Reporters described him as composed and matter of fact. In court, he faced the families of the victims calmly.

"It really wasn't me who did these things," he said. "I was like a robot when the urge came on me."

The spectators exploded. "He's trying to plead insanity!" and "Why are you letting him speak?" Jason Ardison, whose sixty-one-year-old mother had been Seeley's oldest victim, leapt over the banister at him. Seeley had given Ardison several summonses for late-night parties, and had threatened to reveal his gay lifestyle to his mother. "You did this to get back at me!" Ardison shrieked, delirious and sobbing. The judge had him removed and rebuked the gallery. "The accused has the right to address the court."

The next day the families had their turn. Relatives, friends, husbands, boyfriends, stood up to vent their hatred and grief. Each told of a beautiful person, of a life full of promise cruelly ended.

Alexandra Baines' mother was unable to speak.

Her older brother, Douglas, trembled so badly he had to grip the lectern for support. "I slept through my sister's murder," he said. "I could have saved her, but I was drunk and stoned like I was every night . . ." He had to stop and take a minute to compose himself. "So now I'd like to ask you, Mr. Seeley. Your daughter Hannah was best friends with Zandy. We used to joke about what a nosy bastard you were, peeking into people's trash and all. You knew about my problem with drugs and alcohol. You knew my sister had taken care of me, gone to meetings, researched a hundred different places and finally when they put me in lock up, given up her weekends for six months to visit me." At that point, he began to sob convulsively. His friends tried to lead him away, but he shook them off. "Tell me the truth, Mr. Seeley," he said. "When you were planning this, did you know I would be so strung out that I wouldn't be able to wake up to defend my sister? Did you know?"

The courtroom went dead quiet. All eyes turned to Seeley, who had been standing with his head bowed. He nodded slightly. "I knew," he said softly.

Sentencing was a formality. Everyone knew that Seeley had made a deal in which he agreed to plead guilty and make a public statement of contrition to spare the families the pain of a trial. His lawyer, Abner Fried, a famous civil liberties attorney, had driven a hard bargain, saying that Seeley would only plead guilty if his life were spared.

He was sentenced to eleven consecutive life terms to be served in isolation at Otter Point Prison, a maximum security institution that housed the most dangerous criminals in the state of California. He would be locked down 23 hours a day, with an hour alone in the exercise yard. He would be allowed no visitors, except his lawyer, no reading matter, other than the Bible. No TV, radio, or Internet.

Seeley's family was hardly mentioned in the trial stories. Because of death threats, neither his wife of twenty-five years nor his daughters had attended the trial.

But his pastor, the Reverend Manfred Kellner, had been at his side every day. "Arnold Seeley was my friend," Reverend Kellner told reporters. "I prayed with him for the victory of his daughter's soccer team. I looked up to him, sought his advice. I put him in charge of our counseling program, advising troubled families and young married couples. And all the while he was planning his evil crimes."

Reverend Kellner said that Arnold Seeley's arrest had been "the blackest day of my life." He had felt a deep sense of betrayal. "When I saw how much suffering this man had caused I questioned my belief in a just, merciful God. I cried out in hatred for bloody retribution.

"But the blackness passed and I came to realize that this was a test, not only for me, but for our community. Could we find comfort in faith? Could we heal and forgive?"

He urged the people of Robbinsgate to reach out to the Seeley family. "Let us not seek to appease our thirst for vengeance on the innocents." He organized vigils at the Seeley house. Nobody came. He invited Rose Seeley and her daughters, Hannah and Rachel, to Easter Services. But they had already left Robbinsgate. At a service covered by all the local stations, he lamented their absence. "Easter is a time when the basest elements of our human spirit—greed, betrayal, and murder—undergo a mystical transfiguration into resurrection and eternal glory." He prayed that Hannah, Rachel and Rose would not "wander alone with their pain."

I found pages and pages about worldwide reaction to the crimes. Seeley had not only made a whole town crazy, he had brought out the insanity in others. Prison authorities reported that he was getting an average of a hundred marriage proposals a month from all over the world. The prison e-mail had been so overloaded they were considering giving Seeley his own address.

Loretta Napoli, a widow from Erie, Pennsylvania, was writing a book about what she said was "the true story of Arnold Seeley." Soon after her husband's death, she said she had awakened on a cold winter's night to find Seeley standing at the foot of her bed. She was frightened at first, but he reassured her and after they talked for a while she realized that he was "the most misunderstood man in the world."

Talk shows scrambled to book her. "Condemned men develop unusual powers," she told Oprah. "Like many men serving long terms, Arnold has developed the ability to transport his spirit over prison walls. While his body languishes in a cell, his soul comes to me in human form. We have been joined together in a telepathic ceremony. We were married in the eyes of the higher power." Every month she picketed outside of the prison, demanding conjugal visitation rights. People in the audience stood and applauded, screamed, "Good luck, Loretta!" and "You go, girl!"

I typed: *Arnold Seeley's daughter*. There was a page of sites about *Rachel Seeley killed in burning crash* . . . I read the first one: "The daughter of convicted rapist-murderer Arnold Seeley was killed when her car went off the 101 Freeway outside of Pismo Beach, California, plunged down an embankment, and burst into flame."

That was Hannah's sister. Another tragedy.

I found a Hannah Seeley, who had been burned as a witch in Salem. Another Hannah Seeley had been head of the public library in Racine, Wisconsin, for "40 devoted years."

The AP had a story, DAUGHTER'S DNA NAILS SERIAL KILLER. It told how police had surreptitiously obtained Hannah Seeley's soccer shorts from the Robbinsgate High Athletic Department and had linked her DNA with material taken off the victims. Its prurient ring had attracted scores of other papers as far away as New Zealand. DAD UNDONE BY

DAUGHTER'S JUMPERS.

There was only one story about Rose Seeley, Hannah's mother. After twenty-five years of marriage, she had filed for divorce on the grounds of "non performance of conjugal services occasioned by spouse's incarceration." A *YouTube* clip showed a small woman, trembling like a sick bird, besieged by reporters on the courthouse steps. "Arnold was a good husband and an affectionate father to our daughters," she said. But the crowd screamed insults and court officers escorted her, sobbing, to her car.

The city of Robbinsgate had sued Rose Seeley for the proceeds of the house she had just sold for $233,000, saying, "this monster's family should not be allowed to profit from his crimes." The suit had been dismissed, the court ruling that the sale of a home did not represent profit from an "illicit activity." But before the house cleared escrow it was destroyed by fire. "Arson," the Robbinsgate Chief of Police said. "I doubt if we'll ever find the perpetrator."

A hand shook my shoulder. "Still here?"

Detective Willis was standing over me. An hour had gone by. She bumped me with her thigh. "Move over, honey, I gotta finish my Sudoku."

Herrera was waiting for me at the elevator. "Messed up, huh?" he said. "And I thought my old man was bad because he farted in front of the TV."

It Happens Again

H errera dropped me a block from my building. As I got out he lowered his window. "People are gonna think you got bags of crack in your house. Watch out some knuckleheads don't make a run at you."

Maybe it was what he said, but I felt eyes on me.

The yellow crime scene ribbon had fallen on the ground in the parking lot. There was no one around the fat crack lady's place. No sad *cancionnes* coming out of the Mexican apartments.

The girls were watching TV in the living room, their suitcases by the door. "The news was here, all three channels and Fox," Naomi said. "Hannah wouldn't come out of the room, so they talked to us. It'll be on at ten."

They slammed the front door on their way out.

My bedroom door was closed. I knocked softly. "Hannah?"

Hannah opened it a crack. "You're such a slob."

She had made my bed, swept the dust balls out of the corner, folded my clothes, even put bookmarks in the books I had dropped on their spines.

My hand was starting to throb. "This might be infected," Hannah said. "Did they give you an antibiotic?"

"They were too busy trying to make me confess I was the drug lord of the Fifth Ward."

"Did they say anything about me?"

"They found your driver's license," I said, handing it back to her.

"Anything else?"

That was my opening. I could say: *They said you were the daughter of a serial killer.* But I couldn't get it out.

Instead I said, "They think you're my mule." My knees were watery again. "I think I have to lie down."

The sheets were cool. Hannah slid in next to me and put a cool hand on my face.

"You were very brave last night," she whispered.

It got very cold in the room. We turned off the AC and opened the curtains. The sun turned orange in the grimy sky. A dull metallic gleam came off the buildings in the medical center.

"I'm hungry," she said.

"Mexican or ribs?" I asked.

"That the choice?"

"On our budget, yes."

"Someplace quiet."

There was a barbecue joint with picnic tables on Kirby. We sat in a dark corner, speaking in whispers, although there was no one near us to overhear.

"I have a conditional acceptance to Southwestern Law school, but I have to finish my last semester," she said. "I have to do a lot of writing."

"So you came to me."

"I have to take The Modern American Novel and American Presidents. Plus write an essay for law school."

"How'd you know where I was?"

"You gave me your home number, remember? Your mother told me."

"My mother doesn't know where I work."

"I went to the college neighborhoods where I thought I might run into you."

"Did my mom give you my cell number?"

"Yes."

"So why didn't you call me right away?"

"I was afraid you'd blow me off."

"Like you did to me?"

"I thought if I saw you I'd have a better chance."

"Because I'd swallow my pride just to get your body."

"Well, you don't have to be bitter about it."

A car drove up the alley, catching her face in the brief sweep of its lights.

"So you drove all the way from LA just to get a couple of essays done," I said.

"I like road trips."

"And when the job is done you'll take off and I'll never hear from you again."

"You never know," she said. "I might decide to go for a Ph.D."

"You'll pass your orals."

She sighed wearily.

"Bad joke," I said.

She patted me indulgently. "They're all bad."

"Okay, so you don't love me for my coruscating wit."

"Tell me what coruscating is. Maybe I do."

"But we still have the same deal."

Another sigh. "Same deal."

"You'll grit your teeth and think of Jesus."

"Does Mr. Fragile need reassurance?" Her hand came out of the darkness. Her fingers stroked the back of my neck, sending a chill down to my toes. "Can we go home?" she said. "I'm worn out from your emotional needs."

She gave me the keys to her little blue VW Bug. "You drive." She was asleep by the time we pulled out of the parking lot.

I'll tell her when we get home, I thought.

Houston is a big town, but it shuts down after eleven. The only people out are drunks, whizzing down broad, empty boulevards that run straight to the horizon. Houston was named the "Fattest City in America" three years running. Every other store on Kirby was a restaurant. Their signs went dark as we drove by.

I touched her leg. I could feel the warm flesh under her jeans.

High beams appeared in the rearview mirror, blinding me. I waved my hand over the mirror, but they kept coming, bearing down on us.

They were going to hit us.

I tensed and yelled, "Hannah, watch out!"

The crash knocked me off the seat. I hit the ceiling and came down hard, my forehead bouncing off the steering wheel. I blacked out for a second, blood pounding in my nose.

Hannah was still half asleep. She reached for me. "Peter—"

"They rear-ended us," I said.

In the side mirror I could see a black Escalade roll to a stop. Rage roared through me. "Assholes!" I threw open the door and stepped out. The Bug's rear end was crumpled like a squashed paper bag.

The driver's door opened. A black guy slid out, ducking behind the door, pulling a stocking mask over his head. Another guy came out of the passenger door, moving low.

I screamed. "Lock your door, Hannah!"

I jumped back behind the wheel and slammed the car into first, but took my foot off the clutch too quickly. The car bucked and stalled. In the side mirror I saw them coming. I turned the key, revved the car, and released the clutch. Easy, *easy* . . .

A man in a stocking mask appeared at the window, gun in hand.

"Peter!" Hannah screamed.

The Bug lurched and shuddered. I gave it gas and it took off.

The other guy was running alongside us. I turned to cut him off and felt a bump.

"Get down, Hannah!"

I flinched, but there was no shot. In the mirror I saw him kneeling next to his partner, who was writhing on the ground. I had sideswiped the guy in our attempt to get away.

I ran every red light on Kirby. Tires squealed and horns blared at every intersection. Blood poured onto my pants.

"Shit! Me and my little baby bloody noses."

"They're not chasing us," Hannah said. "I think we're

okay."

"You *think* we're okay?" I said. "That's rich. That's really funny."

She pulled at my arm. "You'd better call that detective."

I was calm inside, but outside I was ranting.

"What for, they're not gonna do anything. I'll just have to spend another three hours down there with McVickers, acting like they jacked us because we had a ton of heroin in the back seat and it's part of the Crips versus Nerds drug war that's devastating Houston, film at eleven."

She squeezed my knee. "Call him, Peter. He has to know."

"Okay, okay. I know I look crazy, but deep down I'm totally under control."

I pulled onto one of the quiet side streets by the Rice campus and called the extension on McVickers's card. It rang forever until a tired voice answered. "Robbery."

"Detective McVickers there?"

"Detective McVickers will be in at eight-thirty tomorrow morning."

"He told me to call," I said. "My name is Peter Vogel."

A moment later he came back on. "I'm going to conference you through, Mr. Vogel. Go ahead, Detective McVickers."

A voice croaked, "This better be good."

"I just got carjacked. That good enough?"

I could hear McVickers's heavy nasal breaths as he listened. "Okay," he said when I finished. "Don't go home. Go over to Main by the Medical Center. There's a Holiday Inn. I'll call ahead."

"I can't afford a hotel."

"City of Houston'll take care of it," he said. "Go there and put the chain on the door. And don't go back to your place until I figure out what's goin' on."

I Used You

I drove down Fannin Street, past the Medical Center. "World famous, state of the art," I said. "Anderson Cancer Center. People come from all over to be cured here. Like it's Lourdes or something."

Hannah looked out of the window. She was amazingly cool, as if this kind of thing happened every day. But I was split in two, the calm calculating one watching the crazy one who couldn't shut up.

I had gone my whole life without ever really raising my hand to anyone. There had been a couple of shoves on the basketball court, a wild drunken roundhouse right at a party, which hadn't connected. Once in middle school a kid had threatened to beat me up because I had grabbed his girlfriend's ass during band practice. But it hadn't been me. The first trumpet, a vicious prankster, had moved over into my second trumpet seat while I was getting the music, grabbed her ass in the reeds section, and slid back. It was a mean trick because this kid's brother was a notorious *cholo*. Even the tough guys wouldn't fight him for fear of retaliation. He waited for me in front of the school, but I snuck out the gym entrance. He sat on his bike outside my house, but I went around to the back alley. My mother saw him through the window and harangued me with questions until I told her what was happening. Without missing a beat she ran out and berated the kid. *"You get out of here before I call the school."* I was mortified. Next day I slunk back to school. Everybody knew my mother had protected me and the kid decided the universal ridicule was punishment enough, so after a few shoves he left me alone.

Now I had stabbed somebody, hit somebody with a frying pan. And they had ended up dead.

I had never been afraid of anything but humiliation. Now I feared for my life.

I didn't have much of a history with women. I had pawed at a few girls and a few of them had pawed back. There had been some "this was a really bad idea," even a few "this was cool, let's do it again." One hot fall afternoon day, I picked up an Australian girl on campus. After a quick grapple on my horsehair couch she ran out and I thought she had taken off, but she came back with a 12-pack of Trojans. She made me dinner, even moved my car. She went nuts when I touched her. But two days after she left I could hardly remember what she looked like.

Hannah had brought chaos into my life. What had started as a jerk-off fantasy had turned into an obsession. It wasn't enough to have her, I had to liberate her, hear her screams of ecstasy, have her lay, panting gratefully in my arms. I had to get inside her, read her thoughts, feel what she was feeling.

When she disappeared, I sank like a stone. There were nights when I thought it would be okay if I just didn't wake up. But when she reappeared, the torture started all over again.

"Pediatric Hospital," I said. "Cold. Glass and steel. Like a corporate HQ. Would you take your baby there for tender, loving care?"

Nurses' aides, black and brown ladies in blue uniforms, waited at the tram stops.

"Weird city. It's a medical Mecca, but has the highest obesity and murder rate in the country."

Outside the hotel there were hospital shuttles with wheelchair lifts. People hurried through the lobby carrying take-out bags.

"Detective McVickers called," I told the clerk.

He checked us in with a worried look.

We had a room with twin beds. I grabbed the room service menu.

"I love room service," I said. "The carts with the Bunsen burners. Those beautiful blue flames. The little bottles of ketchup and mayo." I was speeding, but I couldn't put on the brakes. "Maybe it's not the hotel room. I also get hungry after sex and near-death experiences."

She took a shower while I gorged myself on chicken tenders. When I went into the bathroom it was all warm and misty. The towels had her smell on them. When I came out, she was in bed with her eyes closed. I slipped in next to her and slid my hand between her thighs. She clamped her legs shut.

"Some girls fake orgasms," I said. "Some fake sleeping. What do you fake?"

"Both." She pushed my hand away. "The police told you, didn't they? That's why you were down there so long."

She had known all along, but hadn't said anything.

"I was lost in Googlespace," I said.

"And now you know all about my soccer shorts."

She rolled off the bed and stood at the window, a naked silhouette.

"I used you," she said.

"I knew it wasn't love at first sight."

"You're lucky it wasn't."

I realized I had quoted her father. "I mean . . . I thought it was for the papers."

"They were part of it."

"I bought your story totally," I said. "Most people have never read a novel and suddenly they have to write a paper about Henry James. They panic."

"I definitely panicked," she said. "They were stalking me . . . trying to kill me."

My heart jumped, like there was a trampoline in my chest.

"Who?" I asked.

"I don't know," she said. "Oh, God, look at your face." She took my wrist. "Your poor hand is shaking."

"Vitamin B deficiency," I said. "I'm not as chicken as I look."

She stood over me and put her hands on my shoulders.

"You should just get up and leave after what I did to you."
    "Maybe I will. But first I want to know what you did."
    "It's an ugly story."
    "I can take it. I'm an English major."

Life With Father

Hannah drew the thick drapes over the window, as if she didn't want anybody to look in. Or maybe she didn't want me see her. Her voice came out of the darkness, full of self-loathing.

"I was Daddy's little girl, you know. I could do no wrong, and I loved it. I did things to please him. Like play soccer. I'd watch him on the sidelines cheering and I'd play harder just to make him happy. He loved that I was an All Star and could even outrun some of the boys. He loved that I was good in math and science. Better than the boys at everything, he said.

"I never noticed anything weird. We were just a normal family. But after it happened, I started remembering things. He wanted everything a certain way. Like dinner—if it was meat loaf, it had to be with mashed potatoes and not French fries. He was always criticizing my mom. If she was wearing a certain dress, he would make her go back and change her shoes. He'd never raise his voice. He'd be like, are you sure you want to wear that? And she would run in to change. My sister, too. She couldn't do anything right."

"And you?" I asked.

"Not me," she said. "He never picked on me. He would hug me and give me a little kiss on the forehead when I did something good, like score a goal or win the math prize. I loved it when he hugged me like that. Happy, honey? he'd ask with his arms around me. Happy Daddy, I would say.

"We couldn't watch TV at dinner or on school nights. He said the government used television to make people stupid, especially women, so they could sell them all this stuff they didn't need. He said women were gullible and easy to fool.

"Once I came home during the day and my mom was

watching a soap. She jumped out of her skin. Don't tell your father, she said. And I laughed because I thought it was funny the way he would get so upset about little things like French fries and TV shows. My mom laughed, too, but made me swear not to tell.

"It was only after it happened that I realized how scared she must have been. He kept the door locked when they went to bed. I can't imagine what he was doing to her. Sometimes I think about how unhappy she must have been. And I just want to ask her: why did you let him do this to you? If you had come out and told the world, maybe none of this would have happened. Then I realize I'm blaming her like everybody else did."

She paused, looking bewildered, then continued. "He told me he wouldn't let me grow up weak and helpless like other women. He said I shouldn't trust anybody, especially boys, because they all wanted one thing and would say anything to get it."

"Did you listen to him?"

It was a trick question, but she didn't catch it. "Oh, yeah, I was totally brainwashed. If a boy asked me out I would think, no I can't do this to Daddy."

Had I been her first? She was so good it was hard to believe. I remembered Katz telling me: "Women are experts by instinct. It's the men who have to learn."

"I remember the day I had my first period," Hannah said. "He came into the kitchen with a big smile, walked right up to me and slapped me hard in the face. I started to cry. I didn't know what I had done. Mom brought me a Kleenex. It's just an old wives remedy for your first period, she said. He won't do it again."

That ordinary little man with the skimpy goatee.

"I thought I was happy," she said. "My friends' parents drank and did drugs. I knew girls who had to deal with a stepfather who molested them or a jealous stepmother. I actually felt sorry for them. Then it happened."

She came out of the shadows and flopped down on the

bed next to me. "I was at soccer practice waiting for him to pick me up. The parents came for other girls. Nobody offered me a ride. I called home, but there was no answer. Called my mom's cell. No answer, but a few minutes later she pulled up. My sister was lying in the back seat with her legs drawn up like she had cramps. I was getting some things for your father, my mom said. "What things? I asked her.

"Toothpaste, shaving cream, a change of socks and underwear," she said.

"Is he okay?"

"He's okay," she said.

"Is he in the hospital?"

"No."

"Where is he?"

"In jail," she said.

Hannah rolled over and buried her face in the pillow. "And that's how I found out that my father had murdered my best friend. Oh, yeah, and ten or eleven other people."

She sat up and looked at me with a crooked smile. "What, no joke?"

"Not for this," I said. "I can't even imagine what it would feel like."

"And I can't tell you. It was as if my emotions got turned off. I don't think I felt anything. Maybe one day it'll all come rushing in on me and I'll crumble. But for that whole time I just existed. I know I ate and slept and got dressed and did something all day. I know I didn't think about it that much. I know Reverend Kellner was the only person who even tried to talk to me about it, but I don't remember what he said."

"Did you see your father?" I asked.

"Once. The police wouldn't let my mom visit him because they thought she was an accessory and wanted to keep them apart. My sister refused to see him so I went to the jail in Riverside by myself. They brought him in all shackled and manacled in an orange jumpsuit. These big deputies stood over him, glaring."

"I saw that picture," I said.

"When he saw me his face got all squinty, like he was trying not cry. Thanks for comin', honey, he said. I've been thinking about you. I don't remember what we talked about, but I guess I teared up, too, because he sobbed—*Hannah!*— and tried to get up. They slammed him down in the chair. I could see they hated him and just wanted an excuse to push him around.

"'Don't be angry at me, honey,' he said. 'I'm not human anymore. They made me different.' Then they started to drag him out. He was trying to tell me something. 'Ask Abner,' he said."

"And you haven't seen him since," I said.

"No. I didn't go to the trial. We tried to stay in the house, but the calls and the letters and the e-mails got so intense. Then, one night somebody shot out our windows with an air pistol.

"Reverend Kellner offered us sanctuary in the church. He organized this meeting for us. He said when the people saw what we were going through, their hearts would melt. Boy, was he wrong. Some of the victims had been in the congregation and the families freaked out. Dougie Baines got hysterical and this deputy told us to leave. Dougie followed me out into the parking lot, screaming in my face."

She smiled bitterly. "I told him, you're just pissed off 'cause I wouldn't go out with you. That was kind of a cold thing to say, but I wanted to get back at him. Nobody ever stopped to think how I felt. Zandy was my best friend. But some people heard and it really turned them against me. The deputy said we'd better just get out of town for a while.

"They found us a cheap motel in Rialto. It's mostly Mexican and the people there didn't know who we were exactly. We had a room with twin beds and took turns sleeping with each other. The beds were small, but we never touched. We hardly spoke, just brought food in and watched TV. The only thing I remember was my mom saying, well, now we can watch any show we want."

"Did you ever talk about it with your mom?" I asked.

"Not one word. We were walking on eggshells around each other. We never even mentioned his name.

"My sister Rachel was starting her second year at UC-Santa Barbara. Her boyfriend came to pick her up. She took her suitcase and started to leave without saying goodbye. I tried to hug her. Call me when you get settled, I said. She turned on me, her face all twisted. Call you? she said, almost spitting in my face. Are you kidding? I'm never going to speak to you again.

"It all came pouring out. I was always jealous of you, she said. You were Daddy's favorite and I was plain Jane hiding in the corner, hoping nobody would notice me. I never felt I even belonged in this family. But now I'm glad he liked you better than me. It proves you're as fucked up as he is."

Hannah's eyes widened, reliving the astonishment. "I was blown away. We were never close, but I didn't think she hated me that much.

"She got into the party scene at school. After her accident there was a blogger who said she would get loaded, climb on the table, and start screaming: *I'm a serial killer's daughter! Better stay away from me!*

"I was the only person at her funeral. I sat in the crematorium with the organ playing until they came out and gave me the package with her ashes."

"Your mother didn't come?" I asked.

"Oh, God no. My mother doesn't want anything to do with this."

"I guess she took a lot of abuse."

"They persecuted her. If this was the 1600s they would have burnt her at the stake. People said she was Daddy's accomplice. That she had made friends with the victims and that's how he got into their houses. They were like, how can you be married to a man for twenty years, sleep with him, have sex with him, and not know anything about him?"

"How did she deal with that?" I asked.

"She ran away. Went back to live with my grandma in

Oregon. I was going to visit her at Christmas, but she wrote me not to come. She had a new life now and wanted to forget everything that had ever happened and everybody she had ever known."

"Even you?"

"Especially me. She had this little joke when people would compliment her on how good an athlete I was. The babies got switched in the hospital and some tall, skinny mom got stuck with the dumpy, clumsy one. She would say it with a smile, like she thought it was cute. But when I started seeing that smile in my memory, it was resentful, almost hateful.

"So now I find out that my dad's a sex murderer and my mom and sister hate me. Pretty funny, huh?"

"At least you don't have to feel guilty about not calling," I said.

She looked at me in astonishment. But then laughed. "Good point."

It was like the gloom had broken for a moment. The room was quiet. The air conditioner hummed. It was almost restful.

She sat down in the corner and drew up her knees. "I had a half-ride at Stanford for soccer," she said. "But I got a letter from the coach suggesting I redshirt my first year. They didn't want the distraction of a mass murderer's daughter at midfield. Can you imagine the trash talking?

"I decided to get out of there, escape to a place where nobody knew me. So I transferred to Napa. It's kind of an obscure school in wine country. I thought I could hide for a year or two and people would forget. Women's soccer was like a club team. The coach was excited to have me and the year started well."

Her breath caught in her throat. "Then I started getting these e-mails. There would be news photos of my dad with a noose or bloody knife drawn around his neck. Stuff written in black crayon: *You bitch cunt slut, you'll die a thousand times for every woman your father killed*.

"They'd send bondage photos of women all tied up and say: *This is you when we find you. Only you'll be dead.* Believe it or not, it wasn't that big a deal. After it happened I had gotten calls and e-mails and letters, everything from sick jokes to death threats. But this was different. It got worse. They would send two or three different messages hundreds of times until my e-mail crashed."

"Why do you say *they*?" I asked.

She paced in and out of the shadows, running her hand through her hair. "They, he, she, it . . . I don't know. I knew if I complained, my identity would come out. I tried to ignore the e-mails, but they got scary and real personal. They would say stuff about my sister and my mom, like whoever it was knew a lot about my family. Finally, I couldn't take it and went to campus security. I just wanted to know how they had found me. The security guys said all you had to do was put H. Seeley next to the name of any college in the UCs, and put a dot e-d-u after that and you'd get my e-mail address. They couldn't wait to get me out of there. It was like I was contaminated and they were afraid to touch me.

"The coach tried to help. He would take me for coffee after practice. But then he started to talk about my dad and I got creepy vibes."

She moved like a wraith in the gloom. "I changed my e-mail account to a different name. I used A. Baines at first, after my best friend. That worked. They stopped for a while. Then the phone calls started. A shrieking voice with a lot of static and howling like in a horror movie. Always on a different caller ID so I'd have to listen to it for a second before I realized who it was. *You think we're gonna let you go on living, after what your father did,* it would say. *You're gonna suffer what those women did. Only for you it'll be thousand times worse.*

"Reverend Kellner was my only friend, so I called him. He got real nervous. You have to take this seriously, he said. He told me to call the FBI and demand protection. I went to the FBI office in San Francisco. They had a profile of the kind of person who did this stalking. He's a loner, they said. A guy with murder in his heart, but harmless. Your father was a lot more dangerous than any of these guys, an agent told me. He was like, what did I expect after what my dad had done?

"He said I didn't have to worry. Harassers rarely, if ever, acted out their fantasies. The creep wants to see fear, he said. Don't give him the satisfaction. Ignore him. I told him I was thinking about changing my name. That's not necessary, he said. Give it some time. He'll get bored and go onto something else."

"But he didn't," I said.

"Not at first. He kept doing it four or five times a day. I would scream at him, don't you have a life? But then I got numb to it and just listened. After a few minutes he'd run out of steam. I'd hear him breathing hard, like he'd been running real fast.

"One day there were no calls. A week went by. I couldn't believe it. The FBI had been right after all.

"But he had switched to my suitemates. He had their cell numbers and e-mails. He'd call them and say: *Do you know who you're living with? If you don't throw her out that means you're a bitch like her and you'll get the same treatment.*"

There was a knock. "Housekeeping." The door opened and a little Mexican lady peeked in. "Turn down?"

"Not right now," I said.

The door closed softly.

Hannah shivered. "Crazy city. You're either broiling or freezing."

I couldn't think of anything to fill the silence. After a moment she started talking again.

"My suitemates kicked me out. They needed an excuse, so they said I should have told them who I was. I asked Reverend Kellner if he and his wife would put me up for a few days during winter break because I had no place to go. But he freaked. He was like, you can't come here. They burnt your house down. There's no forgiveness here. If I take you in they'll drive me away. I guess I started to cry because he got real upset and started talking about prayer and redemption and how he had never understood the Book of Job until this happened and that's why we had to have faith, because God worked his will in mysterious ways. I guess I was still crying, because he said I should get settled and he'd come and see me anywhere I was."

Her voice turned harsh. "Meanwhile, I couldn't find any-one else to live with. The whole place was acting like, how dare I bring my crazy shit to their cozy little campus in the hills. So I quit and came down to R. It was a bigger school and I thought I could get lost. I didn't go out for the soccer team because they would find out who I was. I didn't even go into the dorms, but looked on the bulletin boards for a share. That's when I met Mona, my roommate. After a couple of glasses of wine, she said, 'Hannah, I gotta warn you. I'm a real slutbag. I bring guys home all the time.'

"I said that's nothing. Ever hear of the Robbinsgate killer? That's my dad. And she just broke out laughing. Cool, she said. You're worse than me."

The drunken blonde. She had tried to warn me.

"She kept your secret," I said.

"She was a good friend. I didn't want her to get into trouble. That's why I moved out."

"And quit school?"

"I had to do that. They tried to kill me."

She said it in a matter-of-fact tone, like when she had said *I'll let you fuck me.* I tried to keep my tone casual as well. "In school?"

"Where I worked."

"The strip club?"

She got up and started pacing again. "Mona said I was-n't tough enough to be a stripper, but I was all twisted and took the job. It was like I was punishing myself for what my dad had done. In the lap dances I would flirt with guys and lead them on. Even the owner told me I was asking for trouble.

"One night there was a guy in a suit. Young and clean-looking, not like the other slobs. He said he didn't drink, but he would buy me champagne if I would sit with him. That was a big deal because they got a hundred-and-fifty dollars for a ten-dollar bottle of Proseco. We never used our real names. I told him mine was Zandy, short for Alexandra, and he was like, are you Russian? You look European.

"He was kinda cute with a baby face and an innocent look. He smelled of toothpaste and cologne, like a high school kid going on his first date. He said he'd never been to a place like this before and didn't know what had drawn him in."

"And you bought that?" I said.

She came at me, pleading, "I was lonely, I was scared. I had a couple of glasses of champagne. But now that I think about it, I was pretty gullible.

"I had to do another set. When I got up on stage, I turned to look for him, but he was gone. I thought, well, he had gotten whatever he needed. You're not gonna believe this, but my feelings were hurt." She looked lost for a brief second, then said, "They have a mini-bar? I'm thirsty."

"I'll call room service," I said. "Want a beer?"

"Sure."

I ordered six Coronas.

"You gonna drink five beers?" she asked.

"I've had a rough day."

She stood there looking at me with her hands on her hips. When she was quiet like that, I couldn't guess what she was thinking.

"At closing there were always creeps hanging around," she said. "We'd wait while the bouncers cleared out the parking lot. I was walking to my little blue Bug when he jumped out from behind a car. He was all polite and nervous. 'I've been waiting for you,' he said. 'Can I buy you a cup of coffee or just drive you home?' I told him I was tired. He begged like a little puppy. 'Oh, c'mon, just a cup of coffee, we'll talk for a while.' I said thanks, maybe tomorrow. Then, he grabbed my arm." She winced at the memory. "His hands were big and rough, like they belonged to somebody else. I pulled away. He came after me. 'Wait up, Hannah,' he said.

"It was like an electric shock ran through me. He knew my name. This wasn't just an accidental meeting. He had planned the whole thing.

"I screamed and took off. I fell out of my heels I was so scared. I ran down an alley shrieking at the top of my lungs. Heard him chasing me, breathing hard, but it was really the sound of my own footsteps, my own breaths.

"I hid behind a trash can and called Mona. She was bombed and with some guy, but she came down right away. I told her a customer had jumped me. I felt bad about lying, but I was afraid she'd kick me out if she knew a maniac was stalking me because of my dad."

"Are you positive you didn't tell that guy your name was Hannah?" I asked.

"Positive."

"Maybe he asked one of the people in the club what your name was."

"They would tell him Zandy. It was the only name I used."

"Okay," I said. "So this guy came to the bar to kill you. But I thought the FBI said these guys didn't act out their shit."

"Maybe they were wrong. Or maybe this was a different guy."

"So now you're telling me there's a gang out to get you?"

"Fuck you! I'm not telling you *anything*."

She jumped up and put the light on. "Where's my bag?" She found it under a chair and started throwing her things into it.

"I'm just playing devil's advocate," I said.

She went into the bathroom and slammed the door.

"You can't stop the story now," I called. "I'm just about

to make my appearance."

She came out and pushed me aside.

"I'm sorry, Hannah," I said. "I guess I just don't want something so horrible to be true."

She yanked the door open, but jumped back with a cry of fear and clutched my arm. "Peter!"

The waiter, a pudgy, dark little Indian was standing there with a tray of beers and a tentative smile.

"Room service?"

Hunted

"**L**et me go," she said.
And I should have, right then and there.
None of this would have happened.

Can't blame myself. No one can foresee the future. I wanted to protect her. But now I think she might have been better off without me.

Anyway, I ran down the hall and caught her by the elevator. "Don't make me feel guilty for driving you away."

She sagged. "You won't feel so guilty after you hear the rest."

Back in the room, the waiter set down the beers and looked up nervously. "Gratuity included, sir," he said, and slid out, closing the door so softly I heard the lock click.

She watched as I opened a beer. My hands shook as I tried to cram a lime wedge down the neck of the bottle.

"You poor thing." She lurched as if someone had pushed her, and caressed my cheek. "Why did I get you into this?" Then stepped back, as if surprised by her impulsive gesture.

We were in a strange dance. Come together, and step back. And do it again, as if for the first time.

"I've done a terrible thing to you," she said.

"What?"

"I was afraid to be alone. Afraid they would come in and get me. I needed somebody I could call at a moment's notice."

"So you picked me," I said.

"I lured you into my sick, warped world. I used you for my own protection."

"Why me?"

"I saw you checking me out in class."

"I wasn't the only one."

"No, but I knew I could handle you."

"Why?"

She took a breath. "You won't like this."

"I'm an English major, remember?"

She came closer, looking into my eyes as if she wanted to see me when she said it. "You reminded me of Dougie Baines."

"The drunk who slept through his sister's murder?"

"Dougie had a crush on me from when we were kids. He was always moping around the house when I came out. He'd call me sometimes and keep me on the phone for hours. I tried to be nice because he was Zandy's brother, but it got to the point where I couldn't stand him."

"So I reminded you of a guy you couldn't stand?" I said.

"You're skinny like him. Hair flopping over your face. Moony look in your eyes."

"Moony?"

"I'm not a writer like you, okay. Sometimes I don't use the right word. "

"Moony is the right word if you mean *moony*."

She raised her hands as if to ward me off. "Okay, okay."

"So this whole deal about the papers was just a ruse."

"No. I needed the GPA, too."

"So I did double duty, tutor and bodyguard."

"In a way."

"And you paid me off with occasional sex."

"It wasn't as cold as that," she said. "I was actually having fun and that's what made it so bad. It would have been better if you were repulsive."

"Thanks."

"I wanted to tell you the truth, but I knew you would dump me and then I'd be alone . . . I was afraid, Peter. I know that's no excuse."

She rolled off the bed and went back to the chair in the corner, as if she wanted to get as far away from me as possible. "I was shopping one day and I got a big package of spinach ravioli because I knew you liked it. And I felt terrible."

"Because I liked spinach ravioli?"

"Because you thought you were in a relationship. You were so sweet when you tried to convince me how great those boring books were. When we were in bed you'd be all hot and going crazy. I knew you were into me and I wanted you to be happy, but all I could think of was that I had to keep you there until Mona got back. I knew I was being unfair to you, but when that guy grabbed me outside the club, I realized I might be putting you in danger."

"So you took off without telling me."

"If I told you I was leaving, you would have asked why and then I would have made up some kind of lie. Running away seemed like the best idea."

"Okay, so you went to LA. Then what?"

"I had aced my LSATS and gotten a provisional acceptance from Southwestern," she said "No way I could change my name and drop out of sight now. I told them I had been sick the last semester and they said they would let me take classes and I could finish my degree in summer school. What's the matter?"

I realized I had been shaking my head, remembering how I had physically ached with loneliness.

"Nothing," I said.

She looked at me quizzically, but continued. "I looked on Craig's List and found a share on Rossmore Street in Hollywood with two other law students. One of them was an older guy from Pittsburgh, the other a Korean girl. They didn't know anything about me and I didn't tell them.

"I got a hostess job at a steak place not far from my apartment. I'd go to work and come right back to my room. Then, I'd sit by the window to see if anybody had followed me. Weekends, the girl stayed with her cousins in Koreatown and the guy went rock climbing with his friends. My building didn't have a doorman and there was never anybody in the lobby. I'd step away from the elevator when the door opened so I could run away if there was anybody inside.

Sometimes I'd walk up the stairs and check my floor from the landing. I'd put a strand of hair under the door knob so I could see if anybody had tried to get in."

"Strand of hair . . . cool."

"Yeah, I must have seen it in a movie. But even after all that, I'd freak every time I went in. It was a small apartment, but it seemed like a dark cavern when there was nobody around. I'd turn all the lights on and blast the TV.

"The weeks went by and nothing happened. But that made me more paranoid, like I knew it was just a matter of time. I would drive down my street a few times to see if there was anybody outside. I knew I couldn't hide. My little blue Bug stuck out like a sore thumb."

"You should have gotten rid of it," I said.

"It was a high school graduation present," she said. "My dad gave it to me for getting into Stanford. I loved that car." She tugged at her hair. "Stupid, huh? Don't say anything. It *was* stupid."

She pulled back the curtains and looked out the window. "Coming home one night I saw this banged-up old pickup. There was a man sitting inside, wearing a baseball cap. He was probably a plumber or something, I thought. But just to make sure, I turned the corner and drove around for a few minutes and then came back. He was still there, watching me in his side mirror as I drove up.

"I parked in the alley behind my building, but went in the front way. I wanted him to see me go in, so if I left I could go out the back and he would think I was still at home."

"You had it all planned out," I said.

"Your mind starts to work. You think about what you'll do if this or that happens."

She crouched by the window, reliving that moment. "It got dark. I saw the cell phone screen glowing in the pickup. A little while later, a Domino's car pulled up. The delivery guy passed a pizza through the window."

She drew the curtains quickly and turned to me, her face ghostly white in the shadows. "Maybe it was totally innocent, like he was on his lunch break or waiting for a friend, but that pizza thing freaked me out. I had to get out of there."

"So you came back to me."

She looked at me earnestly. "I had nowhere to go. No one to turn to."

I reached for her, but she stepped back.

"Don't forgive me, Peter. That'll make it worse."

She turned away.

"I called your house," she said. "Your mother told me you were in Houston. I sat by the window watching the truck and tried to talk myself out of it. It was stupid to take off on a wild goose chase. What if I couldn't find you? Or if I found you and you told me to take a hike?"

"Why didn't you go to the police?" I asked.

"And tell them what? I've been getting death threats? They'd say duh, you're the Robbinsgate killer's daughter, what do you expect? A guy tried to attack me outside the bar where I work as a pole dancer. Double duh, strippers get hassled all the time. There was a guy parked outside my house in an old pickup. I know he was watching me because he had a pizza delivered to his car. Right—pepperoni or meatball?

"I got my stuff and went down to my car. I thought they might have somebody watching the back, but the alley was empty. I drove east on the 10 Freeway and followed the signs all the way to Houston. I drove straight through, stopping for naps at rest stops."

"That beer's gonna explode if you keep shaking it," I said.

She put the bottle down on the table. "I thought I'd gotten away. But that guy in the bar must have followed me from LA."

It was starting to make sense and I didn't want it to. "He came in right after you did," I said. "I turned him away because it was couples only. Then he came back with a drunken girl, who he dumped as soon as he got in. Next thing, I saw him talking to you."

"He asked me was that a Cosmo or a Pink Lady I was drinking," she said. "Drop dead, I told him. He laughed and told the bartender 'back this high-class lady up'. It was stupid to take a sip of the drink he had bought me. In a second I knew he had slipped something in it. In Health Ed they said if you've been drugged, make yourself throw up before you pass out. I tried to get into the bathroom, but he came out of nowhere and grabbed me. C'mon, Hannah, he said, let's get outta here."

I was ahead of her. "He knew your name."

"As soon as he said it I knew he had been sent to kill me. Like the guy in the parking lot. The guy in the pickup. I knew, but I was so woozy I didn't care. I let him drag me. I was ready to die. I had tried to imagine how those women had felt when my father . . . Now I'm gonna feel it, I thought. Now I'll know what it's like before you die. And then you appeared. You saved my life, Peter."

I remembered the Nightmare's sad look when I said, "I don't have a beef with you, man."

"You do now," he had said.

The phone clanged like a fire alarm.

It was Herrera. "I'm downstairs," he said. "We've got some pictures to show you."

Stung

The lobby at Police Headquarters was empty. A cop dozed by the metal detector.

A janitor with a stoic Andean face pushed a vacuum around the Robbery Squad. An elderly black cleaning lady emptied trashcans from the cubicles.

In one cubicle, a chunky blond guy whirled around in a swivel chair like an antsy little kid.

McVickers was in a corner office staring into a computer. He drummed his fingers while I told him Hannah's story. When I finished he shook his head. "You want me to believe that someone has mobilized the criminal community of Houston to kill this little girl?"

"It's the truth," I said.

He squinted at me so tightly his eyes disappeared. Then he slid a stack of photos across the table. "These the boys who tried to jack you?"

It was two black guys in the front seat of a car. One was leaning forward, forehead on the wheel, like he was sleeping. The other had his head down like he was looking for something on the floor.

"I don't know . . ."

"Take a good look," McVickers said.

Closer shots showed wounds in the backs of their heads. Ribbons of dried blood down their necks.

"A twenty-five caliber makes a nice, neat hole," McVickers said. "But you gotta have a lotta confidence to use it on two players like this. You gotta be a professional."

There were photos of a black Escalade on a turnoff on the 59 Freeway.

"That the car?" he asked.

"Could have been," I said.

"Killer was in the back seat. He tells them to pull off, he has to take a piss or something like that. Whole thing takes three seconds. One-one-thousand—pop in the back of the driver's head and pop to the other guy. They didn't even know what hit 'em. Two-two-thousand—two more pops to make sure they're done. Three-three-thousand—my man strolls outta there."

"Who are these guys?" I asked.

"Freelancers," McVickers said. "There are people in this town who'll do anything for money. Nobody'll miss 'em, but we don't want the word to get out that you can shoot people in H-town and walk away like nothin happened. Take another look."

Just for show I riffed through the photos again. And shook my head. "I didn't see their faces."

McVickers nodded. I could see he didn't believe me. "Those boys had electric cable and duct tape in the back seat, Peter. So maybe it wasn't a simple jacking. Maybe they were hired to snatch you and your girlfriend."

"She isn't my—"

"Maybe they tie you up and take you where somebody's waitin'. Torture and slow death, Peter. That's how the cartel punishes people."

"I don't have anything to do with any cartel."

McVickers' eyes hardened. He slid another stack of photos across the desk. "See if you can find the guy who tried to grab your girlfriend in the bar."

It was a rogue's gallery of white thugs. Ponytails, tattooed faces, elaborate mustaches. I got to the middle and there he was. "That's him. A little younger, but it's him."

"Robert 'Sonny' Doane," McVickers read. He hunted and pecked on the computer. In a few seconds the printer started spitting out sheets. "Sonny's from Needles, California. Know where that is?"

"Up in the desert by the Arizona border."

McVickers read his record. "Possession with intent, starting when he was still in high school. Two terms in Juvie.

Assault and robbery, felonious assault, assault with a deadly weapon, attempted murder. Impersonating a federal agent. He and his boys had a little trick. They'd get phony badges and raid the meth labs, pretending to be narcs. By the time the dealers realized what was happening, our boy Sonny had the drop on 'em."

He looked back down at the sheet. "His last charge was for running a meth lab of his own in Big Bear. Incarceration at San Quentin. He became an enforcer for the White Supremacist Movement so they moved him to Otter Point."

"Arnold Seeley is at Otter Point," I said. "They could know each other."

"No way. Seeley is in isolation in the Special Housing Unit, and Doane was in the population. Even if Doane were put in solitary at SHU, they would never cross paths. Inmates in isolation aren't allowed to fraternize."

McVickers rose, wincing, as if his back bothered him. "Did you know that your roommate, Michael Kohler, was expelled from the University of Arizona for drug dealing?"

My heart fluttered, then started pounding again. He watched me for signs of agitation, but I couldn't stop that goddamn thumb from trembling.

"That's a campus thing," I said. "College stoner dealing to finance his habit."

McVickers took a pint of Wild Turkey 101 out of a drawer. "Kohler was arrested with three-hundred kilos of marijuana and eleven pounds of crystal meth in the trunk of a rental car. The only thing that saved him from a prison term was that the car was rented in someone else's name."

"That's not possible," I said. "They would never have taken him in the program."

"Mr. Kohler forgot to mention his little brush with the law on his application. But they know now." He poured a shot into his Houston PD coffee cup. "We checked with Narcotics. Kohler has made six sales to an undercover officer out of your apartment." He slid a photo across the desk. "Recognize this guy?"

It was me in our living room, seriously trashed.

"Cell phone shot taken by the undercover," McVickers said. "Don't bother tryin' to think back to who it was. These boys—or girls— blend right in."

I remembered those nights. Everybody chipped in twenty bucks. Mike came out of his bedroom with a couple of joints. We giggled a lot and went out for burritos. In the morning we'd get wrecked again and go to the zoo.

"It was just a bunch of stoned-out people with the munchies," I said.

"That's not what the DEA thinks," McVickers said. "There's a string of meth labs along the Tex-Mex border. Kohler bragged to an informant that he was a local distributor for the Cancun cartel. So the feds made him a target. DEA thinks they're onto a cross-border deal, but they need a lotta players to turn it into a cartel thing. So they're lookin' to add you and your girlfriend to the cast of characters."

"But I was just a guy who lived in the same apartment and got high with him a couple of times."

"That story won't play anymore," McVickers said. He poured himself another short shot. "Task Force grabbed Kohler with a car full of meth early this evening. They put that together with the break-in at your place and subsequent double homicide. Added another possible double homicide of the two boys in the Escalade and came up with a big time drug war, which is exactly what they need to justify their investment, you understand?"

I understood. Hannah and I were part of their scenario. I tried to keep the desperation out of my voice. "Look, I know what you think, but I swear—"

McVickers cut me off with a wave of his hand. "As we speak, Kohler's being questioned in another part of the building. They're gonna put him under the hot lights and tell him he's facin' ten years in a Texas pen. They'll tell him he's a suspect in the murders. Then, they'll offer to take six months off his sentence for every accomplice he gives 'em. That boy'll start squealin' like a rusty gate. He'll lie like a rug to save his ass. He'll give them the people he's dealin' with first and when they ask for more, he'll start makin' shit up. Before you know it he'll be tellin' tales about you and your girlfriend. You'll be stuck tryin' to prove a negative, Peter. Guilty until proven innocent is not a good place to be, 'specially in Texas."

"But I had nothing to do with this," I said. "He can't implicate me."

"Implicate," McVickers said. "Another nice word. I remember the first time you came in you used the word farfetched." McVickers took a sip and grimaced. "I happen to believe the only thing you're guilty of is losin' your mind over a piece of ass, but that can get you in just as much trouble as a double homicide. Anyway, just between you and me . . ." He leaned in and lowered his voice, as if someone was listening. "Only a guy who was thinkin' with his little head would believe your girlfriend's story about people tryin' to kill her."

It was insane, too ludicrous to laugh at.

"You think Hannah is a courier for a drug ring?"

"She shows up and all hell breaks loose," McVickers said. "When the smoke clears we got four dead thugs and a dealer fleein' town with a car full of meth."

"You think she was bringing something for Michael? She doesn't even know him."

"Don't say that too loud 'cause she knows you and you know him, which makes you the link to the conspiracy. Kohler made numerous sales to an undercover officer in your presence. And now that a convicted meth dealer tried to kidnap her—"

"You mean Sonny Doane? She doesn't know him, either."

"That's what she told *you*. But it seems kinda suspicious, don't it, that she comes runnin' to you and then an hour later he shows up and tries to snatch her? Tailed her all the way from LA, she says. Maybe he did, maybe he didn't, but we know what happened next. He tried to grab her in the bar, but you stopped him. That night two boys tried to bust into your house. You chased 'em and somebody cut their throats. Then the players in the Escalade tried to jack you. When that didn't work, somebody shot them execution style." He took a short slug. The booze was making him talkative. "What if that somebody was Sonny Doane? You say he came down here to kill your girlfriend to get even with her dad. Don't try that in court. A Texas jury knows cartel trash when it sees it. The Mexican mafia uses white boys like your roommate to mule cocaine, marijuana, and methamphetamine across the border. When they have a problem they hire a white boy like Doane to solve it. A Texas jury can be easily made to believe that you and our girlfriend were low-level players. Especially when they find out who her dad was. Bad-seed-grows-poison-plants kinda thing."

"The truth will come out in the end," I said.

"But the end can be a long time comin'. They can arrest you on Michael Kohler's say-so. They love lockin' up white boys on narcotics charges. Makes 'em look like equal opportunity law enforcement. DA can set your bail so high you can't make it. Get you a Public Defender with such a big caseload it'll take weeks before he gets to you. Put you in a cell with a known sexual predator to make you confess."

"But I have nothing to confess."

"Spend a few weeks in an eight-by-eleven cell with a three-hundred-pound rapist and you might change your mind. First thing that happens is you can't close your eyes 'cause you're afraid he'll grab you when you drop off. Sleep deprivation makes people do strange things . . ."

It was good cop/bad cop and he was playing both roles. Trying to scare me into confiding in him.

"You're wrong about me," I said.

"Okay, say we are." He held the bottle up to see how much was left. "When a cop makes a mistake he doesn't say oops, sorry, let me make this right. He covers his ass, Peter. There are guys in jail right now who didn't do a damn thing. I put a few of them in myself. I'd just as soon not do it again, but it's like a doctor whose patient dies. You don't lose sleep over it."

"Can you at least put a cop in front of our room tonight?"

"I'll put the National Guard out there if your girlfriend tells me about Sonny Doane."

"But she has nothing to do with him."

He shook his head slowly. "Then I can't help her. I stretched the rules puttin' y'all in that hotel. I told my bosses you were potential informants. Now I have to go back and tell them I wasted the city's money. They're gonna be really pissed about them chicken tenders."

"Herrera," he hollered. He took another slug and leaned over me so close I could see the bloodshot streaks in his dungaree eyes.

Herrera stumbled out of a cubicle with a furtive look, like he'd been going through somebody's desk.

"Take Mr. Vogel home," McVickers said.

"I can't believe you're just going to sit here and let them kill Hannah," I said.

He held the empty bottle over the trash can and dropped it with a crash. "We solve homicides, Peter, we don't prevent them."

No Exit

errera's car reeked of booze. He hugged the
wheel, steering with his body. When we got to
the hotel, he missed the driveway and bumped
over the curb.

The lobby was full of weary faces, exhausted from a day
with sick relatives. One man sat alone. Blond buzz cut, steel
rim glasses, gym shoulders hulking under a blue dress shirt. I
had seen him before. Maybe he was one of those cops I had
passed at headquarters. He was speaking with quiet urgency
on a cell phone and when he caught my eye he turned away.
It was probably a normal reflex. Still, I lingered at the newspaper rack until some other people came in and jumped on
the elevator. I got off at four and walked up the back stairs,
straining to hear voices. At the seventh floor I stopped and
listened, but heard nothing. The door creaked as I opened it.

Two young guys in suits were standing on either side of
the elevator. One of them turned.

I spun so quickly I lost my balance and fell backward
down the stairs. My head bounced off the bottom step. The
pain burned everything out of my mind. I watched the door
inch open. Had to get up. They were coming after me. Get
up! Get up! I rolled over, pulled myself up and jumped to the
next landing. My ankle buckled. I dragged myself to the next
landing, jumped down half a flight, hitting hard on my knee.
Steps clattered down the metal stairs. I lunged for the banister and jumped, taking three steps at a time until I got to the
mezzanine.

Somebody was making a speech in a banquet room.
Laughter came from behind the closed door.

I limped into an alcove and watched the landing. Nobody
came down. Had I been running away from my own foot-

steps? My own fevered breaths?

I stumbled to the balcony overlooking the lobby. It was quiet, everybody going about their business. The guy on the cell phone was gone.

No point in reporting this. There were no witnesses. Security would see some hyperventilating weirdo with a wild story of being chased by two guys who had vanished. They'd check and see we were suspected drug dealers put in the hotel by the Houston PD. Case closed.

I hopped to a house phone and called the room. After a few rings my stomach dropped. They got Hannah, I thought. She was lying dead in the room, with the phone ringing. I felt a surge of relief. Okay . . . it was over. They had gotten her and would leave me alone.

"Peter?" It was Hannah, breathless. "I was in the shower."

I was flooded with remorse, which faded fast, replaced by some kind of dread. My moods were changing so quickly I didn't know what I was feeling.

"Did you put the chain on the door?" I asked.

"No. I was worried I wouldn't hear you."

"Do it now. I'll be right up. I'll knock three times, then twice."

"What's the matter?"

"Three times, then twice," I said.

I took the elevator back up to seven. Nobody was in the hall. Maybe they were whispering behind a closed door, watching me through the peephole. Maybe it had just been two random guys waiting for the elevator. I got a bucket of ice out of the machine, knocked three times, then twice.

Hannah opened the door and lifted the chain. She had a towel wrapped around her head like a turban. The room was so dark you could hide in the corner.

"You take too many showers," I said.

The fear had leeched the strength out of my bones. I fell onto the bed.

She switched on the lamp. "What happened to you?"

"I fell on the steps and twisted my ankle."

She raised my pants and poked at my ankle. The pain shot through me.

"I've had a million of these," she said.

She took the liner out of trashcan and filled it with ice. Then, propped my foot up on the pillows.

"I found that dude who hassled you in the bar," I said. "He's a killer and an ex-con. McVickers thinks he was after you on some drug thing."

"Why drugs?"

"One of my roommates was dealing. McVickers thinks you were in on that, too."

"That's funny."

"You've got a weird sense of humor," I said.

"Does McVickers think I killed those two boys, too?"

"He thinks they broke in to get something you had brought from LA. He says he won't protect you unless you become an informant. He thinks I'm lying for you. He says I lost my mind over a piece of ass."

"You did."

She lay next to me and closed her eyes. "I was thinking about Mona before. Right now she has just finished screwing some guy she hardly knows. She's beating herself up for being such a slutbag. But tomorrow night she'll be wondering what shade of toenail polish to wear when she goes out. Right now your friends are doing shooters in some bar, wondering which party to go to . . . and you and I are in hell."

All I had to do was get up and limp out. She would be too proud to try to stop me. Once I got through the door it would get easier with every step.

"We'd better order dinner before room service closes," I said.

She sat up and grabbed her bag. I thought she was going to run out again, but she was just looking for something.

"Do you think they can send up some Tampax?"

"How do you want it cooked?"

She gave me that long, inscrutable look again.

"I know, I'm a clown," I said.

She lunged awkwardly and put her head in my chest. "Don't talk." She wrapped her skinny arms around me, squeezing harder and harder until I got the message.

We did it quietly. Like screwing in a girl's room late at night while her parents are sleeping down the hall. With the covers over our heads, we lay silent and intertwined, growing inside each other, clutching tighter and tighter.

When it was over, we lay side-by-side, holding hands. It was quiet except for the beating of our hearts.

"I forgot about it for a while," I said.

She rolled away from me.

"What would you have done if you never met me?" she asked.

"Katz is going to Emporia College in Kansas, to be chairman of the English Department. He offered me a Teaching Assistant stipend while I was getting my degree. He said my BA was a Bachelor of Angst and I'd need an MA, or Major Asshole degree, just to teach high school."

"I'm sorry I messed up your plans," she said.

"I didn't want to be an English teacher anyway," I said.

I ordered a big meal—steaks, desserts, and a bottle of wine. It came with a discreet knock.

Through the peephole I saw the same Indian waiter. I opened the door, but kept it on the chain.

"Room Serv—"

"I know, I know," I said. I looked down the hall to see if there was anyone behind him. He followed my eyes, then turned back, his tentative smile fading.

The sight of all the food I had ordered made me queasy. "This is a fat man's meal," I said.

He misunderstood. "Oh, no, sir, this is for you. Room 736."

· Hannah jumped up from the bed, laughing.

And then I was laughing, too.

On the Run

T he hydraulic whine of the garbage trucks woke me. It was dawn. Hannah was kneeling on the bed staring down at me.

"I got a text from Reverend Kellner," she said.

She showed me the message: "HOUSTON POLICE CALLED. PLEASE GET IN TOUCH WITH ME ASAP."

I jumped up like I'd been awake for hours. That scumbag Mike had been talking. McVickers had warned me.

"We'd better take off," I said.

We were packed in minutes. I gave her the steak knife off the room service cart and took one for myself. "Fake low, then slash their eyes," I said.

"You know self defense?" she asked.

"No. That just seems like a good thing to do."

I made her wait at the door while I got the elevator. A bellman was dropping copies of *USA Today* by the doors. He saw the knife and froze. "I don't wanna get hassled goin' to the elevator," I said.

A maintenance guy pushing a waxer along the lobby floor stopped to let us pass, and I realized I was still holding the knife. Outside, a tour bus waited, motor rumbling, driver asleep at the wheel. In the parking lot, couples, paunchy and grumbling, threw bags in their cars.

A muggy gray mist settled like beads of prickly sweat. I was startled by a voice. "Bayou is boilin'. It's gonna be a scorcher today . . ."

A leathery old man in a Texas Longhorn cap had been walking behind us all this time and I hadn't seen him. "It's pourin' down rain in N'awlins," he said.

"What's it like in Tulsa?" I asked.

"Heavy rain acrost the Southwest," he said, walking on

to a Dodge Ram pickup.

"Why do you want to go to Tulsa?" Hannah asked.

"I don't. But he was following us. He could be one of them."

She turned to look at him. "That old man?"

"Why not? It could be anybody."

On the 45 heading for San Antonio, her ringtone went off. It was "Imagine" by John Lennon.

She answered and listened for a long time, looking at me in agitation. "No, no, that's not what happened," she said into the phone. "They have it all wrong. No . . . Peter saved my life . . . I'll put you on speaker." She held the phone out. "This is Reverend Kellner."

It was a younger voice than I had imagined. "Hi Peter, I'm Fred Kellner. I've been talking to Detective McVickers of the Houston Police Department. He thinks Hannah is involved in some kind of drug-related homicide situation."

"I know. It's surreal." I hated that word. Katz had devoted a whole class to a tirade against it.

"I told him it just wasn't possible," Kellner said. "But he said you and your roommate . . ."

Hannah jumped in. "Peter had nothing to do with this. They were after *me*. I ran away from them, but they followed me to Houston."

"Who followed you, Hannah?" he asked.

"I told you I don't know who."

He spoke in the measured tones of someone trying to stay calm. "You did, Hannah, I remember. But I spoke to the FBI after you saw them. They said it wasn't unusual for the families of criminals to be harassed like this. It was terribly sad, of course."

"A man tried to kidnap me in a bar," Hannah said.

"Yes, Detective McVickers told me."

"Then, they tried to break into Peter's apartment. And the next night they tried to run us down on the street."

"Yes I know. Detective McVickers thinks this might have something to do with the drug thing."

"Detective McVickers is wrong," she sobbed, looking into the phone as if she could see him. "Don't you believe me?"

I had never seen such emotion from her. What had really gone on between them? Had her body been developed when she was thirteen? Those breasts, those lips. Her father had kept her in a virginal, trusting state . . . She would be easy prey . . . Clerics were notorious lechers . . .

"Where are you now, Hannah?" Kellner asked.

"On our way back to LA."

"When you get to California give me a call," he said. "I want to see you. Both of you."

Texas Goes On Forever

S even hours later, we were just clearing San Antonio. There was nothing but yellow dirt, scrub and stunted hills. The sun set with a pinkish glow. It was like being on Mars.

We had been the only car on the road for hours when I saw headlights blinking behind us. They would disappear as the car drove to the bottom of a grade and reappear as it came to the top.

They kept getting closer.

Somebody was bearing down on us. I floored the Bug. I was going 85, but the headlights kept getting closer.

The pink glow was breaking up into gray. There were no towns, no gas stations on this stretch, not even a rest area.

Then it was behind us, bearing down. It was an 18-wheeler, barreling along in our lane. I switched to the right to let it pass. The trailer swayed as if it were empty. It came up alongside. The driver was a dark figure. I could only see driving gloves on the wheel.

The Bug whined and rattled up a steep grade and wouldn't go any faster. The truck stayed abreast of us, going at exactly the same speed. It was a trucker's prank, pinning you in your lane, not letting you get clear. There was a sharp curve ahead. I stepped off the gas pedal and tried to hold the road without braking. The truck slowed down along with me. All he had to do was slide into our lane and give us a bump, and we'd go flying off the shoulder down the embankment, bouncing and flipping, then bursting into flame.

The curve sharpened. The back end started to drift. I fought the wheel to straighten out. If I turned too much I'd go into a spin and hit the truck, maybe get jammed up in its undercarriage. But I couldn't hold the road. The Bug bounced onto the shoulder.

"What are you doing?" Hannah screamed.

I jammed down on the brake with the heel of my shoe. The Bug skidded on the sandy shoulder and came to a jolting stop. It shuddered and stalled. A gust of burning rubber blew into the car.

"I must have fallen asleep," I said.

"Do you want me to drive?" she asked.

"No, I'm okay now."

The truck was already far ahead of us. I pulled out and kept at a safe distance. Then it disappeared around a bend and we were alone again.

Maybe it had just been a bored trucker. A hot surge of hate ran through me. I felt as if I could kill that bastard, shoot him down in cold blood and not care about his wife and babies.

We got back on the road. Exits led to twisty dirt trails that seemed to go nowhere. Then, the landscape thickened. We passed gutted houses and stripped barns. Corrals with broken rails, tumbleweed rolling. City lights sparkled in the distance. El Paso 29 miles. El Paso 17 miles. A bridge, a skyline, the muted roar of passing traffic, and we were in the city.

We pulled off for gas in the barrio. The Mexicans looked at us without interest. A few exits down we hit a big, cheerful barbecue restaurant. A matronly waitress with a red-checked apron called me "honey."

"I think we're safe," I told Hannah. "Nobody knows where we went. We were alone on the road so I know we weren't followed."

She dug into her bag and handed me some crumpled twenties. "My treat."

A few hours later we came to a billboard: WELCOME TO NEW MEXICO, LAND OF ENCHANTMENT. Then the roads got black and we had only our headlights to show the way. Occasionally, I'd see lights in the mirror and sweat it out until they disappeared, or a car roared past us.

Shapes loomed against the sky. Our brights hit an exit—D . . . BUSINESS DISTRICT . . . GAS, FOOD, LODGING. We followed a dark road for a mile. Just as I was starting to get nervous we came upon a festive strip of restaurants and motels, neon splashing patterns across the road.

A Holiday Inn was all lit up. Through a picture window we could see people dancing in the bar.

Across the road was a Motel 6. The office had a plain Protestant crucifix on the wall. A pale clerk put down his Bible with a smile. "Welcome travelers."

He gave us a bare room with a narrow bed. I went out and moved the car so I could see it from our window.

A naked bulb burned over the bathroom mirror. My hair was cowlicked at odd angles. Scraggly patches of beard crawled on my face. I hadn't brought a change of clothes. My socks stank. I rinsed my underwear in the shower.

Hannah huddled on the bed in the light of the TV.

"I got another text from Reverend Kellner," she said. "He wants to know where we are."

"We're somewhere in New Mexico," I said.

She texted.

"He wants to know how long it'll take us to get to California."

"He doesn't trust me," I said.

"I'll tell him we'll be there tomorrow."

I sat by the window, peeking out behind the drawn shade at the car. When I started to nod I would jerk my head back up to stay awake. After a few hours of this, my neck stiffened.

"Come to bed," Hannah said.

She drew the covers up over me.

"Go to sleep," she said. "I'll watch."

California, Here We Come

For hours there was nothing but Navajo on the radio.

"We're on another planet," I said.

Signs told us we were entering reservations. Casinos swam like mirages in the glare. Even at this early hour, the parking lots were full of old heaps and pickups.

We turned off the radio and drove on, lulled by the hum of the tires. We passed through heat shimmers and under sudden outcroppings of yellow rock. In the middle of nowhere there would be a hamlet of trailers, bungalows, and gutted shacks. Cannibalized cars and rusty refrigerators. Satellite discs sprouting from the poorest roof. No sign of life.

"Could be Indian reservations," I said. "The remnant of tribes massacred by the Cavalry?"

She didn't answer.

"I'm talking to myself again," I said. "Like the sound of one hand clapping."

"You talk when you're nervous," she said. "I shut up."

MapQuest sent us onto Route 17 toward Arizona. The road was a straight line to infinity. There were billboards in the desert: 40 ACRES FOR SALE.

"Who would buy land out here?" I said.

As if in answer to my question we passed a bungalow a few hundred feet off the road. More car carcasses. A basketball hoop drooping from a pole. A tattered clothesline. No satellite dish on the roof.

"There's somebody who really wants to be alone," I said.

"Maybe he's hiding," Hannah said.

"Sitting in the dark with a half gallon of Jim Beam and a shotgun pointed at the door."

Going north, we hit switchbacks, steep grades, deep

descents. The sky was cloudless and pale blue.

"It's like we're inside an Easter egg," I said.

She was looking out of the window. "What?"

"Nothing. I'm tripping."

I checked the rearview to see if we were being followed. For miles we were the only car on the road again. In a country of three-hundred million it didn't seem possible that we could go hours without seeing another human being.

"We're not real anymore," I said. "We're in someone's Second Life."

"Want me to drive?" Hannah asked.

The rocks turned reddish brown. The landscape had a tame, resort feel. Outside Flagstaff, we passed stands of evergreens. There were log cabin motels, RVs hogging the road. Asian tourists hurried out of a Burger King and onto a tour bus. They moved in lockstep, like figures in a video game.

Just beyond the WELCOME TO CALIFORNIA sign there was a mile long line of trucks at the weigh station. CHP officers waved us with mechanical gestures through the fruit check booths.

Hannah punched out a number. Kellner's tense, boyish voice came over the speaker. "Where are you?"

"Outside of LA," Hannah said. "We can stop at Robbinsgate."

"No, no, don't come here. I'll meet you . . ." He paused for a moment, picking a place. "Just before Palm Springs, around the Marengo Casino, there's an outlet mall. It's at the Cabuchon exit. I'll be waiting in the food court."

Heading into the desert, the pickups and RVs were replaced by gleaming sedans—Lexuses, BMWs, fancy SUVs—heading for Palm Springs. Wind farms stretched to the mesa, blades turning slowly. The freeway was smooth and freshly blacktopped. The sun sparkled on the cars in the Marengo Casino parking lot. Up the road, the low sandstone buildings of the Cabuchon Mall seemed to go on for miles. We finally found the exit. Cars weaved through the lot, coming and going.

We got trapped in the flow of humanity. Women—pushing carts, juggling shopping bags, dragging toddlers—came at us. The entrance narrowed into an arcade. People pushed in behind us, anxious to get in. There were men— husbands, boyfriends, even some grandpas along for the ride. I checked the crowd for a lone male, maybe two, keeping a discreet distance.

It was a high-end outlet—Armani, Ralph Lauren, Eddie Bauer. Hannah took my hand. "C'mon." She was excited about seeing Kellner. A flush burned under her sallow skin.

The food court was at the end. Bored teenagers slouched behind the counters. Listless Mexicans in oversized uniforms dragged brooms and dustpans. The floor was slick with ketchup and mustard.

A man waved to us from a table in the back by the restrooms.

"There he is," said Hannah, pulling me along.

He was slight and balding, A pinkish scalp under sandy hair. Blue dress shirt tucked into khaki Dockers. Watery bloodshot blue eyes, like he'd been crying. He reached for Hannah like a blind man. His head came up to her chest. It was like she was hugging a little boy. I watched to see how long his hand would rest on her back, how tightly he would press her to him.

"I've been worried about you, Hannah," he said. And then turned, squinting me into focus. His hand was small and soggy. "Thank you for bringing her back safely, Peter."

A Divine's Intervention

She had to lean forward to make herself heard. Reverend Kellner pushed his chair closer. They were nose-to-nose, just the two of them. I was forgotten. He never took his eyes off her. When her story was over, he sat back and clasped his hands, like he was about to pray.

"That man outside the strip club," he said. "He could have been the kind of pervert who hangs around those places."

She looked at him in alarm, realizing he doubted her. "But he knew my name."

"I know, I know," he said gently. "So did the man in the bar, you said."

"I said?" She sat back abruptly. "You don't believe me."

"I believe you heard your name."

"But you don't believe it really happened. You think I imagined it."

He took a breath. "You're suffering for an atrocity you didn't commit, Hannah. What's being done to you is almost as bad as what your father did."

"Almost?"

"Do you know the Old Testament decree, 'the sins of the father shall be visited on the sons to the third generation'?"

"You know I don't."

"These things happen in a modern context and we don't recognize them as prophecies fulfilled."

"You mean God is punishing me for what my father did?"

He raised his hand to calm her. "God doesn't punish, He *corrects*. You feel that somehow you should atone, don't you?"

"I feel ashamed," she said.

"But you can't make restitution. And so you can't find relief or redemption. It festers in you. It won't go away."

Some kids ran by us, screeching and chasing a balloon.

"I keep thinking about Zandy," Hannah said. "How weird it must have been when she saw him standing over her. There was a second when she trusted him because he was my dad. That moment of hesitation was all he needed. He always had some way of tricking them into letting him in."

"I know," Kellner said. "I've had many dark nights about this."

Hannah blinked. Tears glittered on her lashes. "I know her room. If I close my eyes now I can see everything in it. I can see Zandy. When he tied her up she knew she was going to die. I try to imagine how that felt . . ."

Kellner shuddered. She stopped.

"I'm sorry."

"You've taken his guilt upon yourself," Kellner said. "Like your poor sister and your mom. But it's worse for you because he loves you. You are probably the only thing in the world he ever loved. You love him, too. And you feel even more guilty for your anguish over his suffering."

He sounded more like a shrink than a pastor.

"Sometimes I do worry about what they're doing to him," Hannah said. "But then I get angry and I feel he deserves everything he gets."

"You say that, but you don't mean it," Kellner said. "You hate yourself for not hating *him*."

She put her hand over her eyes.

"You must go to him, Hannah," Kellner said. "Confront him with your feelings." He leaned forward again and took her hand away, gently, so he could look into her eyes. "You're his victim, too. You have to come to terms with what happened. You need closure so you can move on."

She held his hand and searched his face. I knew that look, obsidian-black eyes boring into you.

"I swore I'd never see him again," she said.

"He told me."

She stared. "He told you?"

"I go up there once a month," he said. "I've started doing outreach with some of the prisoners. Alcohol counseling, Bible study. It has healed me to touch the humanity in these lost souls. I've spent a lot of time with your dad."

"Oh, my God," Hannah said. "Oh, my God!"

"I'm the only human contact he has," he pleaded. "I couldn't just drop him, even after what he did. He's in a terrible place, Hannah. If the people who wanted him executed saw where he was and how he is being treated, they would at least know that he is enduring a fate worse than death."

A man at a nearby table was looking at us. He was young, hair down to his shoulder, a mustache and a soul patch. No shopping bag, a container of coffee. He seemed to be alone.

"He asks about you, Hannah," Kellner said. "They keep him so isolated, so deprived of any human contact that it makes him delusional, but he's very clear about you. You're the only person he cares about, Hannah. I don't think he feels a moment of regret for your mom or your poor sister, but he worries about you. He always asks me: do you think Hannah will ever forgive me?"

I sat back so the man could see I had noticed him.

Kellner gave me a sidelong look, as if I were reacting to what he had said.

"I've tried to get him to let Christ into his life," he said. "Oh, I know how naïve that sounds. Idealistic young minister waving the Gospel in the face of a mass murderer. But your father is one of God's creatures, Hannah. What he did is somehow part of a plan. We can't know what that plan is. That's where faith comes in."

I sensed the man looking at me. Could be innocent. Maybe he thinks he knows me. It's a food court, a harmless place. I returned his glance. That's normal, too. But this guy was doing everything he could not to see me.

Kellner raised his voice, as if he were trying to regain my attention. "I know how hard it is to keep our faith in this world, how we struggle with disbelief. Sometimes I feel that the souls of those who died are looking down at us with compassion. That they want to tell us somehow that our real life will begin when our time on earth is over."

The man I'd been watching pulled his chair back. He had to pass our table on his way out, and kept his face averted.

Kellner turned just enough to include me. His neck was scraped raw from shaving. "But sometimes that vision fades. Those shining faces disappear and blackness rises up around me. In the wind outside the church I hear the mocking laughter of the damned, Hannah."

"I feel that blackness," Hannah said with a desperate look. "Is that God's punishment or my insanity?"

"You can't know," Kellner said. "You can only hope that your faith can become so strong that you won't have to question. That when your time comes Alexandra will be waiting to take your hand. And then, your soul's mission will be clear."

His hand was like a baby's paw in Hannah's grasp. She let go and sat back.

I watched the man leave the food court, then lost him in the milling crowd.

Kellner moved his chair next to Hannah, urging, "He's done unspeakable things, but he's not the monster you've created in your thoughts. He's a pathetic, sick man. And he is still your father."

She turned. "What do you think, Peter?"

"I think family ties are overrated," I said.

Kellner reddened. "You don't have to be flippant about it."

"That's just Peter's sense of humor," Hannah said, and I thought I detected a touch of pride in her voice. "Can we just show up at the prison on visiting day?"

"Not for him," Kellner said. "He's in a special unit.

Abner Fried, his lawyer, will have to arrange an appointment. Fried has some very dangerous political ideas, but he is a strong advocate for your father."

Hannah got up. "I'll be right back."

I had a sudden jolt of panic as she went into the bathroom. Someone could be waiting for her in there. There could be women in on this. How long would it take to push into a stall behind Hannah, grab her by the hair, pull her head back, and slit her throat?

Kellner sniffed and reached for a rumpled Kleenex.

"Do you really believe people are after Hannah, Peter?"

"Yes, since I've been attacked twice myself."

"Detective McVickers thinks those people could have assumed that you were selling narcotics."

"He's wrong."

"How about the other attacks? Do you think Hannah created them out of her own guilt?"

"They were *real* people."

"Yes, but she could be misinterpreting her confrontations with them."

"She isn't."

He blinked and his eyes watered. "Do you know anything about serial killers, Peter?"

"Not really."

"They can't suppress their urges. They're missing a gene of self-control."

What was he trying to tell me?

"They are unique in penology," he said. "Even the most hardened killer has moments of remorse. But serial killers never feel guilt . . . they continue to get gratification by reliving their crimes."

"Well, at least they can't commit any more."

He didn't seem consoled. "They think of each of their murders as a special achievement. They're proud of them. Arnold sits in his cell night after night, reveling in his memories. Remembering each murder, relishing every detail."

"You don't know that," I said.

"Yes, I do." He grabbed my shoulders, as if he wanted to shake me for my obtuseness. He blew a blast of Listerine in my face. "The Hebrew Talmud says that an evil man never feels remorse, even at the gates of hell. Do you see what I'm saying? You can mortify a serial killer's flesh, but you can't get into his soul. You can't make him repent."

"I see what you're saying."

He sat back. "Hannah is a marvelously gifted athlete, you know. We had to put her on the boys' softball team because she was so much better than the girls. And even with the boys she played shortstop and hit cleanup. But soccer was her real sport. She could outrun most of the boys. She took Robbinsgate to the regionals. It was the biggest news in town until Alexandra . . ." He took a fresh Kleenex out of his pocket. "Did you know that all of Arnold's victims were members of my congregation?"

"I didn't."

"I don't think anybody ever made the connection. Of course, I did. I had the disquieting thought that he had gotten his . . . *urges* . . . during services when we were all together. There's something vulnerable about people at prayer." He blew his nose and looked in the Kleenex. "I knew them all very well. And their families. We dedicated pews to them and put up mosaics and created a little arbor on the grounds. After a while we ran out of ideas for memorials."

He rubbed his nose hard with his knuckles.

"Are you a Christian, Peter?"

"I'm not religious."

He nodded. "God sends the Devil to test us. He hides his face and waits . . . Oh, here comes Hannah. Don't say anything to her about this."

He jumped up as she returned. "Are you all right, Hannah? I didn't upset you, did I?"

"No, no." She took his hand. But the spell was broken. Her eyes were opaque again. She turned to me, impatiently. "Let's go."

On the way to the parking lot, Kellner got a bloody nose.

He was apologizing as Hannah walked him to a bench. "No big deal, I get these all the time."

She made him sit with his head between his legs. "Make sure he keeps his head down," she said to me. "I've got a sure cure."

Blood dripped onto his shoes. "No big deal. Allergies. My nose starts to itch and I keep rubbing it. And I rub it so hard I break a blood vessel." A strange, bronchial sound came out of him. It sounded like a cough or a gasp, but when I crouched for a better look, there were tears trickling down his face, mixing with the blood.

"I see their upturned faces," he sobbed. "When you're in the pulpit they look up to you. They're called the flock and you're supposed to be their shepherd."

"You can't blame yourself," I said.

"Hannah was such a sweet, innocent little girl. When she made a good play she would run off the field to her dad with her eyes shining."

"Maybe you should stop going up to see him."

Hannah returned with a wad of napkins and a handful of lemon wedges. "This always works," she said squeezing the lemons onto a napkin and sticking it up his nose.

We stood over him until the bleeding stopped. He followed us out to the lot, dry-eyed and docile. Hannah showed him the bent fender where the Escalade had rear-ended us. We shook hands. He hugged her with a sad smile.

"Your father and I will talk about your visit when I see him. We'll share some small portion of joy."

In the side mirror I saw him watching us as we drove away. Then he was swallowed up in the surge of shoppers.

"He thinks I'm crazy," Hannah said.

"It's easier that way," I said.

"Where is Otter Point?"

"Way up north by the Oregon border. We don't have to go."

"Yes, we do. We need proof."

A Tahoe pulled in behind us. The driver looked like the

guy at the food court. Didn't mean anything. It was an outlet. People came and went. But I had to know.

Halfway down the ramp I jammed on the brakes and turned sharply. The Bug's back-end flew out. Tires screeched behind us. We flew over a grass divider and skidded across the access road in the path of oncoming traffic. Horns blared.

Hannah screamed, "Peter!"

I bumped up a grassy hill to the station. Then things got tranquil. It was like we had traveled to another world. People were gassing up. No one looked at us.

"See," I said. "It's like it never happened." I turned off the engine. "I just wanted to see if we were being followed."

"Were we?"

"I don't think so."

But when I got out, my knees shaking, I saw the Tahoe on a ridge overlooking the station, waiting.

Sleepwalking

I took the lug wrench off the spare and tossed it into the back seat.

"What's that for?" she asked.

"Just in case. You drive."

I couldn't tell her. I wasn't sure. As we pulled back onto the ramp the Tahoe was gone. Maybe it had been just another coincidence. Life was full of them. Coincidence is the mother of religion, Katz said, because it confers false significance on random events.

But then the Tahoe appeared again, dawdling in the right lane. Hannah pulled out to pass it.

"Hold it," I said. "Don't pass him."

The Tahoe's right-turn signal blinked. He pulled off onto the shoulder and we drove past.

"Okay, speed up, let's get out of here," I said.

I watched in the side mirror as the driver got out of the car and shaded his eyes.

"What's the matter with you?" Hannah asked.

"I think this Tahoe might be following us. Floor it. Let's see what he does."

She downshifted and the Bug leaped forward. We were up to 85 in no time, but cars overtook us like we were standing still.

"Is it a black Tahoe?" Hannah asked, looking in the rearview.

"Yes."

"It's behind us."

I caught him in the side mirror. That turnoff had been a ruse. He had speeded to catch up to us, then dropped back behind other cars.

"Okay," I said. "I'm still not sure."

"What should we do?" she asked.

"Pull off at the next rest stop."

We drove for a while until a sign came up.

"Rest area seven miles," I said.

"I see it," she said.

"This might be the guy who I thought was checking us out in the food court. He was at the table next to us."

"I didn't notice."

In no time, the rest area ramp was on us.

"Okay, moment of truth," I said.

She turned off. "He's following us," she said.

I knew exactly what to do. It was as if I'd been saving this plan in my unconscious for years. "Pull up to the bathrooms and let me off. Then, go all the way to the end. Get out and look in your bag like you're checking to see if something's in there. Then walk up the hill into the trees."

"Where will you be?"

"I'll be up there, watching to see if he follows you."

"What if he does?"

"We'll know they're still after us."

"And then what?"

"I don't know."

I took off my Lakers sweatshirt and wrapped it around the lug wrench.

"What are you going to do with that?" she asked, alarmed.

"I need something."

She stopped in front of the main building. I waited until the Tahoe drove by, then got out, taking the sweatshirt. She drove away without a word. The Tahoe had pulled into a parking space. She drove past it to the end of the rest area.

I watched from the alcove of the Information Center. A few wisps of white smoke came out of the Tahoe's tailpipe. He had turned off the motor.

I went around to a door at the back and stepped out. I was behind the building, he wouldn't see me. I ran across the road and up a little hill to a thicket separating the rest area from the freeway. From here I could see the entire parking lot. I watched as Hannah fussed in her bag. The Tahoe door opened. It was definitely the guy from the mall.

I stayed low and ran along the tree line. Hannah crossed, carrying her bag. Tahoe Guy walked after her, texting into a cell phone.

Hannah walked up the hill into the thicket. Mr. Tahoe stopped at the foot of the hill and looked up, as if he were trying to figure out what to do. Then he walked up after her.

I dropped onto my stomach. The grass was cold and muddy from the sprinklers. Hannah trudged up the path past me and disappeared over the crest of the hill. Footsteps crackled in the leaves. I stuck my face in the wet earth. The guy's Timberlands came up the hill. He was taking measured steps, trying to muffle the sound.

I had a mouthful of muddy leaves, but couldn't spit them out. He passed without even looking around, he was so intent on Hannah.

I slid the lug wrench out of my sweatshirt. He had stopped at the crest of the hill, trying to decide what to do again.

He wasn't far away. Two big steps would get me there. I'd have to give him a good shot to knock him down. Then I'd stand over him with the lug wrench and make him tell me who he was and who had sent him.

I got up on my knees. His head turned like it was on a turret, looking right and left to see if anyone was around. I put my hands on the ground and pushed off. My foot came down on a branch. He started to turn. I lunged, wrong-footed, and swung. I was aiming for the top of his shoulders, but caught him in the back of the neck.

"Shit!" he called out, stumbling forward.

I switched feet and swung from the heels, aiming for his head. There was a thud. He grabbed his head. "Ahh . . ."

He went down on one knee and held up his hand, like he was asking for a timeout.

"Hold on," he said.

I swung level and hit him solid in the back of the head. He went down on his face. I stood over him and clubbing anywhere I could hit.

He swiped at my ankle.

I tripped.

He rolled over and went to his belt. He had a gun! I jumped at him swinging wildly. He put his hands over his face and I hit him in the ribs, swinging until his hands came down. Then swinging again and again. Watching his face come apart.

I don't know how many times I hit him. I swung so hard I lost my balance and Hannah grabbed me to keep me from falling on top of him. He was staring straight up at me, a few leftover breaths gurgling in his throat. His eyes were closed and swollen blue. Blood poured out of his nose and mouth. His hair was caked with blood.

I couldn't catch my breath, couldn't feel my feet.

Hannah held me under the arms. "Don't get it on your shoes."

I pulled his jacket back with the lug wrench. There was a big automatic in a holster.

She found something in the leaves. "His wallet." She opened it. "Oh, God, no!"

Hannah showed it to me. A shiny badge. Drug Enforcement Agency.

She gave me a baffled look. "Why?"

My answer came quickly, easily. "Because those morons thought you were a mule for a Mexican mafia meth ring, that's why."

A cell phone rang out "Reveille" from under the agent's leg. I grabbed it, flipped it open, read the display. There was a text message from a number with a 909 area code: DID YOU GET THEM?

"He must have reported that he was following us," I said.

I didn't have to think. It was like some kind of sociopath inside me controlled my actions. "Maybe we can make them think Doane did this."

I took the phone. Hannah watched over my shoulder as I texted back:

LOST THEM. BUT PICKED UP DOANE. HE MUST BE FOLLOWING THEM, TOO. WHAT SHOULD I DO?

I waited. No answer. I went cold with fear.

"I didn't follow a code or something. They know I'm not him. I outsmarted myself like I always do . . . I'm just a big-mouthed wiseass."

Hannah pulled me. "Let's go."

"Yeah, yeah. Better take his wallet. It has our prints on it."

"The phone, too," she said.

"Yeah, the phone." I forced myself to look down at him. "Can't leave any trace that we were here. Our DNA is all over the place. Can't do anything about that."

She pulled harder. "Let's go, Peter."

A few steps down the hill and we were in a clearing. People were fussing in their cars, chasing children. Someone could have seen us. Someone could be calling 911 on a cell phone.

My clothes were muddy. I had blood on my pants. My sweatshirt was bloody from the lug wrench. But nobody looked twice. Nobody turned to watch as we drove away.

Stuck

We drove for a while and then I realized something. "They probably have his phone on a
GPS."

"Throw it out the window," Hannah said.

"Can't. It has our DNA on it. Pull over."

She slowed and bumped onto the shoulder. I put the
phone on the floor between my feet and clubbed it with the
bloody lug wrench. It came apart like a plastic toy.

"Take out the SIM card," she said.

"What if it keeps transmitting?"

"Break it into small pieces. We'll scatter them along the
road."

I took the phone outside and knelt by the car, banging
like a maniac. Then, I collected all the pieces and put them
under the front tire. Hannah backed up and drove over the
pieces, but they were too small to crunch. I left one plastic
fragment on the ground and got in. She had methodically cut
the SIM card into a little pile with her nail scissors. As we
drove I flicked one piece out of the window at a time.

"What about his wallet?" she said.

We pulled off the road again. The agent's DEA ID had
his name—Noah Frayne—and a photo of him, beardless and
callow. There was a MasterCard, Discover Card, a California
driver's license, a business card with NOAH FRAYNE,
PRIVATE INVESTIGATOR.

"I guess he used that to fool people," I said.

Hannah cut the cards into pieces. The leather wallet was
worn bald in spots. She ripped it to shreds with the scissors,
then held up the badge.

"We'll have to take this and flush it down a toilet or
something."

"Water doesn't wash DNA off."

"It'll be in a sewer, Peter," she said. "They'll never find it."

It was made of tin, flimsier than I thought a badge would be. I tried to fold it, but she slapped my hand.

"Leave it, you're just making it harder to flush."

She peeled out onto the road, speed-shifting to fourth.

"Don't go too fast, they'll pull us over," I said.

I wrapped the lug wrench in my sweatshirt. "Can't let it touch the car. It's got his DNA on it."

"You've got DNA on the brain," she said.

"That's how they caught your father. He'd be cheering you at Stanford right now if it hadn't been for DNA."

I felt a hot flush of shame. I touched her arm. "I'm sorry, Hannah."

She shook her head, all business. "You're right. We'll have to be more careful than he was, that's for sure."

A few miles on we came to a sign: NELSON'S TRADING POST, DATES AND GIFTS AND INDIAN BLANKETS. Hannah pulled off in front of a wooden western-style building. She was back a minute later.

"Would you believe they wouldn't let me use the bathroom. Said it was for employees only."

"Let's come back tonight and burn the dump down," I said.

Her laugh was strangely gleeful. "We might as well. We can do anything we want now."

We came to a sign for Redlands. "I can stop here," Hannah said.

"Too close to home," I said. "Might see someone you know."

Robbinsgate was the next exit.

"We can go to St. Paul's," I said. "Ask Reverend Kellner if he'll let us flush a dead cop's badge down the church toilet."

The freeway stretched out flat and endless. We were lulled by the smoothness of road, the placid sameness of the landscape.

"It feels like we're still virtual," she said.

The sociopath inside me had it all figured out. "They'll start texting him in a half hour. Then they'll lose the GPS signal, so they'll start looking for him."

"They'll suspect us."

"Definitely. They'll talk to the Rev. He'll tell them we're going to see your father and that's exactly what we have to do. Go to the lawyer, Abner Fried, in San Francisco. Get an appointment at Otter Point."

She shook her head. "No way we can get away with this."

"We have to try. We can't turn ourselves in and say hi guys, our bad, we killed Agent Frayne because we thought he was the mystery stalker, can we go now?"

I could say it so calmly.

"They have no witnesses, no physical evidence. The only way they can get us is if we snitch on each other."

I could see it so clearly.

"Before this is over they'll put us in separate rooms. It's called the Prisoner's Dilemma. They'll tell you that I said you did it and they'll tell me you said I did it. They'll try to get us to rat each other out."

"We have to stick to our story," she said.

"Yeah. We're in this together."

Her eyes widened as it dawned on her.

"Forever," she said.

Loose Ends

I had to get rid of the lug wrench.

"I'll pull over at the next rest stop," Hannah said. "We can dump it in the trash."

"No good," I said. "As soon as they see that the guy was bludgeoned, they'll look in every garbage can from here to Sacramento."

"Bludgeoned," she said. "You are such an English major. We can bury it off the road."

"Risky. Some passing Highway Patrolman might see us doing it."

The blood on the lug wrench had caked quickly and looked like flecks of rust. I wiped it off with my sweatshirt. "We have to make it disappear."

I still had McVickers' card in my pocket. I started to punch the number.

"Why are you calling *him*?" Hannah asked.

The phone was ringing. "To plant our story," I said.

There was a sudden silence. Had somebody picked up? Had they heard me? Was I on tape?

"Robbery." The voice sounded bored, but cops were good actors.

I asked for McVickers "Peter Vogel calling . . ."

He was on in a second, as if he'd been standing by the phone.

"Mr. Vogel," he said, full of expansive irony. "Where do I find you in your travels?"

"I'm in California," I said. He already knew that from Kellner, I was sure. "We're going to visit Hannah's dad to see if he can help us figure out who's after her."

"Uh huh," McVickers said. "Well what can I do for you?"

"I think Sonny Doane is following us." I heard an echo. Had he put me on speaker? Were they sitting in there looking at the text message that I had written on the guy's phone?

"I think I saw him at a rest stop," I said.

"You're sure it was him?"

"He's pretty hard to miss."

"What was he driving?"

"Ford pickup."

"Where are you calling from?"

"I'm on the I-10 freeway to LA."

"Okay, here's what you do. Don't try to speed away from him. Stay in traffic. Look for signs to the Highway Patrol or Police or something. Go right to the station and tell 'em to call me. Can you do that, Peter?"

"Okay, okay."

"Call me in an hour, no matter what happens."

"Okay."

I disconnected.

"Was that necessary?" Hannah asked.

"It doesn't matter now, I did it. It's now our official story. We have to be careful. No mistakes. Have to think ahead . . . have to consider the consequences of everything we say and do."

"Peter," Hannah said, suddenly frantic.

"I wasn't smart back there. See, my plan was to get the guy to tell us who he was and why he was following us. But even if he had, we would have been forced to kill him anyway, and that would have made it a bigger sin because it was premeditated, whereas now it's just a stupid accident."

"Peter, shut up for a second!"

It had hit her. Her face was scrunched-up like a frightened little girl's.

She was shaking. I put my arm around her.

"Got a knife or anything sharp?" I asked.

"Only my nail clippers."

It was like watching a lunatic through a one-way mirror. The sane me and the crazy me. Only the sane me was that sociopath, calm and lucid, calculating his every move. And the crazy me was behind the mirror, writhing in a strait-jacket, screaming, "HOW DID I GET INTO THIS MESS?"

I jumped out and grabbed her jack. The Bug was light and easy to raise. Sweat poured off me as I removed the right rear tire and put on the spare.

Then I attacked her rear tire with the nail clippers, stabbing at the treads until I had gouged an acceptable hole. I threw it in the back seat and jumped back in.

"Let's find a real garage."

"There's a gas stop a few miles up."

I turned on her. "No, a real old-fashioned garage!"

"You said you wanted to get rid of the lug wrench right away, but now you want to waste time looking for a garage," she yelled back. "You're not making any sense."

"Get off at Loma Linda," I said.

We pulled off past the big self-service Exxons and Mobils. About a mile down the road was a four-pump station with two bays and a sign that read: TUNE-UPS — FLATS FIXED. A kid in greasy overalls with a smudgy face wiped his hand on an oily rag as he walked toward the car.

"*This* is a real old-fashioned garage," I said.

I opened the door to get out, but then it hit me like I had touched a live wire. I jumped back inside. "Drive away quick!"

"What's wrong?"

"Quick!"

The kid watched us bump over the curb.

"Find a mall," I said.

"What's the matter with you?"

"For Chrissake, I'm covered with blood." My voice was hoarse. Had I been screaming? "We'll have to find a Gap or something and buy new clothes."

"I'll ask at the garage," she said,

"No, no, don't you understand? We can't have any witnesses. Can't you see it on *America's Most Wanted*? *Anybody who has a clue to the identity of the cowards who murdered this heroic DEA agent call this number* . . . And that bozo gets on the phone: *A girl in a blue Volkswagen Bug asked for a mall,* he says. They'll figure it out in a second."

She was in a panic. "Peter, don't go crazy on me."

"There'll be a mall down this road," I said. "You can't drive five miles anywhere in the world without finding a mall."

A few miles later it appeared out of the mist like the Magic Kingdom. A beauty with a Northrops, a Starbucks, a Foot Locker, Wendy's, Pizza Hut, Sushi, Thai takeout, even a Borders bookstore. Garden apartments were lined up across the road with signs: FIRST THREE MONTHS RENT FREE. You could move in. Nice little one bedroom. Get a job at the mall. Go back and forth across that road for years and nobody would find you.

"Park around back," I said. "The last row by the dumpsters is employee parking, so there won't be a lot of traffic. Do you have money?"

"I can use my MasterCharge," she said.

"No, no, we don't want any transactions in your name."

"I can get cash at the ATM."

"Yeah, okay. You can always say you were getting it for the trip. But there are security cameras over every counter. They'll have you on tape. They can zoom in and see what you bought. We'll have to risk it. They have a deal on collar tees at Foot Locker, three for twenty bucks. Get Extra Large. Go to the Northrop's. Get me a pair of khakis, size thirty-two, thirty-four. Socks and a package of boxers."

I grabbed her as she got out of the car. "Get a pair of scissors. And a kitchen knife, too. A big one. Get a cutlery set, you know, like we're newlyweds and it's for our new apartment. You're buying the clothes because your husband is coming home from Iraq, if anybody asks."

"Nobody will," she said.

"Just in case some cashier wants to make small talk. Everybody's a detective these days. Say the wrong thing and they get suspicious. Next thing you know, some security guy is following you around the store."

"I'll be cool, okay?" she said.

"Okay."

I ducked down in the seat and watched her walk across the lot. Tall, graceful, and unhurried. She didn't look back.

She was good at this.

Better than me.

Can't Think About It

I was shaking like it was twenty below. A shift was breaking. People in corporate uniforms walked by the car. Burger King, Pizza Hut, Office Depot, trudging like weary soldiers with their heads down. Some tore at cigarette packs. Others muttered into cell phones. If you asked any one of them you'd get a sob story about their lives. They didn't know how lucky they were.

The blood on my hands had dried into a dark stain. But it was still blood.

"Noah Frayne," I said.

McVickers was right. When you caught them by surprise, they didn't suffer fear or pain. They were too busy fighting for their lives.

Everything had happened too quickly. Frayne hadn't had time to think. He hadn't suffered. I hadn't hurt him. I had just taken his consciousness away.

"Noah."

He had tried to be reasonable. "Hold on," he had said.

He was young, inexperienced. Following two people. Where did he think the other one was? As he hiked all the way up the hill, why did he never ask himself: *where did the dude go?*

He was supposed to be trained in surveillance. He was supposed to be alert, with hair-trigger reflexes. But Noah Frayne had let an English major sneak up and clobber him with a lug wrench.

Hadn't they taught him some self-defense technique against an attack like mine? He could have rolled out of the way and jumped up, gone for his gun. But he hadn't been nimble or quick. He had dropped to a knee and said, "hold on." Do you think a guy who just clocked you is going to stop just because you say "hold on?"

I had never won a fight in my life. Now I had killed a cop.

Hannah walked up with shopping bags, a slight swing to her step, like a girl with nothing on her mind.

She opened the door. "You okay?"

"Thinking too much."

She threw the shopping bags onto the seat. "I got you some Dockers."

I stayed low and slipped out of my bloody clothes.

An old white-haired woman in a Burger King uniform appeared out of nowhere and looked into the car.

I tugged at Hannah's arm. "Let's get outta here."

"Why?"

"She saw me pulling my pants down. She's going to her car to call Security."

"For what?"

"For being naked in a car. For flashing her. Who knows? She's a snitch. Everybody's a snitch. We live in a pop culture police state. Katz says they turn you in so they can get on the ten o'clock news."

She gunned the motor and screeched out of the lot.

"Take it easy," I said. "Don't draw attention."

I hopped in the back and slipped on the new clothes. My sweat smelled strange, as if I were another person.

"Did you get knives?" I asked.

"In the Northrops bag."

It was a cheap cutlery set. There were scissors, too, "All-purpose tool," the package said. "Try it on metal . . ."

I slashed my clothes to ribbons and scattered them like confetti out of the window as we drove down the road. Hannah watched me in the rearview. We passed a CHP car, hiding in a speed trap in an alley.

"Shit! He can get us for littering."

I watched out the rear window, but he didn't pull out after us.

"Here's that garage," she said.

The same kid came out with a blank look, as if he'd never seen us before.

"Can you fix a flat?"

While he rolled the tire into the shop I slipped the lug wrench out of the car and laid it gently under the spare.

"I can patch it, but you'll need a new wheel," he said.

I pointed casually to the wrench.

"That yours?"

He picked it up without a look and threw it down an open bay. It landed with a clang.

I got back into the car. "Now they'll never find it," I said.

Act Normal

We found a Starbucks with a WiFi. Hannah hovered over my shoulder as I Googled the Otter Point Correctional Facility.

There was a Statement of Intent. "Otter Point is designed to house the state's most socially and psychologically challenged offenders in a secure, structured setting."

The Home Page showed a postcard photo of a walled compound cut out of the woods of Northern California. "It looks like a college campus," Hannah said.

The buildings were labeled by number—Administration, Main Housing, Hospital, Psychiatric Services . . . Building 9 was the SHU, Separate Housing Facility. It was a low-slung concrete rectangle, separated from the cluster. According to the description, this was for "maximum custody inmates who cannot coexist in the general population." They lived in total isolation, allowed out an hour a day and three times a week for showers. The facility was "fully automated" and operated from a command center. The inmates had "minimal contact" with supervisory personnel. Guards operated doors by remote control and communicated with the inmates by intercom.

"This is where they'll put me if they catch us," I said. "Total isolation because I'm a cop killer."

"How about me?" Hannah asked.

"You'll be in the female version."

She clutched my arm as I clicked on the photos. Empty corridors. Gleaming waxed floors. Guards behind glass doors. Eight-by-eleven cells with bare whitewashed walls. Each cell had a metal bunk, a metal toilet and washstand, a metal desk protruding from the wall. A slit of a window above the bunk let in the light. A slot in the door served as the opening where inmates received food and medication, and where they placed their hands to be cuffed. The exercise room was bare, except for a chinning bar and a mat. The yard was a square, empty space surrounded by high walls. The shower room had whitewashed floors and narrow spigots. There was a shot of an inmate shuffling—cuffed and shackled—down the hall, escorted by guards in thick body pads.

"Is this where my dad lives?"

"Yeah."

There was a link to a PDF: INMATE VISITING GUIDELINES . . . Visiting in the SHU was by appointment only.

I called the 800 number and got an automated operator. I had to supply the name and number of the inmate to be visited. If I didn't have the number I was advised to wait for "Visitor Processing." The Muzak was Country oldies. I sat through Patsy Cline, Loretta Lynn, and Tammy Wynette before a female voice came on. She made me spell Seeley's name twice. I heard the clatter of computer keys.

"Who are you, sir?"

"I'm calling on behalf of Mr. Seeley's daughter."

"We cannot issue an appointment for a visit with this inmate, sir. You'll have to apply in writing to the office of the Warden, explaining why you wish to visit the individual."

"It's his daughter," I said. "Does she need a reason?"

The voice remained polite. "The institution does not recognize familial relationship as automatically compelling. You can have your attorney call on your behalf, sir. Thank you for calling and have a blessed afternoon."

I hung up. "They won't let you visit your own father, but they wished me a blessed afternoon. We'll have to go through the lawyer after all."

Google found a Web page: Abnerfried.com. A photo—a mountain of thick curly hair, thick lips, bulging eyes behind rimless glasses. Going for the Russian Revolutionary look. Quotes from Ralph Nader: "Abner Fried is an uncompromising crusader for civil liberties." *The Nation Magazine*:

"Abner Fried seeks out the most unpopular causes, the most despised defendants . . ." He had represented accused Islamic terrorists, drug dealers, child molesters, serial killers. In an interview, Fried said: "Everyone is innocent. The system that drove them to desperate acts is guilty."

Fried's 800 number rang for minutes until a robotic female voice came on.

"Mailbox full."

I went back to his Web page and found an e-mail address.

"I am Hannah Seeley," I typed. "My father, Arnold Seeley, was your client. I am trying to visit him at Otter Point, but they won't let me. I have to see my dad. Can you help me?"

"You make me sound like a fourth grader," Hannah said.

"I tried to give it a poignant ring."

My e-mail dinged. Fried had replied from his Black-Berry. "If you are Hannah Seeley, who is PVogel23?"

I wrote back. "I'm using my friend's computer."

He replied: "Come to my office, 1230 Stockton St., San Francisco. Bring good ID. I will ask personal ?s. U have to prove u r A S's dtr."

I pressed Reply. "Thank u. In late tonite. Will call in the morning."

I MapQuested San Fran. "We'll take turns driving."

We brought our coffees into the car.

"I should have gotten a muffin or something," I said. "Coffee on an empty stomach gives me gas."

"We can go back," she said.

"No time . . ."

Whose Avatar Am I?

It was trance driving. At dawn, San Francisco materialized, a ghost city in the mist.

"How'd we get here?" I asked.

"We're tired," Hannah said.

"Was the radio on?"

"All night."

"Did they mention—?"

"No."

"So they haven't found him." The scene was vivid in my mind. "Probably late tonight. CHP makes a routine run through the parking area. They see the empty Tahoe. Get out with their flashlights. Call the plate number in. One of the cops walks up the hill. Just a routine check, he doesn't expect to find anything."

She MapQuested Stockton Street. "It's in Chinatown."

The city's weird worlds seemed to flow into one another. We were in a park. Bright green parrots swooped out of the trees onto homeless people sleeping on the benches.

A moment later, groups of haggard gays came out of clubs, blinking in the hazy sunrise and kissing goodbye. Outside of Peets, a black guy with the head of a woman, blonde upsweep, slashes of rouge and the body of a football player, tattooed arms and tapered waist, came out of a doorway with a falsetto plea: "Don't go, baby. Talk to me."

A few aimless turns and we were in the steel-and-glass world of finance. The breeze kicked up a swirl of fast food wrappers. Men in suits, computer cases slung over their shoulders, glared into the car.

Hannah was back on MapQuest. "Montgomery Street. We're close."

We drove up hills and through twisting streets. Teenage

panhandlers surrounded us, banging on the hood. "Give us money, motherfucker!"

A minute later, a pagoda-shaped gate rose above the street.

"Chinatown."

Stockton Street was on a steep hill descending to the morning whitecaps of the bay. Number 121 was a fish market. Old Chinese, white sleeves rolled up over stick-thin arms, poured ice into outdoor troughs. A narrow flight of steps led to a dark doorway. The door was locked. I could hardly read the 1230 on the sooty glass window.

We parked across the street

"It's 6:30. Too early," Hannah said.

A bent old man with a cigarette dangling between his lips came out of a building. Two girls in school uniforms with backpacks and iPods walked by. I ducked under the window.

Hannah laughed. "They're schoolgirls."

"It could be anyone," I said.

Then she was shaking me. "Peter . . ."

Passing Chinese were peering into the car. Had I been asleep? I had a bad taste in my mouth.

She shook me again. "Peter, is that Fried?"

He stood out in this crowd. Basketball tall. A shambling gait, a rumpled suit and a Giants cap, a leather lawyer's bag, bulging with files.

Hannah e-mailed him. "Hi, Mr. Fried. We're in San Francisco." *why Starbucks for Wifi?*

We watched as he fumbled in his pocket for his Black-Berry. He walked past old women poking through mounds of glittering red and silver fish in the market and disappeared into the dark doorway.

A moment later her computer dinged with a reply. "My office in a half hour. Bring coffee."

"You should have woken me," I said. "Any passing cop would have been suspicious."

I put the cutlery set in a Foot Locker shopping bag. My legs wobbled as I got out. I checked the parking signs.

"We're legal."

She laughed. "You're kidding, right?"

A Chinese coffee shop loomed at the top of the hill. Halfway up, my heart pounded so hard I had to stop.

Hannah felt my forehead. "You're all clammy."

"Heart murmur. I get palpitations. My mom sent me for an echocardiogram. Nothing serious, but I run out of gas. That's why I never really made it in sports. I had a good first step, a good jumper, but they said I couldn't make the big shot. It wasn't mental, I was just exhausted at the end of the game. But she never told me and I hated myself for being such a wuss. I had a good swing, too. You saw that."

"Shut up for a second," Hannah said. She hugged me, put my head on her shoulder. I could feel this surge of grief welling up. Like on the beach, trying to run from a breaking wave, going under and being scraped along the bottom.

"We're screwed, Hannah."

"Peter . . ." She pressed her lips against my neck. We stood motionless, incurious Chinese flowing around us. The grief subsided, leaving the dull ache of acceptance.

"Okay," I said.

We got coffee. "You need something in your stomach," Hannah said. So we got three hard sugary buns.

Two dudes came up the street on mountain bikes. No colors, no helmets. Caps on backwards, muscled legs in cargo shorts churning like pistons up the steep hill. One of them could have been the guy in the lobby of the Holiday Inn. They both could have been the young men in suits outside the elevator on the seventh floor.

The door to 1230 was open. We walked up a musty stairway. A light sputtered on the second floor. We passed an acupuncturist and a real estate office. A sign on a smoked glass door at the end of the hall read: ABNER FRIED, ATTORNEY AT LAW.

"This is too noir to be true," I said.

Hannah turned. "What?"

"We're back in somebody's Second Life again. They

have made it a scene out of Hammett."

"Who?"

"Dashiell Hammett. He wrote detective stories about San Francisco. Katz would love this . . . we're postmodern. Life is imitating art."

Fried's waiting room was long and narrow. Several Chinese were jammed together on an old leather couch against the wall, holding blue legal files. I could feel the hostile interest behind their impassive stares. The receptionist—a young Chinese woman with horn-rimmed glasses, barefoot, her skirt so short I could see the edge of her black panties—finished typing on her computer.

"Miss Seeley?"

"Yes . . ."

She pointed to the shopping bag. "What's in there?" She peeked in and saw the cutlery set. "I'll keep this out here, if you don't mind. You can go right in."

We walked down a shadowy hallway, shelves lined with law books.

"Don't tell him about the attacks," I whispered.

The door was open on a cluttered office. Smudgy windows bent the gray light. The sills were covered with dust. Case files hung off splintered shelves and bulged out of filing cabinets. It smelled like a dorm suite the morning after—tobacco, weed, makeout funk. Abner Fried, spectral in the light of a Tensor lamp, was hunched over a computer, his long hairy fingers dancing like spider's legs over the keys.

"PVogel23," Fried said. He had a jagged bass voice that seemed to rattle the windowpanes. "Why 23?"

"Because there were twenty-two PVogels before me, I guess," I said.

He nodded and reached out a long arm. "ID, Miss Seeley?"

"I only have my driver's license," Hannah said, handing it to him.

He held it against the lamp bulb, squinting. "What instrument did your sister play, Hannah?" he asked, then called:

"Lucy!"

Hannah started at the basso crack of his voice. "Flute."

Lucy clicked in on high heels. Fried handed her Hannah's license. "What kind of cookies did your mom bake for the church meetings?"

"Oatmeal raisin."

Lucy handed the license back. "I can't tell."

Fried turned back to his computer. "What was your father's pet name for you?"

"Honey," Hannah said.

Fried shrugged. "This is all public knowledge. Anybody could find this out with a little research."

"Yes, but why would they want to?" Hannah said. She snatched her license out of his grasp so quickly he flinched and recoiled. "Why would anyone want to be me?"

Fried's eyes gleamed slyly. "Someone might want to pretend to be you."

"Why?"

Fried jerked his head at Lucy. "Thanks, Lucy. We don't need you anymore."

Lucy folded her arms. I could see the movie of their lives in her eyes. They were after-hours lovers. She, in that creaky swivel chair, blouse unbuttoned, skirt hiked up. He, on his knees over her, his long, bent back bristling with black hairs, spider fingers traveling blindly over her breasts. He was doing his courtship dance for Hannah and she wasn't going to let him get away with it.

"Somebody could pretend to be you so they could get information out of me," Fried said.

Hannah looked at me in puzzlement.

"Who would want to do that?" I asked.

He swiveled over to me. "Mr. Vogel," he said, and went back to the computer. "Peter Vogel, from John C. Fremont High . . . your basketball team made it to the regional finals."

It was like a cheap card trick. "Okay, you Googled my name. You saw my name on the team roster."

"After you graduated UCR, you were accepted into the

Teaching For America program. You see it's easy to get a certain kind of information, but they haven't gotten to the point where they can enter your brain and see what you know. And that's what they want to do with me."

"Who's they?"

He looked pointedly at Lucy. "You don't want to hear this."

She turned on her heel.

He waited until she had closed the door. Then lowered his voice. "I have to be very careful. They're very interested in what I know about Arnold Seeley's case."

"Who is?"

"Do I have to spell it out?" he hissed. Fried looked at the bag in Hannah's hand. "Oh, great, you brought coffee!"

A Marriage License

"Your father is a victim, Hannah," Fried said. He smiled down at her, baring stained, jagged horse teeth. "You don't mind if I call you Hannah, do you?"

Arnold Seeley's case files were piled on his desk. There were court papers, newspaper articles, photos, DVDs. He saw me looking at the clutter.

"Like my bookkeeping system? I keep everything in hardcopy. The computer is too easy to penetrate. They could hack in and hack out and I'd never know it."

"You mean the government?" I asked.

Fried smiled like there was no need to answer. "It's totalitarian democracy. They maintain the fiction that our rights and privacy are respected, but they control every aspect of our lives. People invest trillions in their myth of democracy. Their whole economy would collapse if the truth came out." He licked powdered sugar off his thick lips. "That's why they skulk around and take incredible precautions. Look what they're doing to you."

He reached across his desk to pat her hand. "Reverend Kellner told me about the people who have been following you."

"He says I'm imagining all this," Hannah said.

"Kellner believes that what has happened to you is part of God's divine plan. It's not. It's a very human conspiracy, carefully planned and executed."

Hannah looked at me in bewilderment.

"Excuse me," I said, "but we came here because we were told you could help us get a visit—"

He waved dismissively. "We'll get to that. Think back, Hannah, this is important. Did your father ever say anything to you about what they did to him?"

"He said I shouldn't be mad at him for what he had done. 'I'm not human anymore,' he said. 'They made me different.'"

Fried sat back with a satisfied look. "Hannah, did your father ever tell you what he did in the Navy?"

"We never talked about it."

"He was a medic," Fried said. "Stationed at St. Albans Naval Hospital outside New York City. He was assigned to a top-secret ward where Navy Seals were being treated to enhance their combat effectiveness. Experiments had established that even the toughest, most motivated of men hesitated before killing certain targets—women, older people, children, their own comrades. This reluctance was imbedded in the Judeo-Christian culture, they thought, and put our fighters at a disadvantage with Asians and Arabs and even certain Europeans, who suffered no such compunctions. They wanted to produce the perfect machine that would kill instantly on command."

"How do you know all this?" I asked.

Fried nodding, conceding, "That's a fair question. After your father's arrest, Hannah, I got an e-mail from a man who had served with him on that ward—Ward Four." Fried tore through a pile of smudged and crumpled papers and held up a printout, triumphantly. "Here it is, in his own words." He cleared his throat, as if he were in court, and read: "Arnold Seeley is not responsible for what he did. He and I were used as guinea pigs, without our knowledge or consent in an experiment by the United States Navy . . ."

I reached for it. "Can I see that?"

He pulled it away. "Privileged communication."

"Why didn't you call this man as a witness?" I asked.

"Two reasons, Mr. Vogel. One: I risked outing him to a very vindictive organization, the American military. And two: At this time, he was a patient in the psychiatric ward of the Fort Hamilton VA hospital."

"In other words, he was crazy."

Fried's insect eyes bulged with indignation. "In other words, he was suffering the effects of mind-altering drugs that were administered to him without his knowledge or consent."

"If it was without his knowledge, how did he find out?"

Fried gave me a grudging look. "He found out by coincidence. After twenty-five years of depression, alcoholism, two broken marriages, and a suicide attempt, my informant committed himself to the psychiatric ward at the VA Hospital. The psychiatrist assigned to treat him had been on Ward Four as a young Navy doctor. The doctor had been haunted by guilt over what he had done. He revealed that my informant—and your father, Hannah—were in a group of five medics who were given the same drugs as the Seals. Their behavior was secretly monitored. After one of the men had a serious breakdown and the other killed his wife and himself, the experiment was terminated, the unit disbanded, and all records destroyed."

Fried leaned forward, his hairy fists clenched. "Do you understand what happened here, Miss Seeley? They altered your father's brain chemistry to the point where he could kill without conscience. He experienced the same sadomasochistic fantasies as so many millions of other men, but where the others suppressed them or lived them vicariously, he acted . . . he *killed!*" Fried jumped out of his chair and pointed over our heads, as if addressing a jury. "The American military made Arnold Seeley a mass murderer and now they want to cover it up."

Hannah winced and trembled, tried to draw into herself.

"Oh, God, Peter, what did I get you into?"

"We're way past that," I said. "Why didn't you plead insanity?" I asked Fried.

"It was a risk we couldn't take," he said. "The DA told me if I went to trial, he would ask for the death penalty. I was afraid our evidence wouldn't sway the jury."

"Because you had no proof that this program ever existed."

"Proof!" Fried's voice exploded, sending a piece of paper fluttering off his desk. "Proof is a legalism, an invention of the power elite. They can create proof and destroy it, as they did with this program." He appealed to Hannah. "Your father was facing a lynch mob disguised as a jury. I couldn't take the chance."

My cell phone vibrated. It was a number with a 713 area code. Houston . . . McVickers.

"You still haven't explained why the government is after Hannah," I said.

"Isn't it obvious?" Fried said. "You were the only one who saw your father after I told him about the program, Hannah. He couldn't give me the names of the other men he served with, or names of the Seals who were on his ward."

"Why not?" I asked.

Fried took a phlegmy breath, trying to calm himself. "Because they were watching."

"I thought a lawyer's communication with his client was privileged."

He looked at me with scornful pity. "Except when they don't want it to be." Fried turned back to Hannah. "They want to find out if he gave any information to you."

"They're not questioning her. They're trying to kill her," I said. "They tried to break into my house. And they rammed our car the next night. One of them is an ex-convict named Robert Doane, who has actually served time at Otter Point."

Fried printed the name, spelling it out. "D... O... A... N... E... The government often hires criminals," he said. "But Reverend Kellner thinks these attempts were some kind of drug hit aimed at you, Mr. Vogel."

"I'm *not* a drug dealer," I said.

"I didn't say you were," Fried said. "Look, I can't explain their methods. They're not supermen. They blunder and make stupid mistakes and then they try to cover them up. But they're in panic mode now and that's when they're at their most dangerous."

He turned back to Hannah. "This is a huge problem for

them. If it gets out they'll be exposed. Every secret program they've ever operated will come to light. They'll be facing criminal charges, lawsuits, broken careers. This is the kind of thing that can topple a President . . ." He leaned forward, confidentially. "I took their deal to save your father's life. But now we can reopen his case, Hannah. We can exonerate him, get him out of that hellhole and into a more humane environment."

"What do you mean *we*?" I asked.

He looked toward the door, as if he was afraid Lucy was listening. His voice dropped to a whisper. "I need a name. One man who was involved in that project and who is willing to talk. Then, I can get a hearing based on new evidence. I can subpoena records and compel testimony on pain of contempt. I can blow this whole thing wide open."

"Why don't you talk to that Navy psychiatrist?" I asked.

"I called him. He had retired from the Navy and was working as a harbormaster in Seattle. First, he claimed ignorance and threatened me with a harassment charge. Then he calmed down and said they would take away his pension or maybe even worse, if he spoke to me. He was scared stiff." Fried sat back, looking at us between his fingers.

"I asked Reverend Kellner to help. The man's a fanatic, Hannah. He believes your father has to suffer the harshest punishment on earth in order to be redeemed in the hereafter. I told him that while he was on his knees alone in that church praying for your father's soul, I would be throwing open the prison doors and leading him to freedom."

"Reverend Kellner has been a good friend to me," Hannah said stubbornly.

"Oh, I know he thinks he's doing the right thing," Fried said. "But he wants to suppress the truth. He has turned the victims' families against me. They've threatened me with lawsuits. I've gotten anonymous calls threatening my life. I had to get a restraining order against two of them—Baines and Ardison." He leaned forward imploring: "You are the only one who can help me liberate your father, Hannah."

"What can I do?" she asked.

"You'll have a half hour for your visit. Don't waste it on family problems. Get him to tell you everything he remembers about his time on Ward Four at St. Albans. Names, dates, anecdotes . . ."

He spoke so quickly and with such conviction that it took me a second to realize: "Wait a second, they'll be taping our visits, too."

"No, no, no!" He shook his head impatiently. "Let me try to explain this. They think I'm a terrorist because of the Islamic charities I've represented. They think I'm a spy for the Chinese because I do immigration work. They've been watching me for years. I never speak on the phone. I have my office and home—and car—debugged once a month. Are you following?"

"Sure," I said. "You think you're Public Enemy One."

Fried nodded bitterly. "And you think you're an enlightened intellectual, but you've been brainwashed by their version of rationality. They muddy the waters up with Special Commissions and Congressional Committees, and you believe their lies without questioning . . ."

He patted his pockets. What was he looking for? Cigarettes? A vial of coke? Finally, he continued. "They have to be so very careful, you see. If they want to tape your visit, they have to convince a judge that you can become a threat to national security. But in order to do that, they'll have to reveal the details of the secret program for the record."

"They said they might not allow Hannah to visit even if she is his daughter," I said.

"I can fix that," he said. "We'll say Hannah is bringing her new husband to meet her dad. They have to allow that by law."

"New husband?" I asked. "Do we have to get married?"

"No, no, don't worry, they'll take your word for it. But just in case they don't . . ." He scribbled an address. "We'll get you a marriage license. Perfect forgery, it'll easily pass a visual inspection, but it'll cost you two-hundred dollars." He

looked closely at Hannah. "You still have the money from
the sale of the house?"

She looked up in surprise.

"Your mother told me she had given you and your sister
fifteen thousand apiece from the sale," Fried said. "I became
very close with your mother in those horrible days, Hannah.
I promised her I would make Robbinsgate pay for persecu-
ting her. Once we have vindicated your father I will be able
to keep that promise. They won't dare bring this case to trial.
They don't want the world to know that the United States
Navy created a serial killer. Any suit I bring will be imme-
diately settled for a large sum. You'll make a lot of money.
We all will."

He passed a piece of paper across the desk to me. "The
Copy Store on Grant. Give them this . . ." He stopped, as if
in an afterthought. "It might not be a bad idea to get an alt-
ernate identity while you're there. In case you have to travel
incognito. Driver's license, passport, credit cards, A new
phone, too, they can do that. It's safe. They use the names
and numbers of people who just died. It will cost you five-
hundred more."

He got up and went to his sooty window. "They're down
there, watching." He came around the desk. "Let's go."

We followed him back down the narrow hallway. The
office was empty. Lucy was gone. Behind her desk there was
a small door in the wall. We had to stoop to go through.
Then we scuttled along a cramped passageway. Fried's tall
frame was bent, almost doubled over. He was wheezing,
short of breath.

"Where are we?" I asked.

"Secret passageway between the buildings. From the
days when this was a smuggler's hideout . . . opium den."

We climbed a spiral stairway to a battered steel fire door
that opened onto the roof. A gray drizzle fell. "There's a
bridge behind the shed," Fried said, still bent over and
breathing hard. "Go across to the building next door. Downstairs, go out the rear to the alley, down to Grant. In the

Copy Store, ask for Harold. Tell him you want a passport photo. Don't pay him. Come back about five-thirty and I'll have all the documents. You can give the money to me. I'll have your appointment, too." He squinted up at the dirty clouds. "Hurry. They may have their spy drones out today."

Arrhythmia

The bridge was a metal ladder laid across the roofs and bracketed in the crumbly tar. The rails were two frayed ropes tied to rusty rods. It was a free-throw between the roofs, about fifteen feet with a four-story drop to the alley below. I held one end of the ladder while Hannah scampered across. Once on the roof, she knelt and held the other end.

"C'mon . . ."

My foot slipped on a wet rung.

"Don't look down," she said. "Walk fast."

The rope rails were loose and soggy. If I reached for one I'd lose my balance. I got on my knees. The ladder shook and swayed as I inched across. I clawed at the ledge and crawled onto the roof on my stomach.

Hannah was laughing. "You wimp."

"I'm here, aren't I?"

The warped tin-plated fire door stuck and squawked as I yanked it open. A few steps brought us to the top landing. Four apartments to a floor, numbers written in faded gilt lettering on splintery wooden doors. Cooking smells and TV sounds.

On the first floor, an old Chinese man was opening his mailbox. He turned as we came down and went back to his letters, as if accustomed to white desperados running down his stairs. We moved through a dark hallway past bicycles and garbage bags, and came out in the alley. Hannah jogged easily. I had to sprint to keep up with her.

The Copy Store was bright red-white-and-blue. Chinese people hugged packages like they were babies. A chubby Chinese guy with horn rims stood behind the counter.

"Passport photo?" he said.

"Mr. Fried sent us," Hannah said.

"I know. Passport photo?" he repeated with an angry look.

I blanked. For a moment I didn't know where I was.

"You Harold?" I asked.

Hannah shoved me. "Yes, passport photo," she said.

He took us into a tiny back room jammed with packing boxes. The air was dense with dust and cigarette smoke. Blood rushed to my head. I stumbled into a Xerox machine.

"Whatsa matter, be careful," he said.

There was a camera in the back, the kind they used in the DMV. Harold gave Hannah a form. "Name, date of birth, address, parents' names, mother's maiden name . . . You—" He yanked my arm. "Come here for photo."

A red mist rose in front of my eyes. I pulled my arm away. "Get your hands off—"

"Peter . . ." Hannah was behind me, her warm breath in my ear.

Harold backed away with a wary look at Hannah. "Whatsa matter, he drunk?"

"No, no, just take his picture."

Harold looked into the camera. "Stand on the line . . . Move to right."

"What's your date of birth, Peter?" Hannah asked.

I froze. This was insane. I couldn't even remember my own birthday. I fumbled for my wallet.

"Move to the right, hurry up," Harold said.

"Wait a second . . ."

"No time, have to do this quick!"

"I said wait a second."

My heart skipped, then thumped painfully. If he opens his mouth I'll smash his face in, I thought.

I took out my driver's license and flipped it to Hannah. "Fill it out for me, I can't think."

"What's your mother's maiden name?" she asked.

"Raise your chin," Harold said. "Higher."

"Wait a second."

"You don't know your mother's maiden name?"

He was mocking me.

It came into my mind like a headline. "Gluck . . . Jesus, what a weird name."

"Okay, finished," Harold said. "You next, Miss."

Hannah was done in a second.

"Okay," Harold said. "I give you marriage license, driver's license. Five Capital One cards, two-hundred-fifty apiece . . . spend, then throw away."

He bumped me with a scornful look. I followed him, thinking how I could grab him from behind, shove my fingers into his eyeballs, and smash his head against the wall.

He muttered in Chinese. His assistant smirked.

"What did you say?" I asked.

"Not talking to you," he said.

Everybody in the store was looking at me. Harold slid his hand over to an aluminum softball bat under the counter.

There was a stapler on the ledge. I could grab it and throw it in his face before he ever got to me.

"Know how to hit a curve?" I asked.

Hannah grabbed my arm. "Let's go!"

Outside, I shook her loose. "Stop pulling me."

She jumped back, staring, trying to see through me. "What's wrong with you?"

"See the way he treated me? He had no respect."

"So what? We'll never see him again."

"I could wait outside," I said. "Come up behind him with a knife . . . or a lug wrench. I'm real good with a lug wrench. You saw how good I am . . ."

Hannah's eyes had silver glints. "It wasn't your fault, Peter," she said. "It was an accident."

A sob was welling up in me. Like when you're a kid and somebody hurts your feelings and you stumble through a vapor of hot tears. For a second I couldn't remember his name. Then it came blurting out. "Noah Frayne."

"Peter, for God's sake," Hannah whispered, looking around. She took my hand, gently now, as if she were leading a sick man or a mourner. "Let's get something to eat."

We went to an ATM. I watched the street as Hannah got money. Indifferent Chinese again, as far as the eye could see. No weird white dudes.

Strands of fog swirled through the drizzle as we walked down the hill to Fisherman's Wharf. No tourists, the dockside restaurants were empty, countermen staring out, arms folded. We found a coffee place under an awning in a courtyard. Hannah twined her arm through mine.

"Make believe we're on a date."

The rain splattered its last drops and the sun emerged for a few minutes of dying light. Two elderly men who looked like twins came out and played old jazz tunes on a guitar and violin. We had a moment of peace.

But then darkness fell quickly. Hannah looked at her phone. "It's almost six."

As we started back up the hill, my phone went off. "Stupid ringtone," I said. "Jimi Hendrix playing the Star-Spangled Banner at Woodstock. Why did I think that was so cool?"

It was that 713 area code.

"McVickers . . ."

"Don't answer it," Hannah said.

"Have to. They probably found the body. They'll get suspicious." I punched on. "McVickers?"

"Am I on your Fave Five, Peter?" He sounded positively jovial. "I've been worrying about you."

"I had my phone turned off," I said. "I was in the lawyer's office getting an appointment to see Hannah's dad."

"How's that goin'?"

"We're going to drive up there tonight."

"Yeah . . ." His voice got far away, as if he had just switched on a speaker. "Seen Sonny Doane lately?"

I nodded at Hannah. They had definitely found the body. "No, actually," I said.

"Just disappeared?"

"Yeah. Now I'm not so sure it was him in the first

place."

"Yeah, maybe it wasn't." There was a silence, as if he were listening to someone. "Yeah, okay. So you're headin' up north."

"Leaving tonight."

"Okay, well, have a good visit. Call me if you spot Doane again."

"Don't worry, I will," I said and punched off.

"Does he suspect us?" Hannah asked.

"He's just keeping tabs. We've got one thing going for us. They'd never think a wimp like me could beat a big tough DEA guy to death. Doane makes more sense as a suspect. Doane is a better scenario for a jury. Can you imagine being a guy who got away with a bunch of murders getting fried for something he didn't do? That'll make a philosopher out of you. Can't you just see his face?"

It was the sociopath's joke. The sociopath's scornful laugh.

Hannah gave me a worried look. "This city is making you crazy. Let's pick up our marriage license from Fried and get out of here."

The blue Bug was under a streetlight. Nearby, two shadows separated and came together, like two people moving restlessly. Couldn't see if they were white and clean-shaven.

"Let's go through the secret passageway," I said.

She looked doubtful.

"I'll make it," I said.

We ducked back into the building. Some Chinese kids passed us on the steps. We walked through silver beams of moonlight to the edge of the roof. Hannah stepped onto the ladder and ran across. I got down on my knees, but then couldn't remember how I had done it the first time. Had I put my knees on first, or reached out and grabbed a rung?

"C'mon," Hannah whispered.

"I'm frozen."

"The longer you wait the harder it'll be."

I swung my legs over and straddled the ladder, sitting on

it, and slid across. Looking down made me dizzy. At the end I had to lean forward and lift my legs until I was lying prone.

Hannah grabbed my wrists and pulled me off the ladder. I lay on my back and watched my heart fly away, a red ball in the darkness.

Hannah shook me. "Let's go."

Fried's building was quiet, everyone gone for the day. The waiting room was dark. A light illuminated the glass door of his office. Halfway down the narrow hallway I smelled marijuana.

"Happy hour," I said.

I knocked. "Mr. Fried?"

No answer.

"Maybe he left the stuff for us," Hannah said. She opened the door. I pushed by her to get in first.

Our cutlery set was on the floor. Someone had torn off the plastic cover.

Fried's shoe was sticking out from behind the desk.

He was lying face up under his chair. His shirt was ripped open, exposing tufts of iron gray hair. A black and blue bruise bulged off his forehead. The carving knife from our cutlery set was jammed in his neck.

I guess I must have sagged, because I felt Hannah's hand on my arm, steadying me. She peered over my shoulder. What if the room was bugged? I put my finger to my lips and shook my head.

A manila envelope on his desk had HANNAH SEELEY written on it.

A legal pad sat on the desk with a list of calls. I looked down at the last name on the list.

REVEREND KELLNER, 11:45.

Smart, Very Smart

For Hannah, crossing the ladder got easier every time. Not for me. I lay flat and it wobbled as I inched across on my stomach. Fear rose like a hairball in my throat and I retched a few hot gobs.

Hannah wiped my mouth with a crumpled tissue. I got off my knees. The lights of the Golden Gate Bridge glittered in the distance.

"I'm okay."

"You sure he was dead?" she asked. "There wasn't much blood."

The sociopath answered for me. "Once they pull the knife, the blood will come bubbling out."

"Who did it?"

"Who cares? We just have to make sure that *we* don't get blamed."

We ran to the squawking tin door. No one saw us on the stairs. No one saw us come out. On the street, Hannah looked in the envelope: State of California marriage license for us. Then the phony IDs: Colorado driver's license with my photo in the name of Anthony Reed; another for Hannah in the name of Florita Evans. Five Capital One credit cards in both names. A faxed appointment sheet from Otter Point Correctional Facility for Saturday, the 8th in the names of Mr. and Mrs. Peter Vogel.

"Our new IDs state we're both twenty-three years of age," Hannah said. "Didn't Fried say they were dead?"

"Young people die, too," I said.

Hannah pulled out a piece of crumpled paper. "What's this?"

Four names had been scribbled crazily, one barely legible. "Looks like he wrote these in a hurry," I said.

The blue Bug pulsed like an alarm button under the streetlight. I stopped short, as if I'd run into a stone wall.

"We can't go to the car. They're still there." My head throbbed in unison with the pulsing car. "We can try to rent another car. But it'll be tough at this hour with no reservation."

"We can't leave our stuff," she said. "The clothes and my laptop—"

"Right . . . can't leave your laptop. It's our only connection to the outside world. Okay . . ." I drew her into a darkened storefront. "We call 911, tell them there's been a murder. Once the cops show up, we walk to the car. They won't dare jump us."

"Okay." She took out her cell.

"Can't use your phone. Your number will come up on Caller ID."

"Okay, a public phone, then."

"If we can find one. But most of them only take credit cards, which means our names—"

"Use one of the Capital One cards."

My mouth was dry. "That connects us with Harold."

She thought for a second. "Go into a restaurant, ask to use their phone."

"Then the restaurant number shows up and they have witnesses. Don't you understand, all paper trails lead to us."

She turned away in exasperation.

"Too bad we didn't think of this in Fried's office," I said. "We could have used his phone."

"I'll go back and get it," she said.

"Cross the roof again?"

Now it was her turn to be irritated. "Can you think of another way?"

She stepped out into the street. "I'll call them from his office."

The sociopath was pounding my chest, screaming, "LET ME OUT."

"That's no good. The cops might show up before you

come down."

"I'll take his Blackberry."

"No . . ." I grabbed her arm. "Your prints will be on his body."

"I'll use his office phone."

"Your prints will be on that, too."

"I'll say I used it in the morning while I was in his office."

"There'll be no record of a call."

"I'll say I picked up the phone but changed my mind."

"Okay, who were you calling?"

She tried to pull away. "There's no time for this, Peter."

I squeezed her arm. "Who were you fuckin' calling?"

"My mother," she said. "I got emotional and wanted to talk to her, but you talked me out of it."

"Okay, that's your story."

I let her go. She ran across the street in long strides, like she was chasing a goal kick. She was better without me. She could take the steps three at a time. Run across that ladder like it was a six-lane freeway.

I moved back against the store window. Shadows mixed and mingled around the Bug as people passed. I tried to time how long it would take her to get across the roof, through the passageway into Fried's office.

A figure appeared at the window of the second floor office. Had she gotten up there that fast or was somebody waiting for her? Was she walking into a trap? I saw her looking out the window. Was she trying to spot the people who were watching? Forget it, Hannah. Dial 911, report a murder, give the address. They'll ask you to repeat it. Don't fall for it. They're stalling to keep you there.

Something whooshed at me like a dive-bombing bird.

It was Hannah, hardly out of breath. "Okay, done."

The stress had smashed my inner clock. I had no sense of time. "What did you do, turn yourself into a bat?"

"I wish." She laughed. She was actually exhilarated. "I told the police Fried was having a fight with a big, tattooed longhair . . ." She stopped expectantly, like a pupil waiting for a "good job."

"Did they ask you for your name?"

"Judy Wu, I told them. She was the goalie on my team."

"Anybody see you?"

"Nobody."

We stood there staring at each other . . . waiting. A police cruiser rolled down the block and double parked. Two cops got out and ambled into the building.

"That was quick," I said.

Everything was happening fast and jerky, like in a silent movie. Figures crossed the window of Fried's office. Sirens whooped and subsided. A paramedic truck came around the corner, lights flashing. Then a few more cruisers and an unmarked car.

A crowd formed in stop motion. I'd blink and there would be more people. Soon the street was filled with gawkers.

Hannah undid the top buttons of her blouse. "Put your arm around me," she said. "Like we're lovers without a care in the world."

In the middle of the street, a cop was directing traffic. "Can we get out of here, officer?" Hannah asked.

He looked down Hannah's blouse and nodded curtly. She got in behind the wheel. Bystanders stepped back as I went around to the passenger side. A large man loomed in the shadows at the fringe of the crowd. I couldn't see his face, but it looked like he had long blond hair.

My hands were shaking so bad I couldn't buckle the safety belt. "I think I just saw Sonny Doane."

The cop waved us out with his flashlight. I put my aching head between my legs, trying to remember if we'd forgotten anything.

Hannah double-clutched and shifted into second. The tires squealed. The Bug lurched forward. People jumped back onto the curb, yelling, "Watch it! You tryin' to kill somebody?"

Our Blue Heaven

W e found a mini-mall with a Popeye's and a package store. Hannah got a dozen legs and thighs. I got a bottle of Christian Brothers Brandy. We dropped a few short slugs on our empty stomachs and were whooping as we drove across the Golden Gate Bridge. "We're outta here! Bye-bye San Francisco!"

My fear broke like a fever. "I've never felt better in my life," I said.

"Me, too," Hannah said.

The 101 flowed to infinity, enticing us into the blackness beyond our lights.

"We're on a tunnel to the cosmos," I said.

"Right to the cosmos," she said.

"Safe and warm in our little spaceship."

"No one can hurt us."

The brandy got smoother with every shot. "Very cool plan, Peter," she said.

"You made it happen. That was the bravest move I ever saw."

"It was your idea."

"Ideas are cheap. Execution is the key."

"That sounds like a Professor Katzism."

"Katzism catechism. I love Professor Katz."

"Me, too."

Her blouse was still undone. The dashboard light sculpted the curve of her breasts. Her long graceful fingers rested easily on the gear knob.

"Lust is eating my bones," I said.

"Is that one of your poems?"

"I have to touch you." I leaned over and unbuttoned the rest of her blouse.

"I'm driving."

"Your vision won't be obstructed." I got on my knees and unbuckled her jeans. "Lift your ass a little." I pulled her jeans down over her butt. "It's better when you help."

"What?"

"It's a line from a movie." I pulled at her panties. She arched her back.

"I haven't taken a shower."

"Good. I'll get to know the real you."

She tried to push my head away, but I stiffened my neck. "I have to do this," I said. And she took her hand away.

I squeezed past the gearshift and ducked between her legs. She eased lower in the seat.

"I can't brake."

"I'll brake with my hand."

"What if the CHP sees us?"

"They'll watch the fun."

I rested my chin on the seat and pulled her into my face. My calf cramped and went into spasms. I tried to stretch my leg. The pain was unreal, but I was there, and I wasn't going anywhere.

I reached under her shirt and held her breasts. I could feel her arms moving, steering. Could hear her calm, measured breaths. My neck was pressed down into my shoulders. I entered her world. I was surrounded by Hannah.

She said "oh," as if someone had just made an interesting point. She slid down further. "Oh," she said louder, as if she'd just heard something she couldn't believe. Her hand came off the wheel and pulled my hair. "Ohhh . . ." She pressed me into her. "Ohhh!" Louder. Somewhere deep inside her there was a fluttering, like wings beating.

She let go of my head and straightened up. I wiped my face on her thigh.

"Hmm," she said, as if she had just learned something.

I ducked out from under the gearshift. My calf was burning. My neck cracked. "Now I know how it feels to be a turtle," I said.

She reached out, her eyes on the road. I put the brandy bottle in her hand. She took a swig and turned the wheel sharply. The Bug skidded.

"Watch it," I said.

She threw back her head and laughed. "Scared?"

She veered onto the shoulder. The Bug bounced down a slope and stopped by a clump of bushes.

"What's the matter, you have to pee?" I asked.

She turned to me, her eyes sparkling. "Your turn, little boy." She pulled her blouse over her head.

"No time," I said.

"If I know you, this won't take long." She put her arms around my shoulders. Starlight shimmered on her breasts.

"Not here. We have to be moving."

"Is that your fantasy?"

"I want to get head behind the wheel like any good California boy."

"Okay, drive." She slid by me, her breasts brushing my face. She pulled my pants down as I got behind the wheel.

"Wait'll I get started."

I turned back onto the road. She knelt on the seat, looking down at me.

"This is going to be easier for me than it was for you."

"Go slow," I said. "I want this to last."

"Hmm," she said. "Popsicle."

She took me in her hand. I felt her cool lips. Slow was wrong. Slow made it happen faster.

"Hmm," she said when it was over. She kissed me with salty lips. "Okay?"

"It was too fast again."

"Oh, poor baby."

"I think I have a problem," I said.

She laughed and wrapped her skinny arms around my neck, hugging me until it hurt. "Yes, you do," she said. "You definitely have a problem."

No Big Deal

W hile it was dark the road was ours. We drove for hours in blissful silence. Then the night began to crumble around the edges.

Grotesque shapes loomed over us.

Hannah looked on the map. "Redwood Highway," she said. "Avenue of the Giants."

Dawn brought the world back. Billboards hawking motels and THE WORLD'S LARGEST SEQUOIA . . . GAS, FOOD, LODGING, FIVE MI. We passed under the giant trees.

"They're just waiting for us to go," I said.

"Who?" Hannah asked.

"The redwoods. We were the last living things created on earth and we'll be the first to go. Remember those big rocks in the desert? Weird shapes like letters or symbols. Puny humans run around, squeaking into their cell phones. And meanwhile the rocks are sending messages into the galaxy. Soon we'll kill each other off and they'll have the planet to themselves."

She stroked my neck with cool hands. "You're thinking about . . . that guy."

"What if his soul is flying around in space? What if he came together with Fried and they're both watching us, because now they're dead and it doesn't matter anymore?"

"I was thinking about my father. What am I going to say to him?"

"That somebody is trying to kill you because of what he did."

It was like being very stoned. Looking at your hands and being fearful that you'd forget how to drive. Then, the signs appeared: OTTER POINT CORRECTIONAL FACILITY, 35 mi. . . . 22 mi. . . . 16 mi. . . .

"Wonder what makes them put the distance signs where they are," I said.

"I'll find out."

She jumped back onto Google on her laptop. "Here it is. Otter Point is what is known as a Control Destination."

The Good Student, I thought. Daddy's little girl. And then was ashamed of my sudden spiteful thoughts.

"A Control Destination is a significant generator of traffic and a focal point of travel in an area," she read. "Distance signs will usually follow an exit ramp. Mileage shown will be the distance to the center of the next community."

"Man is good at organizing," I said. "We get that from the ants, my high school teacher said. We've picked up traits from every species that preceded us. We've got the whole planet divided into grids like a beehive. Latitude, longitude, topography, geography. Every town has a mall and a business center. Red light, green light, Ten Commandments . . ."

Hannah put her cool hand on my wrist. "Peter, you have to try to calm down."

"You know what else that teacher told me? We piss into our water supply and there's so much Prozac and meth and coke and penicillin and every kind of drug that we can't filter it out, and that's why human behavior has changed so much in the last thirty years. It's only going to get worse, he said. And there's nothing we can do about it."

"Peter, try not to let your mind wander," Hannah said.

"I keep seeing my mom making herself dinner, alone in that little house with the TV on in the kitchen. She works for the VA, counseling alcoholic vets. That's how she met my dad. I guess she thought she was going to reform him. When I was a kid I had a shot glass collection. Everywhere we went I'd make her buy me a shot glass."

This is pointless, I thought. Yet I kept talking. "I'm sure she was worried I would turn into an alcoholic. She told me alcoholism was an inherited disease triggered by an emotional incident, like getting cancer from air pollution. She said my dad's alcoholism had been triggered by what he had gone through in the Vietnam War. I used to visit him on Sunday to watch football. He'd be so hung over his hands would shake as he opened the beers. He once asked me: What does your mom say about me? She says you were traumatized by what you did in the war, I told him. He laughed. You kiddin'? The Navy was the best time of my life. I was on a carrier, nobody was shootin' at me. I got a chance to fool around with airplane engines, which I would have done for nothin'. The only thing I was scared of was getting caught smoking Thai stick by the cargo hold. Once a month I'd get shore leave. We'd get shitfaced in Bangkok. For five bucks I could bang a girl who wouldn't look twice at me back home."

Hannah leaned back and closed her eyes. She was thinking about her father, I could tell.

"My roommate Mike had this *sensimillia* weed that was so strong it made you jittery, like speed," I said. "We'd be up all night and then would go to the zoo. There'd be all these nice Houston families and us, a bunch of babbling stoners trying to come down. And what I didn't know then was that there was also a bunch of DEA guys following us. Maybe Noah Frayne was one of them."

Hannah turned. She was listening now.

"The Houston Zoo puts animals in big fenced-off compounds," I said. "Like in their native habitat. So we wandered around, giggling and goofing. We taunted a tiger. It clawed at the fence, snarling, trying to get to us. The DEA guys must have thought we were nuts. Look at these crazy druggies. We got hung up watching these two baboons, a mommy and a baby, grooming each other. Combing each other's fur, picking out ticks and eating them, then smoothing the hair back down. We were like, wow, look how attentive they are, how loving. Then this little brown bunny came sneaking through the thick leaves on the ground to steal their food. The baboons kept grooming, like they didn't know it was there. But all of a sudden they turned with these high-pitched shrieks and took off after it. The mommy chased it and the baby tried to cut it off, like they had been whispering to each other, planning their attack as it got closer. The bunny was squealing in terror. Mommy baboon got a paw on it and ripped a chunk of fur off its back, but it juked Junior and ducked under a hole in the fence. That was it. The leaves flew up in the air as the bunny scampered down into its secret warren. Mommy and baby went back to grooming. Another day in the state of nature, no big deal."

A sign came up: OTTER POINT 5 MI.

"We'll have to find a place to stay until tomorrow," Hannah said.

"It would be weird if Frayne had been in that team of agents. Skulking along behind us. Hiding in trees and whispering into walkies, waiting for us to make the big drop. Then maybe seeing that bunny risk its life for a rotten carrot. And now a couple of months later he's sneaking up on us just like that dumb bunny. Only, he's not as fast. We know he's there. We plan our attack."

"Peter." It came out in a sob. She turned away toward the window. "Don't go crazy on me, Peter. I need you."

We came upon a weathered sign:

MOTEL—CAMPGROUND—SHINGLED BUNGALOWS
FROM THE '50S.

I looked in the mirror as I turned off. Nobody was behind us.

In the office a fat old man with a soft, womanly face was watching a tiny TV behind the desk. I slid him the Capital One credit card. He hardly looked at it. "ID?" he asked in a high-pitched wheeze. I gave him the phony Colorado license. He hardly looked at that. "Goin' to the prison?" he asked.

"Goin' to Portland."

He reached for a Diet Coke. "Got a coupla hours of daylight left." He swiveled his chair to get our keys and I could see he only had one leg.

"He knew you were lying," Hannah said, when we got outside.

"That's okay," I said. "It'll make him think twice about messing with us."

She looked back at the office and I knew she was thinking: That fat old man is going to mess with us?

We had the last unit in the line. A few jalopy trailers were parked in the campground. Nobody around. Our door locked with a button on the scuffed brass knob. A rusty hook on a chain. A stack of takeout menus on the table. Perfect setup, I thought. They wait outside. When the delivery guy shows up, they pay him and take the food. Then, they knock on our door. "Pizza Hut . . ."

"Stay here," I told Hannah. "I'm gonna buy a gun."

"Why?"

"Because everybody has one but me."

I went back to the office. The fat old man was leaning on a crutch, pouring candies into a glass bowl on the counter.

"Any gun stores around here?" I asked.

He didn't even blink. "Pawnshop in Kingston. Picker town twenty miles north." He wrote an address on a piece of paper. "Tell Renay you were recommended by Paul at the campground." He pushed the bowl at me. "Diabetic candy. Can't tell 'em from the real thing."

An Accomplice

T he fat old clerk had printed the directions in bold block letters: 101 NORTH TO KINGSTON . . .
A few miles out of Otter Point we drove through a miasma of cow manure. Fields stretched to the horizon. Black specks moved like ants and it took awhile to realize they were pickers working the rows.

A blue van came up behind us. I slowed down, but it didn't overtake us, just stayed at the same distance, like it was following us. I speeded up. It made up the space. I turned off at the next exit. It drove by, but it might be waiting on a turnoff like Noah Frayne did.

We were on the service road for a winery. Pickups were parked on the shoulder. Burly white guys watched brown men in baseball caps hack at dead vines with rakes and machetes. When we got back on the freeway the van was gone.

The Kingston exit came up fast. No mall or business district. Couldn't see anything from the road. The exit ramp turned serpentine, twisting along humpbacked hills. Like they were trying to hide the town.

We turned onto a street of bodegas and dusty pickups. Mexicans in boots and Stetsons stared into the car. Further down was a grocery sign in Asian characters.

An old stucco building was hidden in a stand of palms. It was divided into three small stores: a check-cashing service with a big red sign for PAYDAY LOANS . . . EL DIA DE LA PAGA PRESTA, a Vietnamese takeout, and a store with a yellow sign: WE BUY AND SELL. There were watches and guitars in the window. A bell tinkled as we went in. We picked our way past boom boxes, bicycles, barbecues, clothing racks . . . A TV image floated like a disembodied head at the far end.

A gravelly voice came out of nowhere.

"Can I help you?"

"Renay?" I said.

A woman seemed to materialize. First a glowing cigarette, then wrinkled flesh hanging off a withered arm, bracelets jangling, rings with large colored stones. A smear of lipstick, wingtip glasses with rhinestone frames, hair the color of pink cotton candy.

"You want guns?"

"How'd you know?"

"You didn't come all this way for a wedding ring inscribed *Elena mi Corazón*."

"Paul at the campground sent us."

"I know." She pulled a chain and the fluorescent light sputtered. She pointed to an old publicity photo under the glass counter—a blond baby-faced man in a white dinner jacket. "That's Paul. Recognize him?"

"We just met."

"He was quite a singer in his day. Worked all the lounges in Reno . . . You wanna knock down a house or a medium sized person?"

Rifles hung from the walls. There were handguns in a display case.

"They're all in good firing order," Renay said. "A *vato* takes good care of his guns. They're the last thing he hocks." She took out a big gold-plated automatic. "Desert Eagle, big fifty. You don't have to hit a guy with this, the wind'll knock him over. Here's a three-eighty, honey." She offered Hannah a small pearl-handled automatic. "You're gonna need somethin' too. You're not exactly traveling first class."

"How much?" I asked.

"Gimme two-and-a-quarter for both of 'em."

She shook her head at the Capital One. "No plastic. I'll give 'em to you for a hundred-and-seventy-five cash."

She watched as Hannah dug the crumpled bills out of her bag. "Your treat, huh, honey? Hope he's worth it."

She took our information off the phony driver's licenses. "Reason for purchase?" she asked.

"Personal protection."

"We'll make that target practice. There's a five-day waiting period, but I'll suspend it if you promise you're not gonna barge into the prison and blow everyone away."

"We're not going to the prison."

She kept writing. "Well, you're not up here to pick grapes." She looked up at Hannah. "You know how to shoot, don't you, honey?"

"My dad took me to a firing range," Hannah said.

"Daddy loves to go shootin' with his little girl." She looked at me. "You've never fired a gun, have you?"

"Never."

"Mama's baby's gonna bring peace on earth."

She showed me how to load the clip. The bullets were heftier than I thought. "This'll go through an engine block," she said. She snapped the clip into the handle. "Wanna see?"

She took us out in the back. In the sun she looked like an unwrapped mummy. She lined up some empty half-gallon vodka bottles on a rusty oil drum and handed me the gun, then pushed Hannah. "Step behind him, honey."

The gun was heavier than I thought.

"Just hold it out straight, arm stiff to keep from shaking," Renay said. "Point and squeeze and make your day."

I pointed at the bottles and squeezed. The gun boomed, jumped and blew the top of a picket off the back fence.

Renay cackled. "Hope nobody's out there buryin' somethin' they shouldn't." She pushed my wrist down. "Beginners aim low. Shoot at his balls if you wanna blow his brains out, although that's really the same thing on a man, right honey?"

My ears were still ringing from the first shot. I aimed low and squeezed. The bottles jumped and shattered. I had to duck the flying glass.

Renay poked my arm. "Fun ain't it?" she said.

My New Best Friend

The Desert Eagle was cold in my lap. I moved the chair so I could face the door and got a stiff neck twisting my head to see the TV. Every time headlights flashed outside, I jumped up to peer through the slats in the blinds. If they came, I would have to shoot through the door. I might hit an innocent guy who was just going to the wrong room. Or even another stupid cop like Frayne.

We'd have to be packed and ready if anything went down. We were registered under the phony names, so they wouldn't know who we were right away. But if they traced the credit cards to Harold, he would rat us out for sure.

The trick was to stay alive and hope there was a way out of this.

"We'd better sleep in shifts," I told Hannah. "You go first. I'll keep watch."

"Put the gun away," she said. "If you go to sleep it can drop on the floor and go off."

"I won't go to sleep," I said.

Conan O'Brien was on TV. Hannah was under the covers, mouth open, breathing through her nose. The Desert Eagle sat on the floor under the chair with the safety on. It took me a second to realize I had been asleep for hours and nobody had been watching the door.

I shook Hannah. Kept shaking after she'd opened her eyes.

"You crazy? Why'd you let me sleep?"

She pushed me away. "You were out like a light."

"So why didn't you stay up?"

"I tried, but I kept dropping off."

"Why'd you put the gun on the floor?"

"So it wouldn't drop and blow your precious dick off!"

"What if they broke in?"

"You'd have time to get it."

"You crazy?" My voice was getting louder. "One push and the door's open . . . You know how dead we'd be?"

"We wouldn't be." And now she was angry, hissing through clenched teeth. "Because as soon I hear a noise. . ." She pulled the .380 out from under her pillow and pointed it at the door. "BANG . . . They're on their way in. They try to shoot back. BANG BANG."

She could shoot me now, I thought. That was a way out of the Prisoner's Dilemma. Shoot me and tell the police I killed Frayne and kidnapped her. It wouldn't help with the people who were after her, but it would get her out of a murder charge.

She put the gun down and lay back with a sigh. "Now what's going on in your head?"

"Nothing."

"Don't lie, I know that look. Some kind of Henry James story about a crazy girl with a gun?"

"Not Henry James."

Then, I was kneeling by the bed. And she was stroking my hair. And I was in bed, drawing her warmth to me.

Then it was morning and the phone was ringing. Herrera or my mom or maybe Kellner, or . . .

It was Paul, the fat old clerk.

"You get a free Continental breakfast with your accommodation."

"I'll get dressed," Hannah said.

Halfway down the porch, a woman rushed by, head down, holding three steaming containers. Inside the office was a pot of coffee and a tray of cinnamon buns, still warm from the oven.

Paul was in his chair behind the counter. I got the feeling he never moved. "Buns are homemade," he said.

"Can I get you one?" I asked.

"No. One bite and my sugar will go through the roof. If I ever want to end it all I'll just eat a few cinnamon buns. Got fresh milk in the fridge back here if you don't want the creamer." He turned in his chair as I walked behind the counter to the refrigerator.

"Did you see Renay?"

He knew we had. He just wanted to talk.

"Yeah. She said you were quite a singer. Showed us one of your photos."

"Jeeze, that thing must be fifty years old. Ever hear of Stan Kenton?"

"Never."

"Progressive jazz. He was big in the '50s. I toured with him . . ." He went into a quick reverie. "Renay was a show dancer, you know. Gorgeous. She was Willie Alterman's girl. Ever hear of him?"

"No."

"He came from Minneapolis. Icepick Willie they called him. Ben Siegel put him in to run the Mapes Hotel. Know him?"

"Bugsy Siegel?"

"Don't call him that to his face. They got Willie on a phony murder rap. Tried to turn him, but he wouldn't talk. Renay waited thirty years for him to get out. They ran that little pawn shop together until Willie died a few years ago. Who you visiting?"

"My girlfriend's father."

"I did three years for heroin," Paul said. "They hated the jazz musicians because we were integrated."

Hannah was all packed when I got back to the room. "I put the guns in the laundry bags," she said.

"Let's go."

As we drove out, the office door flew open. Paul stumbled out on his crutches, his stomach jiggling. "Hey c'mere," he shouted. "You can't take that hardware with you. They search the cars. It's five years for bringing a weapon into a correctional facility. Give 'em to me. I'll keep 'em under the counter for you. Give me your cell phones, too. They'll just confiscate 'em." He gasped and steadied himself against the porch rail. "Be careful around them. They think you're a criminal just 'cause you're going to visit one. They're not on your side. Don't believe anything they say."

Visiting Day

O utside the campground there was a splintered wooden arrow with STATE PRISON scrawled in faded black paint. Ancient handmade signs guided us down a twisty side road. Coming around a bend we had to stop short behind a bus that was blowing billows of black smoke out of its tailpipe.

A big black guard in a green uniform clutching a clipboard came up to the car. His partner, a wiry woman with a ponytail, stood on the passenger side, hand on her gun.

"Name?" the guard asked.

"Peter Vogel."

He looked on the clipboard. "The lady's name?"

"Hannah Seeley," Hannah answered.

"Here to see?"

"Arnold Seeley," Hannah said.

His partner passed a mirror under the car.

The guard stepped back. "I need you to get out of the car, sir."

"Ma'am, step out of the car, please," his partner said to Hannah.

We got out. Two black women in a Grand Cherokee behind us watched with amazed expressions.

"ID?" the guard said.

My hands shook as I opened my wallet. If he saw the phony license we were dead. I could see Hannah fumbling in her bag.

"Open the trunk, sir," the guard said.

He searched the car, the glove compartment, under the seats, rapped on the trunk floor, looking for a false bottom. Found nothing. Paul had saved our lives.

"Both hands on top of the car, sir," the guard said.

"Hands on top of the car, ma'am," his partner said to Hannah.

He searched me from my shoes to shoulders, raised my cuffs and looked in my socks, patted me gently up and down my legs twice. His partner was doing the same to Hannah.

"You search every visitor?" I asked.

"You can get back in your vehicle, sir," he said.

We followed the bus. Hannah stared straight ahead, hands tightly clasped in her lap.

A half-mile down the road the bus jolted to a stop. People got off, cowed and quiet, carrying shopping bags.

A guard rapped on our hood and waved us on. Now we saw it. The low-slung sandstone buildings. The watchtower in the middle of the compound. A sign over the entrance—OTTER POINT CORRECTIONAL FACILITY.

We drove along a chain-link fence that was topped with concertina wire. TV mobile units were parked at crazy angles, as if they had pulled in and everybody had run out.

Two lines of demonstrators were separated by police barriers. One group had signs reading AMNESTY INTERNATIONAL DEATH PENALTY AWARENESS. It was a mixed crowd—students, blacks, the old lefties you saw at every demo. There were signs that read ABOLISH THE DEATH PENALTY. People were chanting "Save Ronnie Perry!"

Across the barricade, a smaller group screamed red-faced curses at them. Guys wearing baseball caps. Women holding toddler's hands. Gray-haired ladies twisted with hate. "Kill Ronnie Perry!" "Burn his ass!" There were signs that said RAPIST RONNIE PERRY MUST DIE! . . . RAPISTS BURN IN HELL!

Local cops stood at both ends of the barricade, tapping their steel truncheons in their palms.

A chunky girl in jeans and a headset ran up. "Wait a second, please. We're taping."

A TV reporter interviewed a woman in a mink coat. Dark, thick brows, red lips, rings and bracelets glittering. The woman looked at us and shrieked. "That's her. That's my stepdaughter."

The camera turned toward us. The reporter ran out, pointing her mike.

"Miss Seeley?"

"Hannah," the woman called. "I'm Loretta Napoli . . . I'm your stepmother."

Now I remembered. I whispered to Hannah, "She's the one who goes on TV and says your father comes into her bedroom every night."

Hannah stared transfixed as Loretta Napoli wobbled up in spiked heels. The cameraman backed up to get us all in the picture.

"Your dad is my husband now, Hannah," Loretta Napoli said. "We were joined in mystic matrimony."

She lunged at me. "Are you a friend?" Her breath smelled like a dead animal. A photo fluttered out of a soiled envelope, a nude shot of her, offering freakishly huge breasts. Her nipples were bright red, as if she had put lipstick on them. She bent to retrieve it and I saw she had a low-cut black dress under her coat. "Give this to him."

"They'll take it away," I said.

She moved in closer with a lewd wink. "Hide it up your rectum."

The camera was in my face. I tried to brush it off.

"Don't touch the lens, dude," the cameraman warned.

"Tell your dad I'll be waiting for him tonight, Hannah," Loretta Napoli called. "Tell him these walls cannot keep us apart."

Hannah took my arm with a dazed look.

A line had formed in front of the gatehouse. Mostly women, black and Hispanic moms, pained and patient with shopping bags and coolers. Some had toddlers pulling on their skirts. There were a few gaudy girls in cutoffs and heels, dressed hot to give the guys something to think about. An orderly group. Even the babies seemed to understand this was no place to cry.

Heads turned slightly and we got quick looks, like what

are these white kids doing here. A guard walked slowly down the line and the heads turned back.

"Miss Seeley?"

He was an older guy, bald with a hard belly and bars on his shoulder. He looked her up and down, slowly so she would get the message. "Come with me," he said.

The other guards were bullies, but he would be the good cop. The one who would use his power to do favors and you'd better do a favor in return.

He walked us to the front of the line, looking hard at the other visitors, daring them to complain. They stared straight ahead.

"This your first time up here, Miss Seeley?" he asked.

She didn't answer. I felt his angry impatience. "We just got married," I said. "I'm coming up to meet her dad."

Guards watched us through a glass window. Tight smiles. I could tell they were talking about Hannah.

The guard held the gatehouse door and announced us. "Mr. and Mrs. Seeley . . ."

"Vogel," I said.

The guards smirked. They didn't ask for our marriage license. It was as if they knew we were lying and didn't care.

The guard behind the desk was a young guy with blood-shot eyes and a football neck. He unfolded a map. "You're here," he said, "and you want to go here." He drew a thick line in Magic Marker. "You'll be walking down our free-way," he said. "Stay to the right of the white line. Administration building will be on your left, power plant on your right."

A bent Mexican lady in a long black skirt waited outside with a guard. "*Siga los,*" he said, and she walked a few steps behind us. The "freeway" went around the perimeter of the prison. Now we were on the other side of the fence. Loretta Napoli was screaming for the camera: "Arnold, Arnold, they can't keep us apart!" The demonstrators were chanting. "Free Ronnie Perry . . ." "Rapists must die . . ."

The road curved and the voices faded. "Administration"

was a two-story brick building with prison vehicles parked outside. The power plant had satellite disks and masses of curled cables on its roof. A sign reading SPECIAL HOUSING UNIT swung in front of a long, rectangular stone-and-glass building that could have been a high school or a suburban office complex. The Mexican lady waited until we entered. We passed through a metal detector into a tiny vestibule. Closed-circuit cameras were poised over us. A guard behind a Plexiglas shield pointed to a door marked VISITORS. A female guard took the Mexican lady into another room and we could see them searching her through the glass window.

We zombie-walked into an office where a guard checked our IDs and handed us a printed pass. "You have a half-hour," he said. "According to federal court decisions, your conversations may be recorded. Arnold Seeley will be in room 19. Make sure you return the pass when you leave."

The door swung open onto a long, empty corridor, floors gleaming. Guards stared out at us from behind a glass window. A voice came over a speaker. "Room 19."

We followed the numbers and came to a panel marked 19. It slid open onto a room with a glass partition. A clock over the inner door read 11:40. The door slid shut as we entered.

Behind the glass another panel slid open. Arnold Seeley, in a light blue jumpsuit, shuffled out with hands and feet shackled. He was even smaller than I thought. Balder, his scalp pasty white, the fringe of hair plastered to the sides of his head, his beard flecked with gray. He walked to the window, his lips trembling. His voice came over the speaker, distorted, metallic. "Hannah . . ."

Shaking, she reached out her hands. "Daddy," she sobbed. "Daddy . . ."

Daddy

Their faces were pressed together against the glass. Their palms were touching. Their tears slid down the window.

"Daddy . . ."

"Hannah, honey . . ."

He looked at me in puzzlement.

"This is my fiancé Peter, Daddy," Hannah said.

He blinked, as if he hadn't understood. "You're getting married?"

Hannah looked uncertain, so I jumped in. "You only have a half-hour, Mr. Seeley, and there's a lot to talk about."

His eyes burned through the glass at me. "Yes, well I want to know who you are, young man."

The sex murderer playing concerned dad. It was nuts, but I played along. "I'll tell you all about myself on the next visit, sir."

He turned back to her. "I've been waiting for you, Hannah."

Tears glittered on her eyelids. "I'm sorry, Daddy."

"I thought you were angry at me . . . I thought I would never see you again."

"No . . ."

"Not that I would blame you, honey. After what I've done to you."

"I'm not angry, Daddy," Hannah said.

His lips quivered. "I haven't spoken to anybody in weeks, Hannah . . . just voices on the intercom. Do this, go here . . . Not a word . . . Except when Abner calls. They have to let me talk to him. Thank God for Abner."

I squeezed her leg so she wouldn't tell him Fried was dead. She brushed my hand away. "But doesn't Reverend

Kellner come?" she asked.

"Oh, yes," Seeley said. He rubbed his forehead with his manacled hands, leaving a red blotch. "Twice a month. I only see him because I have to have some human contact or I'll go crazy. You think he'd try to comfort me, but he sits there with a sanctimonious look and talks about redemption. He says I can't be saved because I haven't accepted my sin. He says prison is paradise compared to what awaits me if I don't truly repent."

Hannah clawed at the window, as if she wanted to get through, to touch him. "Daddy . . ."

"I begged him to work with Abner on my case," Seeley said "Help locate the guys in my unit and convince them to testify. Maybe even shame the Navy into releasing the details of those drug experiments that made me crazy." Seeley sobbed. "He won't do it, Hannah. He says Fried is a legal trickster. If he wins the case, it will be the worst thing that could ever happen to me. If he gets me moved to a hospital, he'll only move me closer to eternal damnation."

"I'll talk to him, Daddy," Hannah said. "He'll change his mind."

"You have no idea what it's like in here," Seeley said. His face collapsed in a mass of self pity. "They hate me, Hannah. They give respect to murderers, drug dealers, then put what they call sexual predators at the bottom of their stupid pecking order. They killed women and children, but they look down on me because I did it with sexual intent."

He said *sexual intent* as if it were the most natural thing in the world. Hannah sat back with a startled look.

"They did it to me, Hannah," Seeley said. "Abner says my brain chemistry was altered, that's why I did it. But these people have no excuse. They're deviant maniacs, every one of them. The guards, too." He looked up at a vent in the wall and said loudly: "Who but a sick pervert would spend ten hours a day in a prison? That poor, misguided woman Loretta writes me letters. They censor them, Hannah. I get them with thick black lines drawn through them. But they let the threats go through."

The clock read 11:44. Four minutes had gone by.

I leaned in and whispered: "We don't have a lot of time."

She winced and shook her head. She wouldn't look at me. Or couldn't. She wiped her eyes with her shirtsleeve.

"Who's sending the threats, Daddy?" she asked.

"Everyone," Seeley said. "The inmates, the guards. The first day I was here there was a note folded up in my jumpsuit. Don't think you're safe in isolation, it said. We can get to you anywhere, anytime . . . I find notes in my food or the laundry. They're under the bench in the workout room. Stuck to the wall in the shower . . ."

Hannah had her head down, eyes narrowed, like she was solving a math problem. "What do they say?"

"That they're going to kill me. What else?" Seeley said. "You cheated the hot shot, they say, but we're going to give you justice. They send all those photos of lynchings and burnings."

"Do they talk about me?" she asked.

"Only Rachel. They said they killed her, Hannah. We ran your little Rachel off the road, they said. I gave that note to Abner and he showed it to the warden." Seeley's eyes bulged with indignation. "He dismissed it, Hannah. He said they were just bragging. He said I was completely safe. I would never come in contact with another inmate during my entire time here. He knows they're planning to kill me. They're all in on it, the inmates and the guards. They have to find a way to do it so the guards won't be implicated. And then when it happens, they'll get respect for icing a 'rapo.' That's what they call me, a *rapo*. I'm fair game. And the ones who did it will be honored in this twisted world."

Hannah sat hunched, head down, waiting for the stream of words to subside.

"It's like a competition between the gangs," Seeley said. "The White Power versus the Mexican Mafia to see who can be the first to kill me. They run this place, Hannah. The guards are intimidated by them and let them have TV, the

Internet . . . anything, so they won't cause trouble." He clawed at the window, leaving smudge marks. "Hannah, please talk to Reverend Kellner. He does outreach in the prisons. Abner says he can be really helpful with the media—"

Hannah cut him off. "They're trying to kill me, Daddy."

"You?" He blinked again, as if he hadn't understood.

"They've tried three times," Hannah said. She reached for my hand, without taking her eyes off of him. "Peter saved my life."

Two Suspects

Hannah skipped the parts about Noah Frayne and Abner Fried. She told him about the e-mails, the threats, the clean-cut guy at the strip joint, the plumber in the pickup. She talked fast and low. The guy in the bar, the break-in, the guys in the Jeep. She didn't tell him they were dead.

The self-pitying wince around Seeley's eyes smoothed out. His lips stopped trembling. He became still as stone.

When Hannah finished, he sat nodding for a moment. "They're such hypocrites," he said.

"Who, Daddy?" Hannah asked.

"The so-called loved ones." He turned to me, sensing my reaction. "Oh, I know what you're thinking. How can he say a thing like that?" A white fleck appeared at the corner of his mouth. "Well guess what? I did them a favor, every single one of them."

Hannah stirred next to me.

"Most families are like a bunch of strangers thrown together," Seeley said. "What husband doesn't wish his wife would just die? Or vice versa? Your mother would have been thrilled if she woke up one morning and I was dead. She had been seeing her old high school sweetheart, the one she dumped to marry me. She thought I didn't know, but I read their e-mails and listened to their phone calls. Even followed them to their secret rendezvous." His lips twisted. "They were holding hands in a dark booth in the Macaroni Grill. They drove by a Day's Inn, but I guess he wouldn't spring for it, so they ended up in the back seat of his car. Bringing back high school memories . . ."

Hannah covered her eyes. "Daddy . . ."

He reached out behind the glass. "She always said"—he

mimicked a screechy, quavering female voice—"I'd leave you tomorrow, Arnold, if it weren't for the girls. Well, what was the first thing she did when I was out of her life? Abandoned her precious girls and ran back to Portland to her first love. And now they're meeting and crying over wasted years and wishing they could be together. But he won't get a divorce, because that would mean dividing the property. And if only his wife would just disappear or just not wake up one morning . . . But they haven't got the guts to make it happen. None of the others did. I was a Godsend to all of them."

"Daddy, please," Hannah said.

"It's true, honey. They were bored, desperate, trapped in the lie of the happy family. Believe me, I know. I heard them."

It took me a second to realize. He was talking about the families of his victims. He had spied on them, eavesdropped, hidden in their homes.

"Most people need a catastrophe to give them a new life," Seeley said. "Well, I was that catastrophe. Look what I did for them? Took that annoying person out of their lives. Made martyrs out of them. They got publicity, public sympathy . . . got a new life in the bargain and they didn't have to feel guilty about it."

"Daddy!" Hannah jumped up and pounded the glass with her fists. "Daddy!"

Seeley rose and reached out to her. "I didn't make the world, Hannah," he cried.

She tore at her hair. "Stop!"

"They're jealous of us, honey," Seeley said. "They know you're the only person in the world who ever meant anything to me. Hypocrites!" He spat out the word. "You see how evil they are? They want to hurt me by hurting you."

"Who wants to hurt you, Mr. Seeley?" I asked.

He gave me a scornful look. "Are you the knight in shining armor?"

"No, *you* are."

"Me?"

"You're the only person who might know who's doing this, Mr. Seeley. Who is vengeful enough and smart enough and rich enough, too, because they've spent a lot of money, so far."

"They all got money," Seeley said. "Insurance or settlements from the town." He stopped with a thoughtful look. "Ardison and Baines got the most."

"Jason Ardison?"

"That little fairy got three million."

Hannah shuddered and bent lower.

"And Baines?" I asked.

"Poor doped-up Dougie got four-and-a-half million."

Hannah put her hands over her ears, but Seeley didn't seem to notice.

"I liberated them," he continued. "Jason didn't have to hide his gay lifestyle from his mother anymore. Not that he did a very good job. She always caught him with the guys he brought home from the bars in Palm Springs. They had a bitter, screaming argument that night. She said he was an abomination in God's eyes and would go to hell. He said he was already in hell living with her."

Seeley smiled at some secret memory. I thought of what Reverend Kellner had said: *Serial killers continue to get gratification reliving their crimes.*

"I was in the bedroom closet and heard the whole thing," he said.

Hannah looked up at him.

"And poor Dougie, the talented boy, the lost soul, everybody's pet project," he said, almost hissing with scorn. "All he wanted was to be left alone with an ounce of methamphetamine so he could speed himself to death. Like a kid who keeps trying to jump off a cliff and somebody always pulls him back by his shirt. Poor Dougie. At the trial he talked about how Zandy had helped him go into rehab . . ." Seeley laughed. "Helped him? She had to get a court order to have him put into lockup. He screamed at her. Leave me alone! If I want to kill myself, that's my business. And now

Zandy is gone. Can you imagine what he's doing with his four million?"

Hannah was almost doubled over, sinking lower and lower until I thought she was going to fall off the chair.

"He might be using his money to hire people to kill Hannah," I said.

"He probably is, the little shit," Seeley said.

"One of the men chasing her is an ex-convict named Sonny Doane, who served time up here."

"I wouldn't know him," Seeley said. "I've been in isolation since the day I arrived. But Abner can check on him. Abner has incredible connections."

"Do you think Ardison or Baines could have met Doane somehow?"

"It's possible," Seeley said. "Jason was arrested for forging his aunt's name on checks. He was in prison somewhere. Dougie was arrested several times. If this man Doane had anything to do with methamphetamine, he might know him."

The panel slid open and two guards stepped in. "Time's up."

I had to hurry. "How about the others?" I asked.

"They're all a bunch of bleating sheep."

The guards stood over him. "Let's go, Arnold."

Seeley blinked. His shoulders twitched. "Thanks for coming, Hannah."

She shook her head, slowly.

"Don't be angry. I know I shocked you. I shouldn't have said those things. I don't know why I did. You mean so much to me, Hannah . . ."

She jammed her fingers into her ears as her father went on.

"I never thought . . . I was so crazy with it. I never thought they would come after you." He raised his manacled hands, pleading. "Please write me, honey. I'll be so worried."

I suddenly remembered something. I took the piece of crumpled paper that Fried had left for us out of my pocket.

"Brian Carey, know him?" I asked. "Charles Rothschild?"

"Sure," Seeley said. "They were in my medic unit at St. Albans."

"Jack Powell?"

A guard put a heavy hand on his shoulder. "Let's go, Arnold, if you want to have another visitor this month."

He rose and they took him by the arms. He looked back as they led him away.

"Call Abner, honey. He can help."

Hannah got up, her knees shaking. Her voice slashed the stifled air. "Abner can't help you, Daddy. He's dead!"

The panel slid shut on Arnold Seeley's startled face.

Giggly

In the corridor, I took her arm.

"I'm okay," she said.

She walked ahead of me, taking long strides. When she got to the glass window she stared at the guards until they looked away. She passed the office right under the sign ALL PASSES MUST BE RETURNED and kept going. A guard came to the door, but didn't call her back.

Outside, we walked through the dueling chants "Ronnie Perry must die! Save Ronnie Perry!" Further down, Loretta Napoli was waiting by the fence.

Hannah walked toward her. "They censor your letters, Loretta," she said in an implacable voice. "They'll never let you see him. No more talk shows for you, Loretta."

I couldn't see her face, but Loretta backed up and drew her coat around her.

"Give me the keys," Hannah said. "I'll drive."

"You're being weird," I said.

She grabbed the keys impatiently. "I just want to get out of here."

She floored it in reverse. The tires shuddered against the hard ground. The female guard jumped back as we drove past. The old, bald guard came out of the gatehouse and raised his hand, but Hannah drove by him. On the road the bus was just pulling out to take the visitors back. She veered around it into the oncoming lane. A prison van coming the other way stopped short, brakes squealing, and she pulled in front of the bus.

We bounced over the back road and were at the motel in minutes. An old man was checking in. Paul handed me the laundry bag over the counter.

"How was your visit?" he asked.

The old man turned to look at me.

"Fine."

"Gonna come back?"

"Don't think so."

"Well, good luck to you and your lady."

Hannah raced the motor as I came out. I put the laundry bag in the back seat.

"Paul says good luck."

"He's sweet," she said, and peeled out of the parking lot. The redwood highway went by, as if in a dream. The giant trees seemed to have turned their backs on us. We drove into the sun and headed north on the 101.

"Okay," she nodded. "I'm better now."

"What do you want to do now?" I asked.

"We could go to Canada."

"They'd search the car at the border and find the guns. Maybe we should drive a while and see if anybody's following us."

"They are. We never see them, but they always seem to know where we are."

"McVickers knew we were coming up here. You think he put some kind of GPS on the car?"

"You've got GPS on the brain."

"Fried knew we were coming up here, too. Maybe they were tapping his phone."

She made a mock serious face. "We're doomed."

"You think that's funny?"

"I guess I've been hanging around with you too long."

"Oh, sure," I said. "I get blamed for everything."

She shoved me, playfully. "Stop whining."

"I just want to know where we're going."

"We could go to Oregon to visit my mother."

"Catch her in bed with her high school sweetheart."

"She'd freak."

We drove in silence. We knew we had to talk about him.

She broke the silence. "He sounds so reasonable when he says that insane stuff. He always seemed logical with his rules and his ideas. It was the only world we knew and we thought it was normal."

"He actually seems to love you," I said.

"I loved him, too. Right up until we walked into that room. But when he started to talk about those people like it was their fault . . . I realized that was what my mom lived with, and my sister, too. But not me. And that was why they hated me. Because he was an evil man put on earth to kill innocent people. But he was always good to me. I guess I'm crazy, too."

"Everybody's crazy," I said. "Look at Kellner."

"He's not crazy. He just believes in God."

"Well, Fried was crazy."

"Remember his face when he looked up at the sky?" Hannah imitated Fried's sniffly voice. "Hurry, they might have their spy drones out today."

"But somebody did kill him," I said.

"With our knife. Remember you said"—she did an imitation, which made me sound like Katz— "Get a cutlery set like we're newlyweds and tell them it's for our new apartment."

"You've inherited your father's gift for mimicry."

"You'd better hope that's all I inherited," she said, and then looked at me in amazement. "Did I just say that?"

"We have to talk about what we're going to do," I said.

"There's a rest area. Want me to pull in?"

"I think I've had enough rest areas for a while."

Bipolar Bear

For hours there was nothing to say. The needle on the gas gauge seesawed around the E. We looked for the next GAS-FOOD-LODGING sign. We passed malls, roadside stands, and sandstone townhouses on the ridge.

Finally, we turned off at a Mobil station. I pulled to the side to watch the people gas up while Hannah got coffee and trail mix at the *am/pm* store. A man pumped gas while his wife squeegeed the windshield and emptied the garbage before escorting the kids to the bathroom. A guy in a dusty baseball cap filled up his Tundra, watching the price click off. A palsied geezer in green golf pants had trouble with his credit card as his white-haired wife sat in the car staring straight ahead like a mannequin. They were teetering on a tightrope of sanity and didn't know it. Underneath them was a pit filled with millions of shrieking demons, red-eyed, fangs bloody, spitting fire, flailing with jagged claws. Only a frayed rope kept them from the horror below. A drunken driver, a murderous burglar, a malignant tumor . . . something human or bacterial or accidental or even natural, like an earthquake that would turn their life to hell in a heartbeat.

I felt very old and empty. It was like I had lived sixty years in the last few days. No distant past, only the very near future.

Out of the corner of my eye I saw Hannah looking at me. "We just can't go on driving around aimlessly," she said. She had something on her mind.

"Staying alive isn't good enough for you?"

"Sitting in a motel with a gun pointed at the door? Taking turns sleeping? Eating fast food in front of the TV until our money runs out? We won't be alive for long if we just do that."

"We won't be alive for long no matter what we do."

"Wow, what's the matter with you all of a sudden?"

"Bipolar. If I hadn't smoked all that weed in college I'd be able to deal with this in a much more rational way."

Hannah looked at me, quizzically.

"That's irony," I said. "Remember Katz covered it? Irony closes on Saturday night, he said. But he got the quote wrong. It's satire."

She hunched grimly over the wheel. "Don't start babbling again."

"Babbling?" My voice sounded weak and querulous in my own ears. "You act like I'm pissed off because the Lakers lost, or I can't find my favorite pants. Anyway, you've got some more crazy shit you want me to do."

She sat back. "How'd you guess?"

"I have one talent in life. Reading your mind."

She patted my leg. "Are we having a lover's quarrel in the middle of this insanity?"

"You're the one who said I was babbling."

"I did. You're right. I'm sorry."

I could have said, *Sorry because I read your mind?* Or, *That's the most insincere sorry I ever heard.* I could have kept the spat going. Instead, I just took her hand and muttered, "Apology accepted."

"Okay. Now don't get mad again." She took an anxious breath. "I think we have to find out who's trying to kill me."

"Why?"

"Because it's the only way we can save ourselves. If we know who did it we can go to the police. We can give them a plausible suspect."

"We need proof for that, or at least some evidence," I said. "How are we going to get it?"

"We could start with Jason Ardison or Dougie. They're plausible."

"How do we get proof or evidence about them? The cops won't help us. Nobody will talk to you."

"I thought maybe you . . ."

"Maybe me, *what?*"

"Maybe you could think of something."

She was the girl on campus again, walking backwards, talking fast.

"If I do, will you let me fuck you?" I asked.

She laughed and jumped on me. She was so amazingly warm in my arms.

"Only if your plan works," she said.

Plothead

We turned off at the next exit and got back on the 101, now heading south. Once again, a plan appeared, as if it had been inside me waiting to come out.

"I'll go see them," I said. "Tell them I'm a writer doing one of those true crime books on the Robbinsgate murders. Interview them, get friendly. Then I'll just casually say that I've been talking to you as well. You're staying at a motel in the area and I've made plans to meet you."

Hannah nodded. "Use me as bait. If it's one of them, they'll come after me."

"Only we'll be waiting. With our guns . . ."

She looked at me with what I wanted to think was sincere admiration. "How do you come up with this stuff?"

"A lotta *Law and Order* . . . a lotta '40s movies . . ."

"But we can't shoot them or we'll be charged with murder. We have to hold them for the police." She stopped with a doubtful look. "But what if they don't come?"

"Then, I'll go speak to the other families."

"What if it's not them?"

"It has to be one of them. It has to be somebody who knows you."

"Somebody who wants to kill me," she said. "But why? What did I do to them?"

"Nothing. It's a way of getting even with your father."

"No," she said with a horrified look. "It's *me* they want. Those e-mails and phone calls . . . they wouldn't go to all that trouble. Why do they hate me so much?"

"You can ask them when we catch them," I said. "When we have them on the ground, our feet on their throats." I liked that image, even though I couldn't see the faces of our captives. "When we have our guns jammed against their heads." I liked that even better.

We took turns driving. My heart was pounding, but I liked it. Whenever we stopped for gas I got a 20-ounce to-go cup of coffee, three sugars, and a splash of milk to make it pound even harder.

Somehow we were eastbound on the 10 Freeway. Somewhere around three in the morning we saw the signs for Robbinsgate. Another GAS-FOOD-LODGING led us to a Holiday Inn Express. I banged on the bell and an Indian girl with long sleek black hair came out rubbing her eyes.

It was late and we looked pretty sleazy. I felt I had to say something. "We've been driving for hours, decided to get off the road."

She shrugged like she couldn't care less. And frowned at the Capital One, like we were low rent.

The room was cold. An industrial wall-to-wall over a cement floor. A chair stuck out at an odd angle so you banged your leg when you went to the bathroom. The toilet had an explosive flush.

The clock said 3:42. "We'll have to wait at least four hours," I said.

She shook her head. "Longer. Can't call anybody before at least nine-thirty."

Fear drifted in and out like a room service waiter. I had been okay for a while, but now I was scared again. "Six hours. I don't know if I'll make it."

"You should try to get some sleep."

The pillows were lumpy. My feet hung over the end of the bed. "I feel like my brain's going to blow a fuse."

She smoothed my forehead. "Too much coffee."

She put on a movie, but the voices echoed inside my head and I made her turn it off. I laid my head on her stomach. It had to be uncomfortable, but she didn't say anything, just stroked my hair until I drifted off. I awoke with a stiff neck and a dry mouth. It was 7:30. I stood under the shower forever, but when I came out, it was only 8:20.

"I'm hungry," she said.

"Let me call first, then we'll go eat."

"Call Dougie."

"You have his number?"

She looked on her phone. "I used to. Oh, God . . ." Her hand shook as she handed me the phone. The name "Zandy" was next to a number.

"Can't use your phone," I said. "There'll be a record of the call."

"The hotel phone."

"There'll be a record of that, too. Of course, if they didn't follow us they wouldn't know where we are."

Hannah tugged at her hair. "God, you're making my head ache. Just call him. I don't care anymore."

I punched the number on the hotel phone. My heart jumped with every ring. I would have to be calm and professional. "Hi, Mr. Baines, my name is . . ."

After about ten agonizing rings I heard a recorded message. "This number has been disconnected and is no longer in service."

A temporary reprieve. "No longer in service," I said.

"You'll have to go to his house."

Go right up and knock on his door. Start my spiel cold, face-to-face. *Hi, Mr. Baines, I'm . . .* I would be too nervous. I'd give myself away.

"Let me call Ardison," I said. "Maybe he has the new number." Could she sense my fear? "That's right," I said. "I'm a coward. And you're stuck with me."

"I wasn't thinking that, Mr. Mindreader."

"Oh, yeah? Then what you were thinking?"

"That I don't have his number and we'll have to call Information. But we can't call Information because there'll be a record of the call. You see, I told you I've been hanging around with you too long."

I grabbed the Yellow Pages from the tray on the bottom of the TV cart, thumbed to the White Pages. "He's probably unlisted, too," I said, almost hoping he was. But there it was—"Dorothy Ardison."

"His mother's name," Hannah said. "He never changed the listing."

I could hardly press the buttons with my trembling fingers. Ardison picked up before the first ring had ended.

"Hi . . ." Like he had been waiting by the phone for someone to call.

My voice got caught in my throat. "Mr. Ardison—?"

A breath . . . Silence . . . Like he was disappointed. "Who is this?"

"My name is Jeremy Katz, Mr. Ardison. I'm a freelance writer doing research on the Robbinsgate Murders. I know it's a painful subject, but I was wondering if you could spare me a half-hour."

"Have you spoken to any of the other families?" he asked.

"No, sir, you're the first. Frankly, your story was so tragic and dramatic."

"When do you want to come?" he asked.

"An hour maybe. I'm staying right in town."

"An hour," he said.

I hung up. "An hour."

"That was smart," Hannah said. "That thing about the drama and the tragedy."

California Craftsman

"**D**on't open the door for anybody," I told Hannah. "When I come back, I'll knock."

"I know. Three times, then twice," she said.

"No, let's change the code. In case they were watching. One hard knock."

"Good thinking."

"Are you making fun of me?"

She came to the door and kissed me. Then handed me the laundry bag with my Desert Eagle in it. "Keep it in the car."

The Robbinsgate exit was a few miles down the freeway. The streets were arranged in a grid, all named after birds. Ardison was on Heron Street, right off Martin.

It was a cul-de-sac, ending in an abandoned field that had gone to weed. Ardison's house had a Civic in the driveway. I had trouble springing the latch on the splintery wooden gate. A narrow path between two rows of high, dusty bushes led to the front door. There was a bell, but it didn't look like it worked, so I banged the rusty clapper. I heard scuffling footsteps, like somebody wearing slippers. The door opened on a slight man in jeans and a white T-shirt standing in the shadows of a gloomy hallway.

"Mr. Katz?"

It threw me for a second. I had given him Professor Katz's name without realizing the possible implications.

"Mr. Ardison?"

No handshake. Just a terse "Come in."

He stopped at a table in the middle of the hallway. In the mirror I saw his face, a little boy grown old under a mop of dyed blond hair. It took me a second to recognize the scarecrow standing behind him, haggard and blinking, like a driver trying to stay awake. That scarecrow was me.

"That's my mother," he said.

I had to squint to see the photo in the gloom. It was in a black leather frame, a glossy black-and-white of a white blonde in a low-cut black dress.

"That's from the '60s when she was in her Lana Turner *Black Widow* phase," Ardison said. "Are you from California?"

"Chatsworth."

"Then you know that every California girl thinks it's her God-given right to be a movie star." His voice had a serrated edge. "That's how she met my dad. He was a gaffer. Know what that is?"

"Electrician."

"Sure, every California boy knows what a gaffer is. Everybody has a relative who worked in the—" he wiggled his fingers giving me the quote sign "—industry."

The living room was cluttered with polished mahogany tables and stuffed chintz chairs. A baby grand piano, its top down, sat in the corner.

"They worked in the studios and lived hundreds of miles out of the city, as far away from the Jews and the fairies as they could get," Ardison said. He picked up another photo off the glass-topped coffee table. A brunette with an enticing smile, bending slightly to show her cleavage.

"This was when she thought she might be Natalie Wood," Ardison said. "The besmirched virgin . . . She was a very sensual person, but would never admit it." He turned to me with a challenging look. "Do you want to hear a dirty story about her?"

"Natalie Wood?"

"No such luck. My mom. She told me this, so . . ." he shrugged, "who knows if it's true. She had an agent, Howard Hirsch. Repulsive man, she used to say. He got her a meeting with the Vice President in charge of Talent at Universal Studios. That was a very big deal in those days, you know. So she went to this man's office on the lot and he closed the door. And they talked for a while about her career. And then he got up from behind the desk and his pants were down around his ankles and he had a huge erection." Ardison turned away, but I could see him in the mirror looking at me. "Her version was that she ran out of the office and off the lot. That was the reason she never made it in the . . ." up went the fluttery fingers, "business." He turned to me. "Can you use that story in your book?"

"I think so."

He took a photo off the mantle. A young blonde in tennis whites. A flirty smile, a lot of leg.

"Men would call her a tease, I guess," he said. "The truth is, she was blissfully clueless. You can have some of these photos if you want."

"Thank you. Maybe one of your dad, as well?"

"He didn't hang around long enough to have his picture taken."

Ardison brushed by me and walked down the hallway to the stairs. "Mom said he left when I was six, but I have no memory of him in this house at all. He married a Vietnamese woman and lives in Banning. He has two daughters, my step-sisters. They've been very nice to me. I was a basket case after it happened, you can imagine. They helped me with the funeral arrangements . . . Gina and Lisa. Gina lives in Cano-ga Park with her two little boys. She had me for Thanks-giving and Christmas. Lisa works for the airlines and she came, too. I was the man of the house so I got to carve the turkey. They're both divorced, of course. Are your parents together?"

"No."

"Of course, no one is. The only person I know who stayed married is Arnold Seeley."

We walked up the narrow steps. There were childish watercolor landscapes on the walls.

"Mom painted those," Ardison said. "She thought she was an artist, too. There were no men with big erections to tell her otherwise."

Upstairs, the house seemed to narrow, as if the builder had run out of bricks. A worn gray carpet. A bathroom and two small bedrooms.

"Did you ever share a bathroom with your mother?" Ardison asked.

"No."

"Don't. That old lady smell . . ." He walked into a tiny bedroom. A floral quilt lay over a single bed.

"Mom never looked for another man after my father left. She'd had enough of that. Oh, I almost forgot . . ." He opened the night table drawer and took out a photo. "You might want to use this."

It was his mother, naked, spread-eagled to her bed, a towel stuck in her mouth, head drooping. Dead as the kid in the dumpster . . . dead as Fried and Noah Frayne.

He watched me. "My good friend Gregory took that," he said casually, as if it were a vacation photo. "We got home late. The door was wide open and I could see a light at the top of the stairs. I ran up to her room and found her. While I was throwing up my seven chocatinis, my very good friend Gregory took this picture and many others with his cell phone. I didn't know he had done that, of course. He was so sympathetic. Got me a Tylenol and a cup of tea. Sat with me until the police came. Then went upstairs and got a few more shots of me standing there, looking down at her. I didn't know, of course, until they showed up on every sick Web site in the world. My good friend Gregory had sold the photographs to anyone who would buy them. Two million hits on my dead mother."

He ran out of the room quickly and was back with another photo. "My good friend, Gregory, again."

It was a snapshot at a pool. Ardison in droopy shorts and a Laker T-shirt. A big smirking kid with shoulder-length hair, tattoos crawling up his arms. He looked like Sonny Doane.

"Mom hated him," Ardison said. "Said he was trailer trash. So am I, dear, I said. I'm the trailer trash of the gay world—no looks, no money, no class. If you want to live this way, why can't you find someone nice? she said. I tried to explain it to her. The bars, the boys . . . I wanted her to see how terminally unhappy I was. I wanted to hurt her because she loved me, you see?"

He went into the hall and threw open the closet. "And all the time, Arnold Seeley was hiding here, listening," he said. Ardison pulled back the coats hanging from the bar, revealing a small shallow space. "The police could never figure how he got in without us hearing him. It was such a small house. I guess he knew that we would be so involved in our little comic opera he could come right up the stairs and we would never notice."

I remembered what Seeley had said in his confession. "I was hiding in the closet." Ardison closed his eyes tightly and leaned against the wall. "He waited until I left and then he came out of the closet, no pun intended. There I was barreling down the freeway with the window open and the radio blasting. Singing along with the Supremes. And all the while he was torturing my mother."

He looked at me imploringly. He fell forward. I grabbed him, my fingers going through his sticklike arm. I tried to steady him, but he fell against me and slid down to the floor.

I got him under his arms and dragged him into his room. It was like a monk's cell. A cot and a table. His head jerked up as I put him on the cot.

"I'm sorry I made you relive this," I said.

"I relive it every day."

He sat up, head in hands. "We only had each other. Oh, we played our little roles. She was Miss Prim and I was the whore of the 10 Freeway. She would deliver her pompous sermons, and I would answer with my little squeak of defiance and go out to the bars in Palm Springs. But I always brought her coffee in the morning. We had breakfast and supper together every day. And we had our shows. She loved *Let's Make a Deal*. Anything where a dream could come true."

He looked up at me. "She was in great shape, you know. Could have lasted another thirty years. And when she got old, I would have taken care of her. That would have been my life."

Somewhere I heard a door open. It wasn't the front door. I could see that from the top of the stairs.

Ardison got up and squeezed between me and the hallway, grazing my arm with a provocative look. "I'm rich now, you know," he said. "I'm a serious socialite. I have boy parties, reign like a Queen. One night I'll bring the wrong boy home—or maybe the boy I've been waiting for—and they'll find me tied up and strangled."

I thought I heard the floor creak, like someone was tiptoeing down the hall from the back door. I took a few steps to get a better look. Ardison blocked my way.

"Scared?" he asked. His eyes had turned ugly. His voice rasped with spite. "You're not a writer, are you, Mr. whatever-your-name-is?"

"Sure I am."

He shook his finger disapprovingly, like a schoolteacher. "Don't lie. If you were a writer you would have been taking notes."

The creaking stopped, as if someone were waiting under the stairs.

"Actually, I'm a documentary filmmaker," I said.

"No, you're not, either," Ardison said. "You're that slut's boyfriend. Reverend Kellner told me about you."

Was his friend Gregory downstairs? Would I have to fight the two of them in that narrow hallway?

"That filthy whore sent you here, didn't she?" Ardison said, his voice breaking. "She wants forgiveness. Well so do I and I can't have it, so why should she?"

"It's not her fault," I said.

"Did she suck you off to get you under her power? She was famous for that, you know." Spittle bubbled out of the corner of his mouth. "Did you know your damsel in distress was the school pump? It all came out afterwards. She specialized in jocks . . . in her basement . . . while her father was out raping and killing."

A shadow fell on the downstairs wall. Somebody was there. I tried to slide by Ardison, but he grabbed my hand. "Leaving so soon? Don't you want to hear the rest of my sad story?"

I tried to free my arm and slammed my hand into his face.

He flew back against the wall. "You little bitch!"

I ran to the steps. Couldn't jump. If my ankle gave out, I was dead.

Ardison came at me, shrieking, "I'm not finished with you yet!" He dug his nails into my wrist. "You're going to hear all about that filthy, rotten slut!"

"Don't call her that!"

I tried to shake him off, but he bit my wrist, snarling like a mad dog.

I shook harder. Couldn't get free. That shadow grew along the wall. My brain was roaring. Harder . . .

He flopped like a rag doll.

I stumbled going down the steps . . . couldn't fall. Slammed against the door . . . something behind me. I kicked at it. I tripped on a chunk of pavement and dove for the gate. Ran around to the driver's side of the Bug. Looked back and saw the door swinging open.

It felt like my heart was trying to crash through the top of my head. I sat there, trying to catch my breath. Slid the Desert Eagle out of the shopping bag and put my hand on the butt. It calmed me, helped me think.

In a second it all came together. Ardison had used his settlement to hire Gregory's jailhouse friends to kill Hannah. That's how he knew who I was.

Fried said the families had been threatening him. He had to get a restraining order against Ardison and Baines. They had killed him because they didn't want him to get Seeley declared insane.

I drove to a gas station by the freeway and called Hannah.

"I saw him. He knew all along I was a phony. I think he had somebody in the house, I'm not sure. I ran out of there."

"Were you scared?"

"Shitting bricks. He's spooky. Fixated on his mother."

"Do you think it's him?"

"I don't know. He has this friend who looks just like Sonny Doane. I just don't know."

"Go see Dougie Baines," she said. "He's right around the corner on Blue Jay Way. Eleven-fourteen, next door to a vacant lot that used to be my house. Maybe he'll tell you something."

"Uh, huh."

I could see her cocking her head, suspiciously. She knew me so well. "What's the matter with you?" she asked.

"Nothing."

"What else did he tell you? C'mon, spit it out."

"Maybe that's something I should say to you."

"What?"

I tried to keep the accusation out of my voice. "Ardison said you were the town pump."

"The *what*?"

"The slut, the class blowjob." I was starting to blurt, but couldn't help it. "He says you did all the jocks downstairs in your basement. That everybody knew about it. That you sucked me off to get me under your power."

"Well, that's no secret."

"It's not funny," I said, trying not to sound whiny.

Her harsh laugh exploded in my ear. "It *is* funny. It's ludicrous. Nice word, huh? You taught it to me."

I could see her eyes getting wider and blacker. "At this point, would it matter if I screwed everybody in Robbins-gate? And my father, too? Because they said we were having sex. That's another rumor they spread."

She was right. My anger melted into shame. "It would-n't matter."

I couldn't hear her breathing. It was like she had put the

phone down and was pacing around that tiny motel room. Looking out of the window at the parking lot, thinking: *How did I get into this? How did I get stuck with this guy?*

"I'll go see Dougie Baines," I said.

No answer.

On Blue Jay Way

Was there any rhyme or reason to the street names? Had they just put a bunch of birds in a hat and drawn them in random order? Cardinal after Heron? And then Blue Jay?

Was there any reason for this stupid town? It had no center. No factories, no railroad stations, no lakes for jet skis. Just a flat, dead field of foreclosed farms off the freeway.

Blue Jay Way was a street of townhouse clones. In the middle was a vacant lot where the Seeley's house had burned. They had put up a wall of splintered beams around the lot. Blackened timbers were strewn across the ditches.

Next door, 1114 Blue Jay Way was going to seed. A red Honda Odyssey with a sideswiped fender sat in the driveway. Dead brown patches dotted the lawn. Somebody had spackled the front door, but hadn't painted it.

I pushed the bell and heard nothing. Shoved my finger into it. One broken ring. A round peephole under the knocker slid open.

A muffled voice. "Yes?"

"Mr. Baines?"

"Yes."

"My name is Jeremy Katz. I'm a documentary filmmaker working on a film about the Robbinsgate Murders."

"What do you want?"

"I'd like to interview you about the case. I know it's painful, but I feel the victims and their families never get their stories told."

"They don't, you're right." The door inched open. "Come in, Mr. Katz, I'll be right with you."

I stepped in to see a guy in boxers running up the stairs. The house had been neat once. A wall-to-wall carpet going bald in spots. A chipped mahogany table by the door with a mirror so the girls could check themselves out one more time before going out. I walked through a curtain of dust motes into the living room. It was another shrine to a victim. Photos of Alexandra Baines—from the squinty buck-toothed little girl coming out of a pool, to the cheerleader, kicking high, blonde hair swinging. The girl with the sweet smile in the simple black dress holding her prom bouquet.

My phone clanged with a text message . . . GET OUT OF THERE! THE COPS ARE COMING.

Something glinted.

I looked in the mirror. Dougie Baines was rushing at me with a baseball bat. I turned and got my hands up. I could see his greasy hair flopping, his pinned eyeballs. The bat slammed into my shoulder. I ducked and took a blow to my forearm. The pain shot through me like an electric shock.

He stepped back and screamed "Motherfucker!" as he swung at my ribs. I tried to catch the bat, but it slammed into my knuckles. He rushed at me, holding the Louisville Slugger high over his head. I grabbed one wrist, but missed the other and the bat came down on my forehead.

I was going black. My knee wobbled. I felt a jarring blow on the back of my neck. I grabbed his wrists. Stuck my head in his chest and pushed. We were frozen for a second, gasping at each other. Then he gave. His foot slid back and we stumbled across the room. He banged into the arm of a chair, yelling "Fuck!" I got my foot behind his ankle and kicked up as hard as I could. He tripped and flailed. The bat flew out of his hands. I slammed him down on the floor and jumped, knees first on top of him.

Eyeball to eyeball, I recognized him. That gawk who had been lurking outside Hannah's house.

The bat rolled away. I grabbed it and pressed down on his Adam's Apple until he gagged.

"It's *you*," I said.

"Go ahead, kill me," he gasped.

I pressed harder. "Why are you doing this to her? It

wasn't her fault."

His eyes bulged. "Her fault?" He clawed at me. I pushed my knees down on his shoulders, pinning him. He jerked his head back and forth, teeth bared, snorting through his nose. "It wasn't Zandy's fault, either. My mom's cancer spread to her liver. It wasn't her fault, either."

I let up on him a little. I wanted him to talk.

"You were stalking her," I said.

"I wanted to see what she was doing," he said.

"You saw her with me."

"Yeah . . . you were as pathetic as I was, always trying to make her laugh. Bet you didn't know she was doing lap dances in a strip club."

"I knew."

"I sat in the dark and watched her dance. She never even knew I was there."

"Then you sent that guy in there after her."

"That what she told you? That how she got you on her side?"

"You did all this out of jealousy," I said.

He writhed under me. "Jealous?" he hissed. He took a groaning breath. "You think I want her?"

"Hannah loved your sister."

"So what? I did, too. I'm being punished, why shouldn't she? Why should she have a life?"

"Because she didn't do anything, asshole." I put the bat in his mouth and pushed down with all my strength. I wanted to crush his teeth, hurt him for what he had done to Hannah. "*You're* the one who's to blame, not her," I said. "You're the one who was too blown out to defend your sister . . ."

My phone clanged with another text message. I pressed harder on his mouth and pushed myself up.

ARE YOU STILL THERE? GET AWAY NOW!

He got up on his hands and knees, blood pouring out of his mouth.

"The cops'll get you," he said. "Both of you. They want her, you know. The DA told me she was part of it. She knew what her father was doing."

Grimacing, he grasped the arm of a chair and tried to push himself up. "Once we get her in jail, she'll never get out, the sheriff told me."

He crawled at me, dragging his leg.

"They'll get her if we don't get her first."

I was at the door. I could hear him behind me, dragging himself along the floor.

I turned and raised the bat. My head was roaring again.

Can't Escape

"Get away from there," Hannah said on the phone.

She was crying. I could see her alone in that room, tearing at her hair.

"But it's Dougie Baines," I said. "He admitted it."

"Get away now, for God's sake. Reverend Kellner called the police."

I had gone back on the freeway and pulled over on the shoulder. "How did he know I was here?"

"I told him. I called him . . . I was scared."

"What did you tell him?"

"What we were doing. What my father said . . . everything. He got mad at me, Peter. You believe that? 'Leave those boys alone,' he said. 'Haven't they suffered enough?' He said if you hurt Dougie he would have you arrested. He was yelling at me. 'Nobody is trying to kill you. You're just taking your insanity out on these innocent boys.'"

"I'll tell him that Dougie Baines confessed," I said.

"He won't believe you," Hannah said. "He'll call the cops and then everything else will come out . . ." She was crying bitter gulping tears, like a little girl with a skinned knee. "He said, hasn't your family done enough? Like I was to blame for what happened to Zandy."

"He was upset. He didn't mean it that way," I said. "Anyway, we need his help. Is he at the church?"

"Just come back, Peter," she pleaded. "Dougie will stop now that we know it's him."

"No, he won't, Hannah. He has no life. Neither does Ardison. I think they're in it together or Ardison knows something."

"Let's just get away from this town, Peter."

"We can't keep running, Hannah," I said. "They're rich. They can hire people to chase us. McVickers said there were people in this world who would do anything for money. They'll keep doing this until they get us."

"I don't care," she said.

"I do. I'm not gonna let them win."

She was quiet now, sitting in that room looking at the end of her life.

"We take turns being brave."

"Let's see what happens when we're both brave at the same time. How far is the church?"

"Only a few miles down the road."

Sanctuary

I doubled back to the exit and crossed the freeway into a time warp. This was what California had looked like before the '30s, when drought raised the Dust Bowl in the Southwest and sent millions of dirt-poor farmers across the country. Before World War II sent the next wave—veterans, young women, a whole generation of people who didn't want to go home again. And in the '60s, when developers bought cheap farmland and created the "California miracle." The road was asphalt with blotches of tar, rocks and dirt pushing through the potholes. Orange groves lined both sides. The breeze carried a citrus fragrance. An occasional house was set back from the road in a stand of shade trees, roses along the borders, berry bushes around the sides.

The road will bend, Hannah had told me, and then you'll see the sign: ST. PAUL'S.

It was set back on a circular driveway and looked like an old Mission with its yellow stucco walls and brown roof. An undigested bit of history popped into my head: *Father Juniper Serra, the Jesuit Missionary, who converted the Indians.* A blue pickup sat parked under a car shelter on the side. The directory read:

WELCOME TO ST. PAUL'S. WEDNESDAY EVENING 6:30 SUNDAY MORNING AT 10. REVEREND MANFRED KELLNER WILL ASK: HOW CAN WE KNOW WHO WE REALLY ARE?

The church was cool. Beams of golden light streamed through the stained glass windows. I walked down the aisle toward the altar. A man sat in a pew, hands clasped, head bowed. It was Kellner, wearing his collar. He turned with a serene smile. "Peter, I'm glad you came."

"We need your help, Reverend," I said. "I know you're

angry at us—"

"I'm not angry. I decided not to call the police." He slid over. "Sit down for a moment."

I banged my knee against the bookshelf on the back of the pew. Kellner smiled. "I do that every time."

I was starting to feel the effects of the fight with Dougie Baines. My fingers were bent and swollen. Hot stabbing jolts ran through my head. I couldn't straighten my neck. But Kellner didn't seem to notice.

"This is my favorite time of day," he said. "Did my morning chores. Made a hospital visit. That's why I'm wearing my clerical—people like you to be official. Had my lunch with the Sunday School committee. In a few hours I'll go home to the blessed burdens of family life. Wife, young children, a noisy house full of cheerful controversy. But this is my time. I can just sit here and feel the spirit. Have you ever been in a church off hours?"

"No," I said.

"It's my only time to commune. The rest of the week, even the Sabbath, I am doing my job. Special occasions, weddings, funerals . . . even holidays are like work for me. Getting through the ritual, reading announcements, the week's events. It's customer service. Even the sermon is a pitch. Here's another reason to buy my product, folks."

"I'm sorry if I interrupted you," I said.

"No, I was praying that you would come." He smiled. "I know how that sounds. There's such a gulf between those who believe in prayer and those who don't. I use the analogy of the cell phone tower. You dial a number and it goes to a tower, which then directs it to the person you are calling. In the same way your prayers ascend and the answer is sent back down to earth. The analogy seems to resonate, especially with the younger people."

"Hannah is in a lot of trouble, Reverend."

He touched my wrist. "Not here, Peter. Let's just sit for a moment longer. This is my time and I'm selfish about it."

He bowed, his forehead touching his clasped hands, his

lips moving. "Will you pray with me, Peter?" he asked.

"I don't know how."

"I'm praying that we find the wisdom to resolve this terrible dilemma that has caused so much pain to so many people."

"I'll pray for that." It sounded like: *I'll drink to that.*

It seemed to go on. Like he was making me wait out of spite. Then, he lifted his head.

"You're a good person, Peter," he said. "I saw great empathy in your eyes for Hannah. Great pain at her distress. You want to save her, don't you?"

I felt a sob coming. "Yes."

"You love her very much, don't you?"

The way she had run to me in the club when Sonny Doane tried to grab her. Her silhouette at the window when she'd said: *"I used you."*

"Yes, I do. Very much."

He patted my hand. "Let's talk about it in my office."

Getting Warmer

O ur footsteps creaked on the nave floor. Like the creaking in Ardison's house. The clattering steps on the hotel stairs, the quick breaths of my pursuers.

"These are our new stained glass windows," Kellner said. "The cross on a bed of lilies. Do you know what lilies symbolize, Peter?"

"No."

"Resurrection," he said. "Resurrection is a powerful symbol. It means there is always hope, even for the most heinous sinner." He looked up at the windows, grateful for their consolation, then said, "We put the windows in a few months ago. We wanted to express our faith in hope and healing . . . and each other. We're not a rich congregation, but we raised the money in one meeting."

"Jason and Dougie must have helped," I said.

"They were very generous, yes."

We walked behind the chancel, toward an office at the end of a long dark hallway. The wall was lined with photos hardly visible in the shadows. A ray of sunlight caught the photo nearest the door. It was Kellner, smiling in his jeans and white shirt, in front of a group of hulking young men. The drab buildings of Otter Point—the SHU, the power plant—rose in the background.

"That's my Bible study group," he said.

"Otter Point," I said.

"You recognize it. Yes. I started the group when I was seeing Arnold. I asked the warden if there were any chaplain visits or clerical outreach. He said this is Maximum Security, Reverend. No repentant sinners here. I asked him to give me a chance and he said he would let me start with men who were about to be released because they wouldn't make trouble."

Kellner's voice swelled in preachy cadence and I realized this was a story he had told from the pulpit many times before. ". . . And I went into the SHU and spoke to the men, got a few to agree to come to a meeting. Men who had tried to kill each other over cigarettes, or homemade alcohol, or some kind of racial affiliation came together for prayer. I called it the Ezekiel Project, from Ezekiel 18:24, which says: *If the wicked one repents of all the sins he committed and keeps all my laws and does what is just and right he shall live; he shall not die.* Come in, Peter." He ushered me into his office and closed the door.

It was small, windowless, the musty smell of books and lemon air freshener mingling uneasily.

"At first the guards wouldn't take the men's shackles off," Kellner said, sitting at a desk arranged with scrupulous neatness, behind a fortress of family photos, toddlers to old-sters. "By the time it was over, my boys had given up alcohol and drugs." His eyes seemed to bulge out of his head. "Some of the younger staff was joining us, guards and inmates praying together."

He smiled, sensing my impatience. "But you're not here to listen to my story. The only reason I mention it is that my relationship with the prison came about as a result of my visiting Arnold. In the midst of all this grief and doubt I found something constructive, do you understand?"

"Yes," I said.

"Did anything constructive come out of your visit?"

"It was good that Hannah saw her dad. But she was very upset."

Kellner nodded. "Arnold refuses to acknowledge the enormity of his crime."

"He thinks the government gave him some kind of drug when he was in the Navy," I said.

"I know." Suddenly agitated, he jumped up and began to pace behind the desk. "I've told him a hundred times that it doesn't matter. He's looking to Abner Fried to exonerate him, portray him as the victim and erase his sin. But Fried is an unbeliever and can only be used as Balaam's ass to deliver God's message . . ."

He stopped, reading his behavior in my startled expression, and went back behind the desk, hands shaking, trying to compose himself. "I thought I could reach him. I've had men drop to their knees in front of me, confessing their guilt, crying out for forgiveness."

"I don't think Arnold Seeley will ever do that."

"No, he won't."

I said, "And even if he did, I don't think Dougie Baines would be satisfied."

Kellner sat back down, clasping his hands so tightly I could see his fingers whitening. "You call him Dougie, as if you knew him."

"I met him once in front of Hannah's house," I said. "He was harassing her, Reverend. He just admitted it to me. He says he was doing it because of his sister, but he really hates Hannah because he thinks she was having sex with other guys."

Kellner was calm now, watching me. "There were lots of rumors flying around at the time, Peter. I didn't believe that one."

"Even if it's true, it's no reason to kill her," I said.

There was a slight smile, a crinkling around the eyes. I was using his argument on him and he knew it.

I kept going. "Jason Ardison hates Hannah, too, and he doesn't even know her."

Kellner shook his head in calm refutation. "Actually, Jason knew the family from church activities."

"Ardison thinks he hates Hannah because of what her father did. But it's just a way of displacing his own guilt for being so into his gay lifestyle that he left his mother alone on the night she was killed. I know I sound like a teenage Dr. Phil."

That trembling smile again. "There are people in this

church who think Dr. Phil should have a stained glass window all his own." He took a breath, like a man facing a difficult task. "What are you trying to tell me, Peter?"

"Dougie Baines is trying to kill Hannah, Reverend. And I think Jason Ardison is helping him."

Kellner winced and tried to rub the headache off his temples. I had seen my mother do that so many times. Then she would pinch her nose and her voice would become strained.

"Hannah has been stalked and harassed and threatened and that's shameful, Peter," he said. "But no one is trying to kill her."

"I'm a witness, Reverend."

Now he pinched his nose. "And how are Jason and Douglas trying to kill Hannah?"

"They've hired these guys. Maybe some drug dealers Dougie knew or thugs Jason met in his travels."

"Did they confess to you?"

"They didn't confess, but they communicated it to me."

"Didn't confess, but communicated," Kellner said with an appreciative nod, as if he were noting it for future reference. "And you think they want to kill Hannah to get even for their loved ones."

Kellner put his head in his hands. Everything got quiet. No birds, no breeze. "These boys are lashing out in grief and confusion," he said. "You're right, they were harassing Hannah. But they're not trying to kill her. That's her invention."

Don't say anything, I thought. Just let him talk.

He opened a small refrigerator and took out a bottle of water. Offered me one. I shook my head.

"Douglas started e-mailing Hannah when her father was arrested," he said. "He wrote the threatening letters, too. But it was the e-mails, hundreds a day for months, that became his obsession. He would write different ones so Hannah would think they came from different people. He's a computer geek. He had some way of using different addresses to send hundreds of e-mails at once."

"You knew he was doing it," I said.

He couldn't look at me. "Douglas came to me after Hannah had left town. He had tracked her to her new school and was blasting her. That was the word he used—*blasting.*"

"Did you tell him to stop?"

"I told him I understood that he wanted to do something to get the pain out of his soul, but this wasn't the way. He admitted that it hadn't helped. He was still as tormented as ever because he knew what he was doing was wrong."

"You didn't tell Hannah or call the police."

He opened a side drawer in his desk and stared into it. "I didn't want to make trouble for Douglas. I knew if the word leaked out there would be another media frenzy." He put a prescription bottle on his desk. "He was clean now, and I thought it might tip him over the edge. Anyway, he promised he would stop and I thought he had."

"And Jason Ardison?"

Kellner picked up the prescription bottle and put it down again. "They give me this for my headaches, but it makes me groggy."

"Jason Ardison," I repeated.

"All right, full confession." He took a breath. "Jason came to see me after the trial. Sat in the chair you're sitting in now, crying his eyes out. He admitted he had been calling Hannah. It was all he did, he said, day and night. He got disposable phones from people in bars so it couldn't be traced back to him."

"Hannah said she changed her number," I said.

"I know," Kellner said. "Jason said he had used some computer program to find her new number and had gotten her suitemates' numbers, too, somehow, by hacking into the university system."

"Jason's old school," I said. "He could never do that on his own. Was he working with Dougie?"

"No," Kellner said. "They didn't even know about each other." He unscrewed the top of the bottle and tightened it again. "Those boys have an ache in them that won't go away.

But they are not trying to kill Hannah."

I got up slowly. "Thanks for your time, Reverend."

He looked up in alarm. "What are you going to do?"

"Tell the police what you just told me."

"That was privileged communication."

"I'm not a man of the cloth. I'm just trying to save Hannah's life."

He reached out to me, like those supplicants in the religious paintings. "Please, Peter. Before you go to the police let me try to settle this."

"How?"

"Let me talk to Jason and Douglas. Try to bring them all together."

"You mean with Hannah? Did she come down with you?"

He clasped his hands, imploring: "Please, Peter, bring her here. I'll get the boys over here. Let me try to make this right."

"She's here," I said.

He watched me take out the phone and punch in Hannah's number. He leaned forward as if he wanted to hear Hannah's end of the conversation.

She picked up right away.

"Peter—?"

"It's okay," I said. "I'm with Reverend Kellner. He wants to talk to you. He says he has a way to settle this. I'm going to come pick you up."

She sounded doubtful. "Peter, are you sure?"

"Hang on, Hannah," I said. "It's almost over."

Bloodbath

S ometimes the best way is also the only way.

The church was empty. No one to see—or hear. No one would remember seeing Hannah's little blue Bug tooling up the quiet country road. And if they did, it wouldn't be enough to make a case. Murder was always a calculated risk. You slashed two kids' throats behind a supermarket and walked away. You shot a couple of thugs on a busy freeway turnoff while cars sped by. A guy came up a hill. You jumped him and beat his brains out. At the bottom of the hill people were taking their screaming kids out to pee. You drove away like nothing had happened.

I went out to the car. The Desert Eagle was still in the laundry bag on the front seat. Big and gold, it would boom like a cannon in the church. I pulled back the slide. Bullet in the chamber, just like Renay had told me.

I put the gun back in the bag and returned to the church. The altar shimmered. The lilies in the brand new stained-glass windows waved gently around the cross.

I was dizzy with fear. The dust choked off my breath. The creaks and squeaks exploded like firecrackers around me.

The door to Kellner's office was half open. A streak of light fell on the photo of his Bible group. I could hear his voice, low and confidential. I slid around the door without opening it. He blinked and hung up the phone, gently.

"Back so soon?"

"Never left," I said. I sat down and put the laundry bag on my lap. "Were you calling Jason and Dougie?"

"My wife, to tell her I'd be late for dinner."

"You're the one, Reverend," I said.

He understood me. It was all there in his frantic look. He

slid his chair back.

"You'll never get to the door," I said.

He got very quiet and watchful.

"I saw your murderers," I said.

I had almost screamed with relief when I saw that photo on the wall and realized I hadn't killed a cop.

"Quite a group of Biblical scholars," I said. "Sonny Doane . . . Noah Frayne . . . McVickers told me about their scam. They would raid meth labs pretending to be DEA agents. Flash the badges, put the cuffs on the dealers, then rob them."

Kellner looked confused. "You know those boys?"

"Intimately. You sent them to kill Hannah . . . and me."

His shoulders were hunched and his eyes were small. "I don't understand what you're saying."

"You hate Arnold Seeley," I said.

"I don't hate Arnold," he said, patiently. "But I feel he will not repent because he isn't truly suffering for what he's done."

"He's in solitary confinement for the rest of his life," I said. "Isn't that suffering enough?"

His face got all screwed up, like he was about to cry. "Let me tell you about suffering, Peter," he said. "I visit a man in the convalescent home. Ed Zwerlin, Jennifer Zwerlin's grandfather. Ed found his granddaughter's bound and strangled body when he came to drive her to work." He blinked and shuddered. "The day after Arnold's arrest, Ed had a stroke. He's paralyzed on one side of his body and has lost the power of speech. He can't move, Peter, can't speak. Doctors say it was his pent-up rage at the injustice of his granddaughter's death that did this to him."

He turned, his voice breaking. "Ed Zwerlin is suffering much more than the man who raped and murdered his granddaughter. Arnold can walk and talk. But Ed Zwerlin is trapped, his anger unappeased."

I rose slowly. His eyes went to the bag. I eased the Desert Eagle out just enough. This will be a cross examination, I thought. And in the end he will be guilty. And I will pass sentence.

"You thought Arnold Seeley was your friend," I said. "But he betrayed and humiliated you."

"It wasn't Arnold. It was *Satan*. He had entered Arnold." Kellner winced and clutched at his head. "They say the devil shrieks with mocking laughter when he enters someone. Satan was laughing at me when I asked Arnold to counsel young married couples. Laughed at me when I preached love and forgiveness, when I led a silent prayer at Easter for the victims. It wasn't Arnold in the front pew. It was Satan. Mocking me."

He leaned forward, earnestly. "The judge said Arnold was legally sane but insane by every other standard. He's a sick man, people said, and you could hear the pity in their voices. I tried to tell them the truth."

"What was the truth?" I asked.

He opened the desk drawer again. "Arnold was possessed, Peter. Before you start to laugh, give me a hearing. There are billions of faithless people on earth, going through the motions of worship. But there are also true believers. We were three-hundred souls down a forgotten country road, but in our little church we could summon the presence of the Holy Spirit. There were times on the Sabbath when our voices would rise up in a cloud. And the Presence would descend to us in a pillar of flame . . .   Satan was in our church and heard our prayers. As the scripture says: *His dominion is in darkness. His mission is to shatter the faith of those who believe*."

Somewhere in my memory the story of Lucifer—the fallen angel—was stirring. It was Sunday school. A young man with thinning hair, neck chafed from shaving, was railing about the devil. We laughed at him to cover our fear and his voice got shrill . . .

Now Kellner's voice got shrill, as if someone was shrieking from inside him. "Satan chose Arnold—the weakest among us—as his weapon. He made him kill in a sickening, depraved way that defied reason. After Arnold's arrest my people came to me in anguish, seeking an answer. Satan is testing us, I told them. They turned away from me. Even my own wife told me if I didn't stop talking about it, they would send us away and I would never get another pulpit."

"So you stopped."

"Yes, I did. In my silence I brooded and I did begin to hate Arnold. I had visions of inflicting the most terrible torture on him."

"You hated his wife and daughters."

"I did, but I struggled with it. I fought my hatred, Peter. I urged Rose to bring the girls to our Easter Service. We were going to sing 'A Mighty Fortress Is Our God.'"

He turned toward the window and sang in a quavering voice:

"Though Devils all the world may fill,
All eager to devour us,
We tremble not, we feel no ill,
They shall not overpower us . . ."

A shadow was spreading across the parking lot. Wheels crunched over the gravel. Kellner raised his voice to distract me. "But Rose took her daughters away. Then Fried arrived with his insane allegations."

"Satan had sent Fried," I prompted.

"Satan, yes."

"Did he send Sonny Doane?"

"God sent Sonny Doane."

He slumped forward, head in his hands. One eye gleamed through his fingers, watching the shopping bag. "One day in our prison Bible group I ended our prayers early," he said. "I told the boys I was going to see Arnold. Their faces got all twisted with hate. *You pray with that rapo scum?* they said.

"Sonny and Noah were in a White Power gang. Their leaders had decided that there would be no sex offenders at Otter Point. They would kill every one until the state stopped sending them. Arnold was a marked man, they told me. They had sent him a message on his first day at Otter Point just so he would know that he wasn't safe, even in the SHU. I was amazed. A message? I said. But he is in total isolation. They laughed. *You think the staff runs this prison? We're in charge here.*

"They had certain guards on their side. Sometimes they had them blast punk rock over his intercom in the middle of the night to wake him up. Sometimes they sent him taunting notes or put dishwashing liquid in his food. They were waiting for the right time to do it. Time stands still in prison. A month is like a minute. There was no hurry."

His face was changing shape right in front of me. His eyes had darkened. His voice rang like it was coming from the bottom of a well. "I should have told the warden they were planning to kill him. Instead, I hoped they would make it a long, excruciating death.

"I had them tell me every time they sent him a note or tormented him in any way. I was in an exalted state. If I had heard that they had burnt him with cigarettes, mutilated him with broken glass, cut off his limbs, prolonged his agony the way they did in the Inquisition, I would have rejoiced."

Was his face crumpling? Was he going to morph into a hideous slimy glob of a *Weird Tales* creature?

"But then I became frightened," he said. "If Arnold died unrepentant, with the devil still choking his soul, he would be condemned to eternal damnation. If I allowed this to happen I would burn alongside him. I had to get Satan out of him before it was too late."

My head was roaring again. Could he possibly believe all this?

"You see, Satan is a proud spirit. He cannot stand to be dismissed. He wants ceremony, so we deny it to him. We don't need magic chants. Real, fervent prayer will drive him away."

His insanity was entering me like an imp, tearing at my mind.

"But Arnold wouldn't acknowledge his sin," he said. "A man who brutally, senselessly, sadistically slaughtered the innocents, insisted that he was the victim and wouldn't pray for forgiveness."

Now his face twisted as he spat out the name. "*Fried—* Fried had lured Arnold away with his promises of salvation on earth."

"So you decided to use Hannah."

"You see, even the most evil man is given one thing to love," he said. "One slender reed to cling to. Arnold truly loved Hannah. It was amazing to see how he would soften when he spoke of her."

"You knew that the only way to make Arnold Seeley truly suffer was to kill his daughter."

I had trapped him. He realized he had said too much. He twitched. Almost flew out of his skin. Then recoiled.

"Not *kill* her," he said forcing himself to be calm. "I wanted her to come with me and talk to him."

"Hannah had a hole in her story that made everybody think she was a liar or just crazy. I mean, why didn't these guys just kill her? They could have done it a hundred places on campus. In the strip joint parking lot. Or her apartment in LA. Sonny Doane could have done it in the bar in Houston that night. He can work real fast when he has to. But a quick death wasn't good enough for you. Your plan was to kidnap her. Take her somewhere. Torture her the way her father had tortured his victims."

He reached out to me. "I meant Hannah no harm, Peter."

"You wanted photos of her being tortured and killed. They were going to record her pleading for life."

"No! I wanted her to talk to her father."

"The prison guards could slip those photos into Arnold Seeley's cell. Put them anywhere. They would spook him pretty good. He'd be afraid to look in his food tray or his laundry. Even his Bible. When he went out for exercise, the photos would be on the floor. When he took a shower, they'd be pasted to the wall. The guards could pipe Hannah's torture tapes right through the intercom into his cell. Play them day and night, he'd never know when. He'd be trapped in his cell, listening to his dying daughter beg for her life."

Kellner reached out a beseeching hand. "I could *never* do anything like that."

Rage surged through me. It wouldn't take much more anger for me to be able to pull the trigger.

"Yes, you could, Reverend. Kill Hannah the same way Seeley killed his victims. Then make him see it and hear it, and know that his beloved daughter had been tortured because of what he had done."

"No, Peter, no!" he cried.

"You would pretend to care. Promise to intercede with the Administration. But then you'd come back and tell him, sorry there was nothing you could do. There was no proof, because the guards would remove the photos and the tape and there would only be his word against the staff. And nobody would listen to a delusional sex murderer. He would cry and beg for your help. And all the while you'd be having your sweet revenge."

"Peter, please listen to me," Kellner pleaded. "I admit I did nothing to stop Jason and Douglas in their vicious pranks—"

"You killed Abner Fried," I said.

He sank in his chair, watching . . . "No!"

"You sent us to see him, and you sent Sonny to follow us."

A vein fluttered at his temple.

"Fried called you after we left his office. I saw the notation on his pad. He was gloating. He was that kind of guy. He had already gotten permission for Seeley to get magazines and newspapers, even buy a TV. He was going to make a big case out of this. With Hannah's help he was going to exonerate Arnold and get him sent to a hospital."

Kellner nodded eagerly. "He did call me. He wanted me to support him. He was going to put together this coalition of scientists and journalists."

"Poor, stupid Fried knew someone was watching him. He took us out the secret passageway and when he got back to his office Sonny stabbed him with a barbecue knife. Am I right so far?"

"You're terribly wrong, Peter," Kellner said. "You're making a case so you can murder me in good conscience."

He was too reasonable. I wanted him scared, pleading, on the edge of confession. It would be easier that way.

"You sent Noah Frayne to the mall," I said. "He was going to flash his phony ID on us. Kill me and take Hannah."

"I hadn't seen Noah for months," he said.

"He was sitting two tables away from us."

"I didn't see him, Peter."

"Sonny and Noah don't do redemptions for nothing," I said. "Did you get the money to pay them from Jason and Dougie? Did you help Sonny and Noah with their meth business as a little extra inducement? Is there a meth lab down in the basement? A church would be a great place for it. Down a quiet road. No one around, except on Wednesday nights and Sundays. No fear of informants or undercover cops. Did Sonny give you a little meth to help you finish your sermon? Did you get to like it? Did you see God? Did he tell you to kill Hannah?"

His expression froze the words in my throat. His lips curled, his eyes screamed hatred. His voice changed, as if the psychopath inside him had decided to drop the pretense. "You can't prove any of this," he said.

"I'll tell the police," I said.

"They won't listen to you. You're a suspected drug dealer, involved in four murders. You killed Noah Frayne. You attacked Jason and Douglas. You threatened me . . ." He smirked like a spiteful child. "They'll lock you up and when the White Power people hear that the man who killed Noah Frayne is in their prison, no power on earth will be able to protect you."

I took out the Desert Eagle. All I had to do was point and squeeze.

He raised his fist. "Kill me and earn eternal damnation. But you won't shield Hannah no matter what you do."

He rose slowly, pointing at me. "Do you know the Biblical story of the scapegoat? Sent on the Day of Atonement to carry the sins of the Israelites away. You are my scapegoat, Peter, sent to absorb my sins and leave me blameless. You are God's message to me that I have done the right thing."

It was so perfect it could almost be true. I had no way out.

But then the words rose up from somewhere—*Noah's cell phone*. It was lying in a hundred pieces on the 101, but Kellner didn't know that.

I slid the Desert Eagle back into the bag. "Won't be needing this after all," I said.

Kellner blinked like the same spiteful child, thwarted and about to burst into tears.

"You texted Noah Frayne," I said. "I have that phone with your text and your number. If anything happens to me the police will get it."

"That means nothing," Kellner said. "Noah was one of my boys. I wanted to know how he was."

"Remember what you texted, Reverend? Did you get them? you asked. The police will ask what you meant. They'll talk to Jason and Dougie."

"Those boys will never say anything."

"They will when their lawyers tell them they can get leniency if they admit that it was your plan, your idea, your prison born-agains. They'll talk to the police, the tabloids, Larry King, Oprah . . . this time it'll be you doing the perp walk in the orange jumpsuit with the cuffs and the shackles and the fat deputies."

Kellner shook like he was having a fit. He raised his arms and screamed: "Sonny—!"

The door flew open, banging against the wall.

Sonny Doane had to duck under the doorway to get into the room. "You should have dumped that bitch like I told you," he yelled at me.

Kellner jumped at him. "Sonny, he has a gun!"

Sonny's mouth dropped, as if he hadn't thought of that.

I got the Desert Eagle out of the shopping bag and lifted it. Keeping my arm stiff the way Renay had told me, I squeezed, but the trigger wouldn't move. The safety was still on.

Sonny lowered his head and charged, so close I could smell his minty breath. I slid my left hand along the barrel and found the safety. His big fist came out of nowhere, clubbing me. The gun jumped and boomed in my hand.

He fell back, screaming, "Shit—!"

A piece of his shirt was blown to tatters, exposing a bloody shoulder.

He roared against the pain and reached down to his ankle with his left hand.

I aimed for his foot. The gun recoiled and drove my hand up against my forehead. Sonny went down on one knee, his hand dripping blood.

Kellner was on his knees, screaming, but I couldn't hear. I squeezed. The gun jumped, but I heard nothing. Acrid smoke burned my eyes.

Sonny stumbled out the door.

I squeezed. The bullet tore through the wall.

He staggered down the hall.

I aimed for his legs, but the gun veered to the left like it had a mind of its own, bullets shattering the photos into a million flying pieces.

Kellner was doubled over on the floor by his desk, blood pouring out of his head, hands clasped, singing: "Oh death where is thy sting? Or grave thy victory?"

He looked up at me with that sickly smile. "In the last moments of my earthly life, I will know what they felt . . . I will know the peace that the Lord granted them, in his love and mercy."

I could hardly see him through the curtain of smoke. And the roaring—like that big semi coming up in the rearview, air horn blasting.

I ran down the hallway, my mind screaming at me. Was Sonny in the church? Were there six or seven bullets in the clip? How many times had I shot? Five? Should have brought the box of shells, so I could reload and blow the shit out of all of them. Maybe he was hiding behind the altar. Bright red blood stained the mahogany pews. More blood on the floor by the door.

Blood on the dirt outside.

Tire tracks swirling like he had skidded on the way out.

The Bug looked lopsided. Had Sonny flattened one of my tires? No, I had parked it on a dirt mound.

If I'd been in his shoes, I would have flattened the tires. I would have had my gun out before I entered the room.

I was a better criminal than Sonny Doane.

And I could kill, too.

Knowing Isn't Enough

T he way out was the way in. A winding country road. A thousand places to hide a car. Blue van backing out of a driveway. Blue van following us down the 101. A million blue vans in California.

What if I came around a curve and Sonny was standing there with a shotgun, his truck parked across the lanes? I'd get out and run, zigging and zagging low to the ground, into the orange grove, going from one row to the next. I'd save the two shots in the Desert Eagle and hide in the trees. He'd think I was running away. He'd be looking straight ahead. When he passed, I'd jump out and run right at him. Get as close as I could before I squeezed . . .

My phone clanged with a text from Hannah: PETER?

I texted back: PACK!

Then I was passing houses and knew I was safe. Sonny wouldn't take a chance on witnesses. A minute later I was across the freeway.

Hannah was waiting outside the Holiday Inn. She got in and I drove to the far end of the parking lot. "Where'd you put my ammo?" I said.

She fished around in her backpack and handed me the box.

I took out the clip. It was empty. "I thought I had two shots left," I said. "If Sonny had come after me I'd be dead right now."

I reloaded, slipping one shiny, stubby shell in after another, feeling calmer as the clip filled up. I put one in the chamber and snapped back the slide. All I had to do now was release the safety to get a quick shot off. Hannah watched, her eyes big, afraid to ask.

"It's Kellner, Hannah. The righteous Reverend and his

merry band of meth-heads."

We drove east, the day dying behind us. She listened quietly as I told her about Kellner and Jason and Dougie.

"I can't believe it," she said. "Reverend Kellner was so good to me."

"He's a religious fanatic. He has fantasies of bloody revenge. Then he feels guilty for them. Then, he justifies them. And they get worse and worse until he convinces himself that God's plan is for you to die so your father can be redeemed."

"How could Dougie hate me this much?"

"How much meth do you have to do before you go crazy? So now you've got all this money and what do you do? You get high, which is just what your dead sister tried to cure you of. So you feel guilty and you get higher and then you decide that it's all Hannah's fault. If she had only loved you as much as you loved her, everything would have been all right."

"But to *kill* me—"

"Death means nothing to them. Jason said one night he would bring the wrong guy back to his place. And Dougie knew he was on his way to a total OD. Kellner kept looking at that bottle of pills, putting it back in the drawer and then taking it out again. He knows when the pain becomes too much for him he'll just take a deep breath and gulp a handful."

"They were good people before this happened. My father took their lives away from them—"

"You were as much a victim as they were," I said. "They had no reason to hate you. If they had killed you, it wouldn't have consoled them. They knew they were doomed, but they kept after you. They couldn't stop."

"Maybe they'll give up now that we know it's them."

"Maybe," I said, trying to keep doubt out of my voice.

Hannah looked out of the window for a long time. Then she nodded, as if she had come to some kind of decision.

"Let's get the hell out of here," she said.

Road Rage

W e drove and drove. Stopped for gas and coffee and drove some more. Outside of Tucson we found a truck stop with an all-night diner and a sign that said FREE WIFI. We pulled the Bug between two gigantic rigs. I carried my shopping bag with the Desert Eagle. Hannah had her backpack.

Truckers were in booths, hunched over laptops. They smiled at us with weary sympathy.

"You should see the other guy," said a guy in a booth. Big blond guy, the light glinting off his steel-rimmed glasses.

"Better go wash up," Hannah said. "You've got blood all over you."

The waitress, a Goth with piercings and tattoos, gave me a dazed look. In the harsh light of the bathroom, I looked like an '80s punk, dust strands clinging to my shirt, oily lank of hair hanging over my eyes. Face smudged, hands scratched, scab of dried blood on my forehead.

"I ordered coffee," Hannah said when I got back.

The waitress brought a carafe and laid a huge cinnamon roll, thick with vanilla icing, on the table between us.

"This is on the house," she said, and ducked away before we could thank her.

"That was nice," Hannah said.

"She likes a guy with a little blood on him," I said. "She would drop everything and come with us right now. Bring her drugs, have smelly, teenage sex with the both of us."

"Calm down," Hannah said, looking around to see if anybody was watching. "What's the matter with you? For God's sake, don't go crazy on me again."

My Jimi Hendrix ringtone went off. *McVickers.*

He sounded surprised that I had answered. "Peter? You

okay?"

"Great. How about you?"

"I thought you were going to call me."

Keep it light. "Oh, yeah. When I thought Sonny Doane was following us. We never saw him again so I didn't want to waste your time."

"Have you spoken to Reverend Kellner lately?"

"Not since we saw him at the outlet mall."

"You said you were going back to see him."

I was getting feedback on my voice. He was recording us. "Never made it—"

"You saw Abner Fried, right?"

"Yeah."

"You know what happened to him?"

"Yeah, we saw it on the news in the motel at Otter Point. It was weird karma, man," I said, playing the college boy stoner. "It's like I was carrying the death virus. To have another guy get offed like that after those dudes in Houston."

"And Noah," he said.

"Noah who?"

"Noah *Frayne*, Peter. Somebody killed him, too."

Time for a little righteous indignation. "I don't know anybody named Noah, okay? I know you think I'm a lying drug smuggler, but you can't blame me for everybody who gets murdered in Houston."

"This wasn't in Houston." The feedback stopped. He had taken me off the speaker. "Let's forget all the other stuff we talked about, Peter. I know Noah was following you."

"I told you, I don't know any Noah."

"I want to help you and Hannah. White Power crews swear an oath to sacrifice their own lives if necessary to avenge the murder of a brother. You're gonna need a friend."

I held the phone under the table. "I think I'm losing you, Detective." Then I disconnected.

"He'll know you did that on purpose," Hannah said.

"So what?" I patted her hand. "He's just trying to scare me."

On the way out I waved to the Goth waitress. She shrugged with a wan smile. The gray-haired cashier looked up from her knitting. "Drive carefully, kids."

On the lot, a dark figure moved like an evil blot around the Bug.

I got the Desert Eagle halfway out of the bag. "Stay here," I said to Hannah.

A trucker in a Stetson and hand-tooled boots stepped into the light. "How is she on gas?"

"Better than a hybrid," I said.

He smiled and walked in my direction, thumbs hooked in his belt. "I'm thinkin' about buyin' one of these for my daughter to take to college."

Hannah moved behind me. "No Peter!" she screamed. "It's that guy in the pickup!"

A motor roared. A little white car sped at us from across the lot.

Hannah ran toward me, pulling the .380 out of her backpack.

"Get in the car!" I shouted.

She fired over me. A flash . . . breaking glass . . .

The trucker reached into his boot.

I got the gun out.

He ducked behind the Bug and scuttled back toward the truck.

I fired. Stupid, I couldn't even see him. The gun almost flew out of my hand.

The white car . . . I turned, blinded by its headlights. It zigged and zagged. I dropped to my knees. Aim low. The bullet slammed into the soft tar. I fired again. The car screeched into a u-turn, speeding back into the darkness.

The trucker in the Stetson was behind the truck. I whirled and shot. The hood ornament blew off, like it was shot from a cannon.

Thumps like faraway fireworks.

Bullets crashed around me.

A screech . . .

The Bug's door flew open. Hannah slumped low under the steering wheel. I dove in, my head slamming into the dashboard. Hannah gunned it across the empty lot toward a line of parked trucks. I tried to close the door, but it swung away from me. Had to fire to cover ourselves. Aimed right because we were going left.

Trucks around us now. A jungle of trucks. Hannah slowed down, looking for a way out.

Headlights flashed. The white car pulled around a corner. Hannah flipped on the high beams. One guy behind the wheel.

"That creep from the strip club," she said.

"Lemme get the door closed," I said.

Too late. Hannah grabbed the wheel and floored it, heading right at the driver in the white car. I tried to steady the Desert Eagle in the crack of the door. Get a shot off . . .

The white car veered sharply away, down a line of trucks. Into the darkness and gone.

"Punk!" I shouted.

"I was gonna crash into him," Hannah said. "Bust him up."

We drove so close to the diner we could see the startled faces in the window.

"We are fucking *bad*," I said.

A blue van rolled out in front of us.

Hannah pounded the horn, screaming: "We're fucking *crazy*!"

It Was Them

Nobody followed us out of the lot.

"Do you think somebody in the diner called the police?" Hannah asked.

"We'll find out."

No flashing lights coming up behind us.

I said, "Are you sure it was the same guys?"

"Of course. Why?"

"Well, you said you only got a quick look at that guy in the pickup truck outside your house."

"I got a real good look at the guy in the club. I had drinks with him."

"Yeah, but you hardly saw him in the car."

"The high beams were right on him. For God's sake, he was coming right at us."

"Maybe he was just driving out of the lot."

"But then he drove right for us."

"Maybe he panicked when we started shooting. Maybe he was just trying to get away from us and we thought he was trying to get us."

"No, no . . ." She squeezed my arm. "It was them, Peter. I wouldn't forget those faces."

"Okay, okay."

I could feel her shaking with silent laughter. "But wouldn't it be funny if we shot at two random guys?"

And I was laughing, too. "That'll teach 'em to stop for a cheeseburger."

She put her arm around me and snuggled close. "Do you think you hit them?"

"No way. That point and squeeze is a lot of crap," I said. "There's more to shooting than that."

"It helps to aim," Hannah said.

"Now you tell me. I was shooting like a drive-by. Good thing this wasn't South-Central, I would have killed a baby and an honor student."

"That's sick," Hannah said.

We laughed ourselves hoarse.

Then the adrenaline ebbed. The bottom dropped out of our euphoria.

"We need a plan, Peter," Hannah said.

Respite

"We need to get lost," I said.

"Where?"

"Someplace. Phoenix or maybe LA. The end of a long street that goes on forever . . . little clone bungalows . . . the kind of street you get lost on trying to find your house."

"And do what?"

"Watch and wait."

"For what?"

"I don't know."

Jimi Hendrix played from my phone all the way across the desert, but I didn't answer and didn't check the voicemails.

"Don't you want to at least see who it is?" Hannah asked.

"I can't think of anybody in the world I want to talk to."

By dusk we were back in New Mexico at the Motel 6. The same desk clerk hunched over the Bible, nodding, lips moving. He looked up with a smile, as if he'd known we were coming. "Have a nice trip?"

"Very nice. Do you have a room?"

"Oh, yes, we always have a room. It's our Motel 6 miracle. No matter how many people come, we never have to turn anyone away."

"Don't need a manger at the Motel 6," I said, and his eyes got small.

"Why did you say that?" Hannah asked, as we walked to our unit.

"Just wanted to wipe that pious smile off his face."

In the room my phone went off again. Hannah came out of the bathroom and grabbed it.

"I'm sick of Jimi Hendrix and the Star-Spangled

Banner." She looked at the screen. "Six-twenty area code."

"Probably somebody trying to sell me health insurance," I said.

"Peter?" It was a familiar voice, but I couldn't place it.

"This is Jeremy Katz."

"Professor Katz." I had forgotten him, the comfortable little man with a scraggly beard, round paunch, pudgy white hands seeming to conduct every word he said.

"I've been calling you for two days. Didn't you get my messages?"

"I've been driving across the desert," I said. "Must have lost service."

"I've been holding that Teaching Assistant job open."

"I'll take it."

"It's a dumpy Division 3 college in the middle of nowhere."

"I'm a dumpy Division 3 kinda guy."

Katz laughed. He loved those half-smart B-movie wisecracks. "I can get you a small stipend and all your classes. You'll probably need to get a job, but we can find you something on campus. Town's dead, but there's a pretty good video store. Nice guy, real film buff. I'm sure he'd put you on part time."

"Sounds great."

"It's a little late, but maybe I can get you into the graduate dorms. You might have to share a room."

"I'm not alone," I said.

Hannah whispered: "Take it! Don't worry about me."

"I'm with Hannah Seeley," I said.

"That hottie from American Short Story? I'm proud of you."

"No big deal. We're just traveling together for a while," I said, glancing at Hannah.

"Tellya what. We have a big old drafty farmhouse. You and Hannah can stay in the basement until you find something. Hannah can help Sara with the kids and we'll count that as the rent."

"Sounds good. When do I start?"

"As soon as you get here."

"Cool."

His voice was full of vicarious innuendo. "You sound like you're having an interesting summer."

Love Rears Its Head

T his is being alive. Your mind is a mystery to you. You have no control over your body. You don't know what's going to happen next.

All of a sudden I had to stick my head in the toilet. I puked out three days worth of coffee and the icing off the cinnamon roll.

Then I was shivering so bad I couldn't stand on my feet and Hannah had to help me to bed.

"Your hands are freezing," Hannah said. She brushed her lips against my forehead. "You're cold as ice."

It was like when I was a kid and I would get the chills and my mother would give me a baby aspirin and pile blankets on me. The next morning I would wake up with an ear infection.

She got under the covers with me.

"Better not get too close," I said. "You might catch something."

"I never get sick," she said.

She pressed against me. Was she was just trying to warm me up? Her breasts shifted against my chest. My legs were numb. I was weak with lust and couldn't think about anything else.

"Did I ever collect for European History?" I asked.

She propped up on her elbow and looked down at me. "Are you turned on by this weirdness?"

"I'm turned on by you," I said. "I wouldn't care if the building was on fire. If burning beams were falling down on the bed . . . if Sonny Doane was standing outside with a grenade launcher."

"Okay, I get it," she said.

She rolled over on top of me. I flinched as she put her

knee between my legs.

"Oops." She put her legs over mine. "I can feel you through your pants," she said.

I pulled her shirt up. Her bare skin was warm and fragrant. I tried to reach under her. "Gimme a hand here."

"Sorry," she said and raised up just enough so I could pull her pants over her ass.

"It's better when you help," I said.

"Isn't that a line from a movie?" she asked.

It Could Happen To Anybody

I dreamt a DVD of a black-and-white noir film, all harsh light and washed-out shadows. It was Kellner and McVickers. They moved in and out of the light. Their voices echoed hollowly like a horror movie. The tape froze in the middle of a scene and then jumped to another.

Hannah sat at a desk in the corner, her face ghostly in the light of her laptop.

I told her, "I had a weird dream. Katz must have planted the content when he was telling me about the job in the video store."

She rose slowly and walked through the grayness like the people in the movie. "I've destroyed your life." She turned the laptop so I could see the screen, which was on Google-news.

MAN SOUGHT IN CALIFORNIA ASSAULTS . . . The son and brother of two victims of the notorious Robbinsgate Killer—and their minister—were attacked today by a man posing as a documentary filmmaker . . .

It took a moment to sink in. "They're after me."

Reverend Manfred Kellner, 43, pastor of St. Paul's Lutheran Church, was found bleeding from a head wound in his office by his wife, Elise, who had been alarmed when he didn't come home for dinner.

A short time later, friends found Douglas Baines, 24, bludgeoned in his living room a few miles away.

An hour after that, paramedics were called to the home of Jason Ardison, 42. He was in his foyer lying at the foot of the stairs with his back broken . . ."

"My brilliant plan wasn't so brilliant," I said.

Hannah tugged at her hair. "I hope they all die! Did you touch anything in the houses?"

"Doorknobs, walls . . . a million things. Ardison was holding onto me like a rabid dog. I slammed him against the wall. I was scared because his friend Gregory came after me. I saw his shadow on the wall. I grabbed the banister. My prints are all over the place."

"But you've never been arrested. They don't have your prints on file." She came at me, holding a bloody baseball bat at both ends. "I found this in the back seat of the car."

"Dougie's bat. I must have put it there. I guess I got nervous about leaving it in the house with my blood and prints on it. Everything happened so quickly I must have forgot."

"That was lucky." She threw the bat in the corner. "We'll have to chop it into pieces." She nodded again, as if receiving orders from her own inner sociopath. "They'll need more than just an ID. They'll need physical evidence."

"They'll find traces of my skin under Ardison's nails. My blood is on Dougie's floor. That must have been why McVickers called. He wanted to get me down to Houston to sneak some DNA samples off a coffee cup."

"Well, you won't go to Houston, then."

"They'll find the bullets from the Desert Eagle, in Kellner's office."

"That's okay," she said. "You bought the gun under another name and I'll bet Renay didn't report the sale."

"They'll know I was in town," I said. "The girl from the hotel—"

"She was half asleep, Peter. She'll never remember."

"The Capital One cards—"

"Fried's the only one who can link you to them, and he's dead."

"They'll have the call to Jason Ardison's house."

"We did it on the hotel phone."

"Reverend Kellner's text messages to you—"

"That was to me, not you," she said. She was pacing again, like when she had told me about her dad. "I'll tell them I was with some guy I picked up on the road. They'll buy that. They think I'm a whore anyway."

I touched her shoulder, trying to slow her down. "It's not gonna work, Hannah. I can't get out of this."

"You will, you will." She threw her arms around my neck, pressing me to her. I could feel her hot tears on my cheek. "I won't let them do this to you."

Then she stopped. "Wait a second." She stepped back with a scornful look. "What are we worrying about? Reverend Kellner can't identify you or the whole insane story will come out. He'll tell McVickers it wasn't you and so will Jason and Dougie. They can't do anything to you, Peter."

"But I killed Noah Fra—"

"No one will ever know. Kellner will keep your secret and you'll keep his." She shook me. "Don't you see? You are totally in the clear."

It wasn't possible. The four in Houston . . . Noah . . . Fried . . . All these people had died, and nobody would be punished for it.

"I'm going to get away with murder," I said.

"It wasn't murder," she said. "It was self defense."

"I was going to murder Kellner, Hannah," I said.

"Don't say that."

"I knew he was setting a trap. Trying to lure you to the church so he could get both of us. I got the gun out of the car and went back inside to kill him. He was melting down right in front of me, screaming about the devil . . . I knew he was crazy and I didn't care. Then Sonny Doane came in. He was right next to me. I was going to kill him, too. I kept shooting, but I couldn't hit him. Kellner was on the floor."

She pressed her hand over my mouth. "Shut up."

We could hear muttered voices in the next unit. Then silence, as if someone was listening.

"I stood over him with my Desert Eagle."

Hannah pressed harder.

"He deserved to die," she whispered fiercely. "They all did. Now shut up about it." She went to the window to draw the shades. Outside, a blue van rolled slowly down the line of parked cars. It slowed in front of Hannah's little blue Bug.

Search Party

After a while, I heard her quiet breathing. I took out the crumpled piece of paper with the names Fried had scribbled.

I Googled *Jack Powell.* Too many sites. I tried *Jack Powell, Navy medic* and up came a news story . . .

MEDIC KILLS WIFE, SELF.

No time to read. I Googled the next name. *Brian Carey, Navy medic...*

Scroll . . . scroll . . .

Thousands of Brian Careys . . . then, an announcement. A memorial service to be held in honor of Brian Carey, former member of the Naval Medical Corps who jumped off the Golden Gate Bridge . . .

No need to search any further.

The blue van was still parked outside. Couldn't see who was behind the wheel. Was it the Army officer who had been outside my house looking for his parade? The blond guy whirling like a pesky kid in the swivel-chair outside McVicker's office? The clean-cut dude in the hotel lobby? The truck driver in the diner, steel-rimmed glasses glinting? Blond buzz cut. Square, thick, football neck. Jock bully spook who had been watching us all along.

Could Fried have been right? Was it a military experiment that had gotten out of control? Did they slip Arnold Seeley the same drug they were giving the Navy Seals? Did he go nuts, like he was on a bad acid trip? So they gave him an antidote, or maybe a strong sedative, like thorazine. He calmed down and they thought he was okay. But then, 20 years later, he was arrested for serial sex murders. Maybe he would have killed anyway, but they couldn't know that.

Maybe Seeley wasn't the only one. Maybe there were

twenty men involved. Maybe one more who went as serious-ly crazy as Arnold Seeley. Maybe an ex-Navy Seal.

Fried was a clown who'd said the FBI had killed Martin Luther King and Dick Cheney had known about 9/11. But he could make trouble. He was the house crackpot for the media, a great foil for the Fox newsies. He wrote a popular blog. People laugh at conspiracy theories, but they secretly believe them. Fried would find willing ears in the media, especially if he had little bit of hard evidence. He'd put in a Freedom of Information claim. Maybe there would be a lot of big names from the CIA on some memos. Maybe even a secret order from Nixon.

How many people died as a result of this experiment? How many serial killers were created? How big a story was it? How many lawsuits? Wrecked careers? How many dedi-cated patriots would spill their guts to avoid prison?

Maybe they sent buzz-cut out to stop it from happening. To shut Seeley up. A sex murderer killed in jail. Easy to arrange. But Hannah would be a problem. As would Fried.

Did he find out that Kellner was after Hannah? Would he have watched them kill her and done nothing to stop it? He had been outside my building on July Fourth. Had he seen those two boys get killed? Or Noah Frayne? And when we went to see Fried, did he run up and kill him, knowing that we would be blamed for it?

Or maybe there were a lot of blue vans on the road. Had I seen the same man all those times or just a different chunky blond guy with steel-rimmed glasses?

Or had there been no experiment? Just a twisted killer who had brought misery to so many people. And a good, devout minister who had been driven insane by the thought that no murderer's punishment can ever fit his crime, that the killer's suffering can never equal the grief he causes.

I opened the door and stepped out, holding the Desert Eagle loosely at my side so he could see it. This time I would stay calm and move deliberately. Raise the gun, arm stiff. Look out over the sights.

And squeeze . . .

The van stuttered and started. The running lights came on. The van rolled forward and went past me. A chunky blond guy was behind the wheel staring straight ahead, holding a cell phone to his ear.

Our Bright Future

Hannah was still asleep. Mouth half open, pupils gleaming under half-closed eyes. I watched her until she stirred. She rolled over and looked at me.

"You'll have to disappear," she said.

"Can't be done."

"Yes, it can. You change your name. Get a new driver's license. New cell phone. Apply for a new Social Security card so they can't find you on the Web."

"That won't stop them. Actually, I know twenty meth-heads in school, flicking bloody boogers at their screen savers, who could hack Socials and account numbers and all kinds of encrypted shit."

"We can stay in that dumpy college town," she said. "Get to know everybody. A stranger will stick out."

"Actually, a scary white guy trying to look normal is normal in Middle America."

"You keep saying *actually*," she said.

"I'm getting back into the academic swing of things."

She reached out to me, opened her arms. "Why are you so far away?"

I laid down next to her and took her hand, just as I had on that night in Houston when this all began.

"Do you think the government really messed up my dad's mind?" she asked.

"It's the kind of thing they do."

"Maybe they killed Fried, too."

"Maybe."

"But maybe Reverend Kellner was right. The devil really did possess my dad."

"That would mean there's a God, too."

She shook her head, hopelessly. "We can't be sure of anything, can we?"

"I'm sure of one thing," I said. "I love—"

She put her finger to my lips. "I'm hungry."

Okay, so she didn't want me to say it. "I saw a Pizza Hut in town."

She sat up, full of concern. "Don't you think it would be safer to call?"

"Don't have to. It's over, Hannah. Nobody's after you anymore."

It was as if she didn't want it to end. "Maybe Sonny—"

"He's a mercenary. What happened to Kellner will take him off your trail. He'll have no reason to kill you. It's me he wants. It's me he was after in the parking lot. I shot him. That's reason enough. But I also killed Noah, his jailhouse buddy. Plus, I can link him to Fried and those guys in Houston."

"What if he finds you?"

"I'll shoot straighter."

She winced and then got quiet, hands covering her face. "You want me to leave, don't you?"

"It's dangerous for you to be with me now," I said.

She stared into my eyes. We were two lovers trying to see into each other's souls.

I said, "I know you're sorry for what you did to me. But that's not a reason to stay."

"You need my help," she said. "You won't make it without me."

"That's my problem. You don't owe me anything."

"You saved my life," Hannah said.

"Didn't do it on purpose, so it doesn't count," I said.

"But what will I do without you?"

I lifted her hands off her face. Her eyes were glistening. I kissed her tearstained cheeks. "Horrible things happen to people, but they survive. You'll get through this, Hannah. The memories will lose their power over you."

"How can you be so sure?"

I tapped my forehead. "English majors are wise beyond their years."

I couldn't read her smile. Was it full of love for me? Or gratitude for my love for her? Or just amazement that I was her sharer, and she mine. And that we would be together at least a little longer.

"Bad joke, huh?" I said.

She draped her arm around me, put her lips to my ear. Her laugh dizzied me in a puff of warm breath.

"They're all bad," she said.

— THE END —

ABOUT THE AUTHOR

Born in the Bronx and raised in Brooklyn, Heywood Gould got his start as a reporter for the New York Post, when it was still known as a "pinko rag." Later he financed years of literary rejection with the usual colorful jobs—cabdriver, mortician's assistant, industrial floor waxer, bartender, and screenwriter. *THE SERIAL KILLER'S DAUGHTER* marks his 13th published book, and seventh novel. He has also penned nine screenplays that have been produced as wide-release films, among them *FORT APACHE, THE BRONX* and *COCKTAIL*. He currently lives in New York City.